Shout Her Lovely Name

Shout Her
Lovely Name

Natalie Serber

Houghton Mifflin Harcourt

BOSTON   NEW YORK   2012

For information about permission to reproduce selections from this book,
write to Permissions, Houghton Mifflin Harcourt Publishing Company,
215 Park Avenue South, New York, New York 10003.

www.hmhbooks.com

These stories originally appeared, in some cases in slightly different versions,
in the following publications:

"Alone as She Felt All Day," *Clackamas Literary Review;* "This Is So Not Me,"
Inkwell, Porter Gulch Review, and *Air Fare: Stories, Poems, and Essays on Flight;*
"Plum Tree," *Gulf Coast;* "Shout Her Lovely Name," *Hunger Mountain;*
"A Whole Weekend of My Life," *Bellingham Review.*

Permissions credits are located on page 227.

Library of Congress Cataloging-in-Publication Data
Serber, Natalie.
    Shout her lovely name / Natalie Serber.
        p. cm.
    ISBN 978-0-547-63452-4
    1. Mothers and daughters—Fiction. 2. Eating disorders—Fiction.
3. Families—Fiction. 4. Domestic fiction. 5. Psychological fiction.
I. Title.
    PS3619.E7359S56 2012
    813'.6—dc23   2011036904

Book design by Melissa Lotfy

Printed in the United States of America
DOC 10 9 8 7 6 5 4 3 2 1

For Sophie, Miles, and Joel
with love and gratitude

All I really, really want our love to do,
Is to bring out the best in me and you.

— JONI MITCHELL

CONTENTS

SHOUT HER LOVELY NAME

Shout Her Lovely Name

May

In the beginning, don't talk to your daughter, because anything you say she will refute. Notice that she no longer eats cheese. Yes, cheese: an entire food category goes missing from her diet. She claims cheese is disgusting and that, *hello?* she has *always* hated it. Think to yourself . . . *Okay, no feta, no Gouda* — that's a unique and painless path to individuation; she's not piercing, tattooing, or huffing. Cheese isn't crucial. The less said about cheese the better, though honestly you do remember watching her enjoy Brie on a baguette Friday evenings when the neighbors came over and there was laughter in the house.

Then baguettes go too.

"White flour isn't healthy," she says.

She claims to be so much happier now that she's healthier, now that she doesn't eat cheese, pasta, cookies, meat, peanut butter, avocados, and milk. She tells you all this without smiling. Standing before the open refrigerator like an anthropologist studying the customs of a quaint and backward civilization, she doesn't appear happier.

When she steps away with only a wedge of yellow bell pepper, say, "Are you sure that's all you want? What about your bones? Your body is growing, now's the time to load up on calcium so you don't end up a lonely old hunchback sweeping the sidewalk in front of your cottage." Bend over your pretend broom, nod your head, and crook a finger at her.

"Nibble, nibble like a mouse, who is nibbling on my house?" cried the old witch. "Oh, dear Gretel, come in. There is nothing to be frightened of. Come in." She took Gretel by the hand and led her into her little house. Then good food was set before Gretel, milk and avocado, peanut butter, meat, cookies, pasta, and cheese.

Your daughter stares up at the kitchen ceiling, her look a stew of disdain and forbearance. "Just so you know, Mom, you're so not the smartest person in the room." She nibbles her pepper wedge, and you hope none of it gets stuck between her teeth or she will miss half her meal.

Alone at night, start to Google *eating disorder* three times. When you finally press enter, you are astonished to see that there are 7,800,000 pages of resources, with headings like Psych Central, Body Distortion, ED Index, Recovery Blog, Celebrities with Anorexia, Alliance for Hope, *DSM-IV*.

Realize an expert is needed and take your daughter to a dietitian. In the elevator on the way up, she stands as far away from you as she possibly can. Her hair, the color of dead grass, hangs over her fierce eyes. "In case you're wondering, I hate you."

Remember your daughter is in there somewhere.

This dietitian, the first of three — recommended by a childless, forty-something friend who sought help in order to lose belly fat — looks at your daughter and sees one of her usual clients. She recommends fourteen hundred calories a day, nonfat dairy, one slice of bread, just one tablespoon of olive oil on salad greens. You didn't know — you thought you were doing the right thing, and you are now relegated to the dunce corner forever by your daughter who is thin as she's always wanted to be.

The fourteen-year-old part of you — the *Teen* magazine–subscribing part of you that bleached your dark hair orange with Super Sun-In and hated, absolutely hated, your thighs; the part that sometimes used to eat nothing but a bagel all day so if anyone asked you what you ate, you could answer, *A bagel,* and feel strong—*that* part of you thinks your daughter looks good. Your daughter is nearly as thin as a big-eyed Keane girl, as thin as the seventh-grade girls who drift along the halls of her middle school, their binders pressed to their collarbones, their coveted low-rise, destroyed-denim, skinny-fit, size-double-zero jeans grazing their jutting hipbones. She is as thin as her friends who brag about being stuffed after their one-carrot lunches.

"It's crazy, Mom. I'm worried about Beth, Sara, McKenzie, Claire . . ." she says, waving her slice of yellow bell pepper in the air.

Google *eating disorders* again. This time click on the link *under standingEDs.com.*

waif low-rise $59.50
100% cotton, toothpick leg, subtle fading and whiskering, extreme vintage destruction wash, low-rise skinny fit, imported

July

Don't talk to your daughter about food, though this is all she will want to talk to you about. Spaghetti with clam sauce sounds amazing, she'll say, flipping through *Gourmet* magazine, but when you prepare it, along with a batch of brownies, hoping she'll eat, she'll claim she's always detested it. She'll call you an idiot for cooking shit-food you know she loathes. "Guess what, Mom," she will say with her new vitriol, "I never want to be a chubby-stupid-no-life-fucking-bitch-loser like you."

After you slap her, don't cry. Hold your offending palm against your own cheek in a melodramatic gesture of shame and horror that you think you really mean. Feel no satisfaction. When she calls you abusive and threatens to phone child protective services, resist handing her the phone with a wry *I dare you* smile. Try not to scream back at her. Don't ask her what the hell self-starvation is if not abuse. Be humiliated and embarrassed, but don't make yourself any promises about never stooping that low again. Remind your daughter that spaghetti with clam sauce and brownies was the exact meal she requested for her twelfth birthday, and then quickly leave the room.

Lovely's Twelfth-Birthday Brownies
    2 sticks unsalted butter
    4 ounces best-quality unsweetened
        chocolate
    2 cups sugar
    4 eggs
    1 teaspoon vanilla
    1 cup flour
    1 teaspoon salt
    1 cup fresh raspberries

Preheat oven to 350 degrees. Butter large baking pan. Melt together butter and chocolate over a very, very low flame or, better yet, in a double boiler. Watch and stir constantly to prevent burning. Turn off heat. Add sugar and stir until granules dissolve. Stir in eggs, one at a time, until fully incorporated and the batter shines. Blend in vanilla; fold in the flour and salt until just mixed. Add raspberries. Bake for 30 minutes. The center will be gooey; the edges will have begun to pull away from the sides of the pan. Try your best to wait until the brownies cool before you slice them. Enjoy!

Later, after you have eaten half the brownies and picked at the crumbling bits stuck to the pan, apologize to your daughter. She will tell you she didn't mean it when she called you chubby. Hug her and feel as if you're clutching a bag of hammers to your chest.

Indications of anorexia nervosa are an obsession with food and an absolute refusal to maintain normal body weight. One of the most frightening aspects of the disorder is that people with anorexia nervosa continue to think they look fat even when they are wasting away. Their nails and hair become brittle, and their skin may become dry and yellow.

Prepare meals you hope she will eat: buckwheat noodles with shrimp, grilled salmon and quinoa, baked chicken with bulgur, omelets without cheese. When you melt butter in the pan or put olive oil on the salad, try not to let her see. Try to cook when she is away from the kitchen, though suddenly it is her favorite room, the cookbooks her new library. Feel as if you always have a sharp-beaked raven on your shoulder, watching, pecking, deciding not to eat, angry at food, and terribly angry at you.

Begin to have heated, whispered conversations with your husband—in closets, in the pantry, in bed at night. He wants to sneak cream into the milk carton. He wants to put melted butter in her yogurt. He wants to nourish his little girl. He is terrified.

You are angry, resentful, and confused. You want help. You are terrified.

"She's mean because she's starving," he says. "How you feel doesn't matter."

"Yes, but I have to live in this house too."

"How you feel doesn't matter."

"Yes, but she used to love me."

"This isn't about you."

Later—after you once again do not have sex—get out of bed, close the bathroom door behind you, close the shower door behind you as well, then cry into a towel for as long as you like. Ask yourself, Is this about me?

September

Take your daughter to the doctor. Learn about orthostatic blood pressure and body mass index. Learn that she's had dizzy spells, that she hasn't had her period for four months. Worry terribly. Feel like a failure: like a chubby-stupid-no-life-fucking-bitch-loser.

When the pregnant doctor tells your daughter that she needs to gain five pounds, your daughter starts to cry and then to scream that none of *you people* live in her body, *you people* have no idea what she needs, *you people* are rude and she will listen to only herself. *You people* (you and the doctor and the nurse) huddle together and listen. You don't want to be one of *you people,* you want to be hugging your frightened, hostile daughter, who sits alone on the examination table. But she won't let you. The doctor gives her a week to gain two pounds and find a therapist or she will be referred to an eating-disorder clinic. You want your daughter to succeed. You want her to stay with you at home, to stay in school, to make new friends, to laugh, to answer her body when she feels hunger.

You watch your daughter watch the pregnant doctor squeezing between the cabinet and the examination table and you know exactly what your daughter is thinking — *Fat, fat, fat.*

Before you leave, the doctor pulls you aside and tells you that your daughter suffers from "disordered eating." She tells you to assemble a treatment team: doctor, therapist, nutritionist, family therapist. "You'll need support; you'll need strategies."

You've never been on a team before. Ask the obvious question: "Eating disorder versus disordered eating? What's the difference?" Get no answer. Try to go easy on yourself.

Knowledge about the causes of anorexia nervosa are not fully known and may vary. In an attempt to understand and uncover its origins, scientists have studied the personalities, genetics, environments, and biochemistry of people with these illnesses. Certain common personality traits in persons with anorexia nervosa are low self-esteem, social isolation (which usually occurs after the behavior associated with anorexia nervosa begins), and perfectionism. These people tend to be good students and excellent athletes. It does seem clear (although this may not be recognized by the patient) that focusing on weight loss and food allows the person to ignore problems that are too painful or seem irresolvable.

Remember, you were always there to listen to painful problems, to help. You kept your house purged of fashion magazines, quit buying the telephone-book-size September *Vogue* as soon as you gave birth to her. Only glanced at *People* in the dentist's office. So why? How? How did this happen to your family?

Karen Carpenter, Mary-Kate Olsen, Oprah Winfrey, Anne Sexton, Paula Abdul, Sylvia Plath, Princess Diana, Jane Fonda, Audrey Hepburn, Margaux Hemingway, Sally Field, Anna Freud, Elton John, Richard Simmons, Franz Kafka, for Christ's sake

You should never have paid Cinderella to enchant the girls at her fourth-birthday party. Cringe as you remember the shimmering blue acetate gown and the circle of mesmerized girls at Cinderella's knees, their eyes softly closed, tender mouths slackened to moist Os. Cinderella hummed Cinderella's love song; she caked iridescent blue eye shadow on each girl while they all fell in

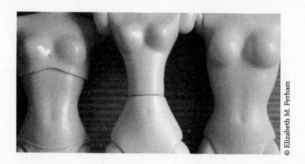

© Elizabeth M. Perham

love with her and her particular fantasy. Know in your heart that even though you canceled cable and forbade Barbie to cross your threshold, you are responsible. You have failed her.

After the doctor's appointment, drive to your daughter's favorite Thai restaurant while she weeps beside you and tells you she never imagined she'd be a person with an eating disorder. "If this could happen to me, anything can happen to anyone."

Tell her, "Your light will shine. Live strong. We will come through this." Vague affirmations are suddenly your specialty.

"I'm scared," she tells you.

For the first time in months, you are not scared. You are calm. Your daughter seems pliable, reachable. During the entire car ride, the search for a parking space, and the walk into the restaurant you are filled with hope. And then you are seated for lunch and she studies the menu for eleven minutes, finally ordering only a green papaya salad. Hope flees and this is the moment you begin to eat like a role model. You too order a salad; you also order pho and salmon and custard and tea. Eat slowly, with false joy and frivolity. Show her how much fun eating can be! Look at me, ha-ha, dangling rice noodles from my chopsticks, tilting my head to get it all in my mouth. Yum! Delicious! Wow! Ha-ha! Ha-ha! Ha!

October

Rejoice! Your daughter adds dry-roasted almonds to her approved-food list. She eats a handful every day. She also eats loaves of mother-grain bread from a vegan restaurant across the river. You gladly drive there in the rain, late at night. In the morning, she stands purple-lipped in front of the toaster, holding her hands up to it for warmth.

> People with anorexia nervosa often complain of feeling cold because their body temperature drops. They may develop lanugo (a term used to describe the fine hair on a newborn) on their body.

Your daughter furiously gnashes a wad of gum. She read somewhere that gum stimulates digestion and she chomps nearly all day. You find clumps of gum in the laundry, in the dog's bed, mashed into the carpet, stuck to sweaters. Seeing her aggressive chewing makes your skin crawl. Tell her how you feel.

"Why?" your husband demands. "How you feel is irrelevant."

"Good for you," your childless friend tells you. "Your daughter shouldn't get away with railroading your family."

"She's an angry girl." The new therapist pinches a molecule of lint from her fashionable wool skirt.

"She called me pathetic-cunt-Munchausen-loser." Where did your daughter learn this language? Your daughter has been replaced by a tweaking rapper pimp with a psychology degree. "What does she mean?" you ask.

The therapist, in her Prada boots and black cashmere sweater, speaks in a low voice. She has very short hair and good jewelry. Stylish, you think; your daughter will like her.

"She means you are making up her problems to get attention, Munchausen syndrome by proxy," the therapist says.

You still don't know what that means, so you volunteer information. "She chews gum."

"They all do."

"I hate that bitch," your daughter shrieks in the car on the way home. "I'm never going back." Remember to speak in calm tones when you answer. Remember what the therapist told you about the six Cs: clear, calm, consistent, communication, consequences . . . you've already forgotten one. Chant the five you do recall in your mind while you carefully tell your daughter that she certainly will go back or else. In between vague threats (your specialty) and repeating your new mantra, feel spurts of rage toward your husband for sending you alone to therapy with your anorexic daughter. Also feel terribly, awfully, deeply guilty for feeling fury. What kind of monster doesn't want to be alone with her own child? During this internal chant/argument/lament cacophony, right before your very eyes, your daughter transforms into a panther. She kicks the car dash with her boot heel, twists and yanks knobs trying to break the radio, the heater, anything, while screaming hate-filled syllables. Her face turns crimson as she punches and slaps at your arms. Pull over now. Watch in horror as she scratches her own wrists and the skin curls away like bark beneath her fingernails. All the while she will scream that you are doing this to her. Don't cry or she will call you pathetic again. Remember that your daughter is in there, somewhere. Tell her you love her. Refuse to drive until she buckles in to the back seat. Wonder if there is an instant cold pack in the first-aid kit. Wonder if there is a car seat big enough to contain her. Yearn for those long-ago car-seat days.

Think, *We've hit bottom.* Think it, but don't count on it. Then remember the last C: compassion.

For some reason, driving suddenly frightens you. When you must change lanes, your heart thunks like a dropped pair of boots, your hands clutch the steering wheel. You shrink down in your seat, prepared for a sixteen-wheeler to ram into you. You can hear it and see it coming at you in your rearview mirror. Nearly close your eyes but don't; instead, pull over. Every time you get into your car, remind yourself to focus, to drive while you're driving, to breathe. Fine, fine, fine, you will be fine, chant this as you start your engine. Be amazed and frightened by the false stability you've been living with your entire life. If this can happen to you, anything can happen to anyone.

When your husband leaves town for business, worry about being alone with your daughter. Try not to upset her. When she tells you she got a 104 percent on her French test, smile. When she tells you she is getting an A+ in algebra, say, *Wow!* Don't let her know that you think super-achievement is part of her disease. Don't let on that you wish she would eat mousse au chocolat, read Simone de Beauvoir's *Le deuxième sexe,* and earn a D in French. Begin to think that maybe you *are* always looking for trouble, Munchausen by proxy. Be happy when she has a ramekin of dry cereal before bed.

Hug her before you remember she won't let you, and don't answer when she says, "Bitch, get off me."

In the middle of the night wake her and tell her that you've had a bad dream. Ask her to come and sleep in your bed. When she does, hug her. Comfort her. Comfort yourself. Remember how she smelled as a toddler, like sweat and graham crackers. Remember how manageable her tantrums used to be. Whisper over and over in her perfect ear that you miss her. That you love her. That she will get better. Know that she needs to hear your words, believe that somewhere inside she feels this moment. In the morning, look away while she stands purple-lipped before the toaster.

When your husband dedicates every Saturday afternoon to your daughter, taking her to lunch, shoe shopping, a movie, use the time to take care of you. Kiss them both goodbye and say with a forced lilt, "Wish I could come too." Quickly shut the front door. Try not to register their expressions, the doomed shake of your husband's head, your daughter's eyes flat as empty skillets.

"Take some *me* time," your childless friend urges. "Get a facial . . . a massage . . . a pedicure. Take a nap, you're exhausted. Read *O* magazine." The magazine counsels:

> *What to Do When Life Seems Unfair*
> *Do you ask, "Why me?"*
> *Or do you look at what your life is trying to tell you?*
> *How you choose to respond to the difficult*
> *things that happen to you*
> *can mean the difference between a life of anger*
> *. . . or joy.*

Instead, take a long bath. Light aromatherapy candles and incense. Pour in soothing-retreat bath oil. Even though it is only eleven o'clock in the morning, mix a pitcher of Manhattans.

Mommy's Manhattan
  2 ounces blended whiskey, 1 ounce sweet vermouth, 1 dash bitters, cherry

Play world music and pretend you are somewhere else. Except of course you aren't. You know you aren't somewhere else because as you were filling the tub you noticed raggedy bits of food in the drain.

Wouldn't she vomit in the toilet? Your daughter must be terrified for herself to leave behind these Technicolor clues. Get in tub. Continue adding hot water. Drain the water heater. Notice as the water level climbs, covering first your knees, then your thighs, and then your chest, that your stomach is nearly the last thing to go under. Weeks of role-model eating have changed your body. Try to love your new abundance.

When your husband and daughter return, you are still in the tub. She slams her bedroom door. Your husband comes in and slumps on the toilet, his head in his hands.

Quietly listen.

"She pretended not to know where the shoe store was. We walked for forty-five minutes. Really, it was more of a forced march."

Say nothing, though you feel more than a dash of bitters; you feel angry and tired of being angry. Stare at your wrinkled toes. You are each alone: your daughter in her room, your husband on the toilet, you in the tub. You're each in your private little suffering-bubble.

"Exercise is verboten," you say. The doctor has given you both this directive.

"I know." When his voice breaks and his hands shudder, get out of the lukewarm tub. Climb into his lap, and put your arms around him. Cling together.

November

Hooray! Your daughter has added whole-wheat pasta to her approved-food list. At the doctor's office, her blood pressure is amazing! She's gained five pounds! *You people* are all smiling. This time in the elevator, your daughter stands right beside you. For days you are happy.

Until you find her in the kitchen blotting oil out of the fish fajitas. When you confront her, tell her that is anorexic behavior, she throws the spatula across the room.

Persons with anorexia nervosa develop strange eating habits such as cutting their food into tiny pieces, refusing to eat in front of others, or fixing elaborate meals for others that they themselves don't eat. Food and weight become obsessions as people with this disorder constantly think about their next encounter with food.

Your daughter claims oil gives her indigestion, the food in the drain is because of acid reflux, you are the one obsessed, you are the one who is sick, she is fine.

You say, "Bullshit."

"Shh," your husband says. "Can we please have peace?" Like a middle-school principal, he calls you into his home office to tell you that she doesn't need to be told every single moment that something isn't right. "Stop reminding her," he says. "Leave her alone. It's hard enough for her without having to faceherproblemeverysingleminute."

He can't even say the word *anorexic*.

Properly censured, return to the kitchen. Your daughter eyes you with smug satisfaction and eats barely one half of a' whole-wheat tortilla—no cheese, no avocado—with her fish. A vise of resentment tightens around you. Anorexia has rearranged your family.

di·vorce [di-vawrs, -vohrs] — *noun, verb* -vorced, -vorc·ing
noun

a judicial declaration dissolving a marriage in whole or in

part, especially one that releases the husband and wife from all matrimonial obligations.

any formal separation of man and wife according to established custom.

total separation; disunion: *a divorce between thought and action.*

verb (used with object)

4. to separate by divorce: *The judge divorced the couple.*

5. to break the marriage contract between oneself and (one's spouse) by divorce: *She divorced her husband.*

6. to separate, cut off: *Life and art cannot be divorced.*

Fantasize about how you will decorate your living room when you live alone, when you disjoin, dissociate, divide, disconnect. Imagine your new white bookcases lined with self-help books:

Wishing Well
The Best Year of Your Life
The Power of Now
When Am I Going to Be Happy?
Flourish
A Course in Miracles
Get Out of Your Own Way
The Upward Spiral
Forgive to Win!
Super Immunity
The Essential Laws of Fearless Living
Feel Welcome Now
100 Simple Secrets Why Dogs Make Us Happy

You're filled with a thrilling flutter of shame. When did this become about you?

. . .

Snoop. Look through your daughter's laundry basket for vomity towels. Stand outside the bathroom door and listen. Look in the trash for uneaten food. Though you want to call her school to see if she is eating the lunch she packs with extreme care every day (nonfat Greek yogurt, dry-roasted almonds, one apricot), don't. When you find her journal, don't read it. Her therapist has told her she should record her feelings, her fears. You are desperate to know what it says. The journal screams and whispers your name all day long. Later, when you are folding laundry and can no longer resist, go back upstairs to her room and find that she hasn't written a single thing. Despair.

Visiting your parents at Thanksgiving, you realize that the difference between your father's overdrinking and your daughter's undereating is slim. Deny, deny, deny. The rest of the family is acutely aware, and between watching alcohol consumed and food left on the plate, your gaze ping-pongs between your daughter and your father. Both start out charming enough. Your daughter sets a beautiful table: plump little pumpkins carved out, their tummies filled with mums and roses, thyme and lavender, slender white tapers rising up from the center and flickering light over the groaning table. But as the afternoon progresses and Grandpa's wineglass is filled and emptied again, the turkey carcass is removed and pies emerge, your daughter's mood fades to black.

"Junk in the trunk," Grandpa slurs, patting your abundant rear as he walks behind you. "Next year, we should all fast." You want to kill him.

Your starving daughter pushes away her plate, her face pinched, disappointed, angry. You can see her mantra scroll across her eyes like the CNN news crawl: loser . . . failure . . . pathetic . . . chubby . . . What she calls herself is neither worse nor better than what she calls you. It's a revelation, and you repeat your Cs: calm, consistent, compassion, communication, calamitous, collapse, cursed, condemned.

At the hotel, your daughter insists on taking a long walk, *stretching her stomach,* she calls it. You and your husband say no. She throws a tantrum and you are all trapped in the hotel room, staring at a feel-good family movie involving a twelve-step program, cups of hot coffee, and redemption.

> *God, grant us the serenity to accept the things*
> *we cannot change,*
> *courage to change the things we can,*
> *and wisdom to know the difference.*

By the next doctor visit she's lost six pounds and she cries and cries. Your body goes cold. You feel like a fool, slumped on the pediatrician's toddler bench, staring at the wallpaper: Mother Goose and her fluffy outstretched wings hovers above you with bemused tolerance and extreme capability. An infant cries in the next room and you yearn for the days of uncomplicated care and comfort.

"I am so angry." Your voice is not angry, it is depleted. You are not as competent as Mother Goose, you are the woman trapped in a shoe with only one child and still you don't know what to do.

Your daughter agrees to go on antidepressants, to help her adjust to her changing body, the doctor says. When you leave the office you drive straight to the pharmacy and then to a bakery and watch her consume a Prozac and a chocolate chip cookie. Her eyes, her giant, chocolate-pudding eyes, drip tears into her hot milk; her hand shakes.

Antidepressants increased the risk compared to placebo of suicidal thinking and behavior (suicidality) in children, adolescents, and young adults in short-term studies of major depressive disorder (MDD) and other psychiatric disorders. Anyone consider-ing the use of [Insert established name] or any other antidepres-sant in a child, adolescent, or young adult must balance this risk with the clinical need.

"It's not my fault," she sobs.

"Oh, Lovely." You shake your head, review the many theories that Google dredged up: genetic predisposition, a virus, lack of self-concept, struggle for control, posttraumatic stress disorder.

"I didn't want this," she says.

"Of course you didn't."

"The voice scares me."

"Voice?"

"My eating disorder. Tells me I suck and it never shuts up, only if I restrict."

Pay attention. This is language that you haven't heard before. Watch. Listen. *Mood swings. Suicidal ideation. Changes in behav-ior.* Be terrified about everything. Ask with nonchalance, "This voice, is it yours?"

She turns away from you. Her skin is the transparent blue of skim milk.

Later, when you are alone, call your husband on his cell phone. He is standing in line, waiting to board a plane. Don't care. Scream into the phone. Imagine your tinny, bitchy voice leaking around his ear while men holding lattes, women with Coach briefcases, students, and grandmas try not to look at his worn face.

"Say it out loud."

"She has an eating disorder," he mumbles.

"Not fucking enough," you shriek, your hands shaking. Until he says it loud, admits it fully to himself, you will not be satisfied. You may have gone crazy.

"My daughter is anorexic. There."

You let it lie.

"Are you happy now?" he whispers.

Oddly enough, you are momentarily happier.

March

She's back. Your daughter dances into the kitchen, holding a piece of cinnamon toast. She wants milk, 2 percent. She also wants a cookie and pasta, a banana, a puppy, and a trip to Italy.

"I want some of those," your husband whispers, nodding to the prescription bottle on the windowsill.

You want this to continue. She may not be eating Brie and baguettes, but she's laughing. Her collarbones are less prominent. She's. Given. Up. Gum.

"The voice is leaving, Mom," she confides. "It polluted everything." She smiles, hopeful and charming, so wanting to please. Even though it may not completely be true about the voice, she wants it to be and for now desire has to be enough. That she talks about the voice without anger or tears takes a grocery cart of courage.

"Quit worrying and watching me so much," she says.

You nod and smile. You will never quit worrying and watching.

Weak spring sunlight fills your kitchen. Your daughter, with a hand on her hip, stands before the open refrigerator, singing. You still are not certain keeping her home and in school is the right choice. A clinic may be inevitable. You've followed advice, you have your team, yet letting go of watching and worrying would require a grocery cart full of courage that you do not have. Just yesterday you checked her Web history and found she'd visited caloriesperhour.com.

"I'm hungry," your daughter says.

You haven't heard those words from her for nearly a year. Grab on to them, this is a moment of potential. Look for more. Remember them. String them together. Write Post-it notes for the inside of your medicine cabinet. *Almonds! I hear me! Two percent milk! I'm hungry!* Dream of the day when your cabinet door will look like a wing, feathered in hopeful little yellow squares.

Then Gretel, suddenly released from the bars of her cage, spread her arms like wings and rejoiced. "But now I must find my way back," said Gretel. She walked onward until she came to a vast lake. "I see no way across..."

Picture *you people:* your husband, the physician, the therapists and nutritionist, family members—all standing across the water, waving, calling; a part of her remains listening on the other side, afraid to lose control, afraid to fail, afraid to drown.

Open your arms wide. Your daughter is getting nearer. Know that it is up to her. Say her lovely name. Know that it is up to her. Shout her lovely name.

Ruby Jewel

WHEN SHE STEPPED off the train, her father honked from the Dodge, three sharp blasts, like elbow jabs to her ribs. His thick arm dangled out the window, the sleeve rolled up, exposing sunburned skin. "Ruby-Ruby, the college gal," he called, a pipe clenched in the center of his grin.

Black land crabs scuttled across the gravel in front of her. Ruby hurried, stepping carefully to protect the Bergdorf pumps her New York aunt had sent along with the tuition check and a little extra walk-around money. "Hi, Daddy." Pabst empties littered the passenger-side floor. She wiped the seat with her hand and dropped the rattling bottles, five of them, into the back before setting her suitcase beneath her feet.

"Cars cleaner up there?"

She leaned over the seat, brushed her lips against his bristled cheek. "Doesn't matter." He hadn't removed his inked pressman's apron, and the cab was filled with his familiar smells. Sometimes, though not this afternoon, the father-odors of newsprint, tobacco, and sweat were rounded out with whiskey or the Lava soap he used to scrub at the ink beneath his fingernails.

Her father shifted gears and the truck lunged onto Beach Boulevard. Outside her window, the Gulf, flat and black as the bottom of a cast-iron pan, stretched away.

"How's Mom?"

"Your mother . . ." His voice trailed off, as if he had something to decide.

Ruby waited, watching the ball of his fist on the gear knob, his biceps flexing each time he shifted. "Is she drawing?"

"No. Nope. She's rearranging the furniture. She's got the couch crisscrossing the corner now. Every goddamned morning I have to double-check where the coffee table is. I'm afraid she might move the john and I'll end up pissing in my chair." His jaw tensed around his pipe stem as he spoke. Everything about him was tight, ready to spring, like a flea. "And, she's pasting Green Stamps to get herself a new dryer."

Her mom could camp at the kitchen table for hours on end, a lit cigarette perched in the ashtray and a sponge resting in a saucer of water to moisten the stamps. Five, ten, twenty-seven booklets filled with stamps and so far all she'd earned was a percolator, a pipe stand, and an electric fan. Ruby rolled down her window and a whoosh of hot air filled the cab. From her pocketbook she retrieved a scarf and tied it over her new hairstyle, short like Audrey Hepburn's in *Sabrina,* only blond.

"The pool nice up there?" her father yelled against the wind.

"I made the dive team." Each morning at practice, she swallowed panic to climb up to the platform, her eyes fixed on the pale, cloudless sky. She pushed off with her toes, flinging herself headlong into it. Fifteen or twenty dives, and every time she thrust herself into the air, Ruby fought her fear. That was worthwhile effort.

"You don't miss the Gulf?"

"I do," she said. It was true. She missed swimming along the shore in Tampa. One mile up the beach to the green-bellied water tower and back again. "I'll swim tomorrow." What she didn't miss was coming home from her swim to laundry on the line, a dutiful pot of something on the stove, another of her mother's pastels, taken from the pages of *National Geographic,* propped on the desk. Kimonos, giraffes, tribal women, sea anemones, the Taj Mahal — beautiful renderings of far-off places. Her mother never drew home. That was before she'd settled on the Green Stamps.

Her father pulled into the Winn-Dixie lot, rumpled up his pressman's apron, and threw it in the back with the beer bottles. "Give me a look," he said, twirling his finger in the air, illustrating what he expected of her.

She pushed her door closed with her hip. "I'm no baby."

"Turn around." He hit his pipe against his callused palm, spilled the hot ashes onto the gravel.

She touched her hand to her neck. While she was tempted to show off the change in her, it was the change in her that would not let her comply.

Her father stared, his gray eyes clear and sharp, his thin lips pressed together in a wry smile. He crossed his arms over his chest as if he had all afternoon to wait her out in the parking lot. This was another thing she didn't miss about home, hot-tempered caprice.

"No," she said, though she did oblige, one haughty half turn, like she was spinning on a dime, before she entered the store.

Bev Richardson stood behind the cash register, her lime-green uniform stretched tight across her bust, fluorescent lighting gleaming off her bottle-red hair.

"Hey, Ruby," Bev called.

"Beverly, you are looking mighty-mighty today." Her father grinned at Bev.

When she smiled back, she trapped a little piece of tongue, like an earlobe, between her teeth. Ruby didn't need to look at her to see the knob of flesh; she knew Bev well enough from all the phony afternoons Bev had stirred canned milk and sugar into her Yuban across the table from Sally, Ruby's mother. Pretending to be a friend, leaving behind an ashtray full of lipsticked filters. Ruby swung her pocketbook over her shoulder, glad she'd dressed up for the train ride, glad to show Bev how well her life was going.

"How's Gainesville?" Bev asked.

"Marvelous," Ruby said, allowing her father to steer her toward the meat coolers. His hands, both rough and tender, rested on her shoulders like they used to when she was a child and he wanted to show her a snowy egret alighted by their clothesline, or when he pointed out the pile of rocks she must paint white and set around the perimeter of their crabgrass yard before she could go swimming. Her father's unpredictable touch unbalanced her now as much as it had when she was young.

Rows of chicken wings, pork butt, and beef ribs glistened beneath the cellophane, blood pooled in the corners of the trays. He selected three thick rib eyes. "Maybe you can get your mother to make some of her famous steak sauce."

Ruby pointed to a fourth steak. "Maybe you'd like to invite the cashier?"

He sucked air through his teeth as if he already had a piece of meat stuck there. "You don't know what you're talking about."

He told Ruby to pick up two six-packs of Pabst and a newspaper and then he made a big show of sliding the steaks on the counter in front of Bev, as if he'd chased down and killed the cow with his bare hands. He dug deep into his pocket to fish out his Florida State money clip and flash through the bills. Payday. Ruby tossed a package of Dentyne on the counter. Boys at her school carried around wads of cash. They spent it on girls. John Douglas had spent money on her lots of times, buying rum and corsages, filling his car with gas for a long drive with the top down. He carried a blanket.

"You buying a gal a cup of coffee with all that cash?" Bev asked.

It used to be "a drink" before Bev joined AA. Ruby wasn't certain how she knew Bev had joined AA, whether her mother had told her in a letter or someone had seen her at a meeting and told her. It was another bit of information that Ruby had collected, piecing together her parents' reality.

"Remember, I am a married man."

"Oh, I remember," Bev said, stroking her finger down the entire row of cash register keys before she punched the 4, 9, and 8 for the steaks.

Steaks were incidental to the stop at Winn-Dixie and Ruby made no move to carry the sack. Teddy held it against his chest, winked at Bev, and then pushed through the door, leaving twenty-five Green Stamps behind.

Clamshells crunched beneath the tires when he turned the Dodge into the lot at the Avenue.

"I thought we were going home."

"You wouldn't deny your daddy the pleasure of one drink, would you?"

Ruby leaned back, prepared to wait as she had so many nights of her childhood when she'd been sent along by her mother so her father would come right home. She'd wait in the truck through twilight until he'd stumble out in the dark, bowing and sweeping his arms in a royal gesture as he held the Avenue door open wide for his little girl to join him. Inside the shadowy bar Ruby would play "Down in the Valley" on the upright piano. When patrons whistled and patted her father on the back, she'd play another, "Frosty the Snowman" or "Greensleeves," her feet beginning to sway back and forth over the sawdust-covered floor. After, her father would pat a barstool for her to come hop up beside him. He'd ruffle her hair, pinch her lightly on the nose while his ruddy-cheeked comrades congratulated him on his fine little girl, and Mr. Goddard, the bartender, popped open a cold grape Nehi, the treat he claimed that he kept in the cooler just for her. With Ruby by her daddy's side, they'd all listen while Teddy recited some poem he'd composed that very morning.

The hours dance on dusky feet,
I learn your lips are soft and sweet.
The hours fly on silken wings,
I learn the rapture your arms bring.
The hours deepen into dawn,
The dream remains but you are gone.

Ruby remembered that poem because his paper, the *Tampa Tribune*, had printed it. He'd thought it was a foot in the door to his own byline and for about a week after it came out he was certain he'd be getting a call. Whenever the phone rang, he made her run to answer it: "Hargrove residence. Whom may I say is calling?"

"Souvenir," he'd named it and her mother had taped it to the icebox. Each time Ruby fetched him a beer or grabbed a banana, she read it. The way he'd recited the poem, his voice scraping over the final words, made her fall in love with her mysterious father. He was a man capable of rapturous thoughts.

Her mother ripped it off one day, then wiped away the tape residue with nail polish remover so all that remained was a dull spot on the icebox she pointed to and called the truth. Ruby hadn't understood what she meant.

Teddy slipped his pipe from between his teeth, and his lips quivered, as if they didn't know what to do with their new freedom. "Come on, Jewel. You're a college girl. You earned a seat at the bar right next to your daddy." With his brows raised in invitation and that trembling smile, his face seemed earnest, eagerly inviting. The face her mother must have fallen in love with. If Ruby had stayed in Gainesville, John Douglas's arm might be hitched around her waist right now as they toasted the start of the weekend with a Cuba libre, everyone's drink of choice. Surely she could have a drink before going home to her mother. No harm in one. She opened her own door and stepped from the truck, smoothing creases from her skirt, hooking her pocketbook over her arm.

It took a moment for her eyes to adjust to the dim light. The jukebox was still there, same as the upright piano. A couple of men hunched over beers at the long L of the bar. The far end held a wheel of cheddar with a wire cheese cutter and a jar of soda crackers. Three or four lazy flies hung over the food. The Avenue smelled of soggy bar rags, stale peanuts, and men.

"Everyone," her father called out. "Look at my Ruby, my jewel." Again he tried to get her to turn around, but she pulled away and bent to wipe the sawdust off her shoes.

Milton Goddard pretended not to believe it was her. He looked up from her leather pumps, past the paisley skirt and peasant blouse. Finally he whistled through his teeth. "Fan-cy."

Ruby smiled, slid onto a barstool. "Hi, Mr. Goddard."

Her father dropped the afternoon edition onto the bar. "Paper delivery." He nudged Ruby. "I consider it my civic duty to edify Milton."

"With the oldest paperboy in the world for a daddy, you must be past drinking grape soda."

"Why, yes, I believe I am. My friends and I enjoy Cuba libres." She tipped her voice up at the end, wondering if Milton knew how to make them.

"*Why, yes? Cuba what?* What kind of horseshit is that?" Her father, hiding a smile at the corners of his mouth, thunked his pipe against his palm.

"Looks like *you* need edification, Teddy." Milton grinned at Ruby.

"We're having shots and a beer. I'll buy you a beer too." Teddy gestured at Milton with his thumb, its nail black and split up the middle from when he'd caught it in the press. "Hell, I'll buy everyone a beer." He threw his arms out expansively toward the two men.

Milton set two shots on the bar and then pulled the drafts. Her father held a glass out to Ruby. She took it, smelled the whiskey, and asked for a cocktail straw.

"Uh-uh. Pour it back, like this." He threw his head back. His Adam's apple bobbed as he swallowed. "Your turn."

She lifted her chin, exposing her neck to the two men, and poured the liquor down her throat. She held back a cough as the whiskey burned its way into her stomach. To hide her watering eyes, she stared at the bar top. A two-dollar bill and a sprinkling of change had been laminated there. She remembered digging at the coins with her fingernail as a child, totaling up the two dollars and forty-three cents in her head every time her father brought her in. It had seemed a tremendous waste. Her legs began to tingle, her eyes cleared, and she smiled.

"How about a roll of nickels?" Teddy peeled a twenty off his money clip and slapped it down. Once Milton complied, he stripped the wrapper from the nickels in one long piece, stacked them in two piles like poker chips, and passed one stack to Ruby. "Let's spin for shots."

"We play word games at school," Ruby said.

Teddy snapped a nickel between his finger and the thumb. The coin caught the light, flickered as it spun. "Of course you do," he said. "I'd expect word games at college."

"I mean tongue twisters. One-red-hen. Two-cute-ducks. You know. I-slit-six-sheets. Seven-sexy-Siamese-sailors. Eight-enor-mous-elephants. Nine-cunning-runts. When you mess up, you have to drink."

Her father raised his eyebrows and expertly spun a second nickel without taking his gaze off Ruby. "This is how we play down here."

She nodded and pinched her own coin. It wobbled, never hit its rim, then fell flat.

"Drink up, Jewel."

Again she gulped. Again her legs and the back of her eyes were flooded with heat. Milton set the bottle in front of them. The tongue twisters were easy. Seated on the sprung couch on the back porch of the fraternity house, her legs bare in her sundress, her friends charmed and laughing beside her, she'd roll them out, crisp and correct every time, then drink anyway.

"You can learn this," her father told her. He pressed his hand around her fingers, showed her how to position the nickel and then snap, as if she were calling over Milton.

She snapped the coin free and it careened in a wide arc on the bar. When it came to rest her father shook his head. "You got me that time." He slapped her on the back, slammed down his second. They were matched, shot for shot.

"What're you learning at that college of yours?" Milton wiped the bar in front of her.

"I'm studying education."

"Here's to elevating the young." Milton raised his beer.

"I keep telling her to elevate higher." Her father dug his fingers into his tobacco pouch and then filled his pipe. He offered to roll her a cigarette.

"No, thanks, Daddy." She took a pack from her pocketbook and tapped it on the inside of her wrist three times. "I've got my own." She wrapped her lips around a single filter in the pack, extracted it slowly. She'd perfected the gesture, always taking enough time for a boy to retrieve a match or lighter before she held the cigarette expectantly.

"Menthols?" her father asked.

She offered one to Milton and he took it and lit a match for both of them. "Sweet. She's got taste."

Teddy scoffed. "Fancy-ass cigarettes do not equal taste. You ever hear what she named her pets? Queenie. Snowball. No imagination."

"Mom liked them."

"Thank God I was there to mix things up."

She laughed. "Mix things up? You renamed every one of those strays Sufchick."

Teddy nodded at Milton. It was true. "Hell if I know what it means."

"They loved you too," Ruby said. "They'd always come."

"I have that effect on puppies and women." He tried to ruffle Ruby's hair and she dodged his reach.

"Damn if it isn't true." Milton laughed, nodding his head.

Ruby rolled her eyes and propped her chin in her palm. It was good to rest. She was surprised by how very, very heavy her head had become. The mailman came into the bar and Milton excused himself, calling out a hello.

"He's a bastard." Her father gestured with his chin toward the mailman. "A sanctimonious, one-drink-a-day bastard with a perfect lawn, the worst kind." Teddy called out, "Drinking on my dime, Phil? Aren't you still on the taxpayers' clock?"

"Nice to see you too, Teddy. Give my best to Sally."

Her father huffed. Ruby smoked. "You have something on everyone," she said.

"That's because I pay attention. Just like you."

She watched in the mirror over the bar as her father plucked a crumb of tobacco from his tongue, then flicked it away. He rubbed his palms over the top of his thighs, stole glances at the men, and let loose a loud sigh, as if drinking and noticing was hard labor. And she supposed it was when a person paid attention to get even, to discover just the right detail to hold against another person. Teddy felt he needed to get a leg up on the world. Ruby paid attention to differentiate herself from her father and her mother. Paying attention would set her free. A long ash balanced on the end of her cigarette. Milton returned, offering a tuna-can ashtray. "So, what'd I miss?"

"I pledged a sorority."

Her father widened his eyes. "Sorority?"

"What do you all do?" Milton asked.

"We meet. The fraternity next door keeps a chicken they can hypnotize." She crossed her legs and twirled her finger in her empty shot glass. "She's a pet and rides around on John Douglas's shoulder. He calls her Meredith. Feeds her Bacardi rum at parties."

"Who is this John Douglas?"

"A friend, Daddy. Meredith's got steel-blue feathers on her neck and one beady eye that gets real mean-looking when she drinks. She's their mascot. A girl I know wears a feather in her ponytail." Without turning her head, she measured her father's interest. He drummed his fingers on the bar expectantly, his eyes sparkled, and she knew to draw the story out slow, just the way he did with his stories.

"What happened to the other eye?"

"Shriveled up like a raisin."

"I send you off to college so you can get one-red-hen drunk?" He dropped his hand onto her shoulder, licked his lips, and laughed loud. "What comes after the red hen?"

"Two-cute-ducks. Three-brown-bears. John Douglas can never make it through that game." She sucked a full drag off her cigarette and laughed along with him. Laughed and coughed at the same time. "I-shit-six-sheets," she sputtered out between coughs. "By nine, he's all messed up" — her father slapped her on the back — "nine-running-cunts, he says. Like it's some amazing thing he's just got to see."

"Whoa." Milton held his hands up as if he were stopping traffic.

Ruby stubbed out her cigarette. She looked at Milton through watering eyes. "People talk like that all the time."

"Charming," her father said. "What about Meredith?"

"Once she's drunk, John Douglas draws a chalk line on the floor and holds her good eye down to it. He holds her head about an inch above the line and everybody watches." Ruby paused. "She stays there for hours, just staring at the white line."

"Chickens are mighty stupid animals." Milton chuckled.

"Poor stupid bird," her father mocked.

"We *put* a circle of empty Coke bottles around so no one steps on her." She looked from one man to the other, her cheeks flushed with alcohol and enthusiasm. "You ought to get one for entertainment here. Draw a chalk line down the center of the bar."

"Remember your mother's chicken?" It had been a long time since Ruby thought about Albertina. "That chicken just wandered into the yard and Sally built it a little pen," Teddy was telling Milton. "She drew more pictures of that damn bird. Studies, she called them."

"Sally is a talented woman," Milton said.

Her mother had loved that bird. She'd claimed chickens were sensitive. Her father kept threatening to roast it on the Italian chicken machine. Food wandering into the yard must be rotisserized, he'd said.

"We set her free," Ruby told them. She and her mother had thrown a suitcase over Albertina and loaded her into the back of the car. She'd squawked the entire drive up the inland waterway until they unzipped the cover and set her free on a deserted stretch of road. Sally brought along five pounds of seed that she spilled to make a trail into the trees. She brought the Brownie too, to take photos of the chicken hurling herself up in attempts at flight. She was a huffy bird. Sally went back twice, but as far as Ruby knew, she never saw Albertina again. "Shouldn't we go home?" Ruby asked.

Her father passed her another nickel. "Keep your sweet self away from this John Douglas."

"I am an adult, Daddy."

He squinted, examined her with his watery eyes now gone dark, the color of thunderclouds. Next he leaned close to her fingers. "Pinch it tight, then let it fly."

How long had they been at this? Her left earring pinched. She opened and closed it against her tender lobe. John Douglas gave the earrings to her on their third date, tiny enamel bumblebees. It seemed like days ago that she'd kissed John Douglas goodbye at the train station and he'd squeezed her arm, hard. Both of them were hung over. "God damn it," he'd said. "Call me JD."

"You gonna blow, puny?" her father asked.

She started to say she was marvelous, only the word was un-wieldy and caught in her throat. It felt as if nickels careened around the inside of her skull.

"You're just like your mother. Sally is what you call a delicate drinker."

Ruby's mother was sitting at home, waiting to welcome her with coleslaw and a pile of clean clothes to take back to college. They'd better leave. Soon.

Milton handed her a clean rag and she mopped her forehead. He slid a pile of soda crackers across the bar to her.

"Sally never could drink," her father continued. "When we lived in the tent, when we were building the house, she'd barely sip brandy before she started complaining about the spins and climbed into bed. Your mother had icicles for feet. Tiniest damn feet"—he held his hands apart—"size four and a half. She'd get shoes in the little boys' department at Sears." He shook his head, grinned around the end of his pipe. The skin beneath his stubble had gone gray and loose as worn flannel.

Ruby shook the pack of Salem cigarettes, tapped it against her wrist, and then finally ripped open the entire side to get at one. She'd outgrown her mother's ridiculous shoes in the sixth grade. She struck a match and inhaled long and full. The smoke came out, wrapped around her words: "We should go home."

"We had ourselves a time. We had your sister, then you."

Ruby played with a nickel on the bar, twisting it back and forth in her fingers. She and John Douglas could be together right now. Maybe they'd have driven to the coast for the weekend. His car, with its soft leather seats, the tiny blue and red lights on the dash, reminded her of a jewelry box. Perhaps they'd have gone out for crab, laughed while the waitress fastened paper bibs around their necks, and then piled crab shells high on the table. With John Douglas, Ruby wouldn't have to hear again about her sister. When she flicked the nickel free, it shot out, glimmering in the faint light, spinning on its slender rim. The longest spin they'd had that night.

Her father watched. "It was losing Joyce that did it." The nickel slowed, teetered, and fell. He dropped his arm around Ruby's shoulder, leaned in, and kissed her cheek. "You were a baby."

She felt the sagging weight of damp armpit on her shoulder. He sipped his beer. "She's something," Teddy said to Milton, and then, staring into the mirror behind the bar, "You're something, all right. You're it." They clinked glasses and he told her to open her pocketbook. She held it beneath the lip of the bar and he swept the whole pile of nickels straight in. "A souvenir. Buy yourself some lipstick."

"Maybe I'll teach John Douglas to spin." She thought about pulling a coffee table onto the porch at the fraternity house and spinning nickels, music and light pouring out the window behind them. She'd tell funny stories about Milton and the crackers, her father's game, all to entertain her friends.

"There's nothing like having yourself a daughter to keep you up. Hoisted me more times than she knows. Now she's grown and gone. High hopes for this one."

Milton held up his beer in salute.

"Thank you, Daddy." She draped her arm around his shoulder and they both slouched over the bar.

"I know we had some ugly times." He scraped his callused hand over his chin, pausing so long she thought he'd forgotten who or what he was talking about. "Your mother and me." Her father kept staring at her in the mirror, his tone slipping into an intimacy that made her uneasy. "Your eyes are nothing like hers."

She busied herself with a tube of lipstick, avoiding him. "We'd better get home," she said, but it came out more like a question than a good idea.

"Make yourself into something. That's all that matters — if you're something and if you're happy. Right, Milt?" But Milton was down at the other end of the bar delivering beers. "I'm hanging on tight to what makes me happy." Teddy chewed on his tongue, working up to saying more. He slid his hand from her shoulder down her arm as if stroking a cat as it passed on its way out the door. "I've been keeping the family together . . . all for you, Ruby Jewel. But you're a woman now."

Looking in the mirror, she saw how they leaned together. Saw that she was drunk. She hadn't thought about what it would mean to arrive home to her mother late and drunk. Just like her father. She applied a second layer of lipstick, dropped the tube into her pocketbook, and spread her hands on the bar to brace herself.

"I love Beverly," he said, his voice flat and even, as if he were asking her to pass the salt.

Ruby's feet slipped from the barstool and one of her pumps clunked to the filthy floor. Outside it was suddenly dark. How long had it been dark? Time tricked you in the Avenue. She remembered how it had dripped past as she'd waited in the Dodge, humming to herself, while inside the bar, time had been different for her father, and now it was different for her as well. Time evaporated like a puddle, so slow you didn't notice till you looked up and all of a sudden it was gone.

"Now that you've said it, what am I supposed to do with it?" She took the pack of Dentyne from her pocketbook, unwrapped two pieces, and held one out to her father. "Let's go."

"Don't you head upstate without coming in to say goodbye now," Milton called after them as she and her father stepped into the parking lot.

Ruby lit another cigarette to clear her head for the drive home. Slumped beside her in the passenger seat, her father whispered, "Loose lips sink ships."

She ignored him, rolled down the windows to blow away the smell of whiskey. The air was cooler now and she breathed it in — the salt, the tarry smell of the baked streets, the cinnamon gum — then started the engine. Her mother would be sitting in the silent house, staring out the window at the line of white rocks that defined their yard. Maybe she'd be watching TV. The quiet grew vast. It was the same numbing, after-the-fight quiet that often filled her parents' house when she was growing up. Her father would scrub his nails with Lava soap as the start of his making-up ritual. He'd scoop Yuban into the percolator, crack an egg into his beer, and drop the shell into the coffee pot. He'd pull out a chair for her mother, a purple smudge seeping out from behind her pancake makeup. They'd eat breakfast like that; the clink of spoons against corn-flake bowls, her rueful daddy reaching out for anyone to hold his hand. When her mother actually took it, the gesture sent Ruby right out the door to swim before school. Her mother would put up with anything.

Ruby sucked at her cigarette, hollowing her cheeks, making her head go light, then lifted her chin and exhaled into the night. Quiet like this brought her to the edge of a gaping hole. "We're a couple of real bastards." She looked over at her father. His eyes were closed and she thought he was asleep. "Hey," she barked, poking his ribs.

"We bought steaks," he said.

She pulled the truck right up onto the lawn and jumped from her seat. The front door was locked. She knocked lightly, calling out in a singsong voice, "Mother. Mother." She kept knocking, gradually with more force. Her father's door slammed behind her. "Mom," she called, her voice an apology. She wanted her mother to open the door to her alone. Her mother had to see her without her father there, as if her being alone would make a difference. As if her being alone would invite forgiveness. "Mommy," she pleaded.

Her father pounded the door with his flat hand. "Sal. Your daughter's home."

The lock clicked and the door swung open. Sally stood there, light spilling onto the stoop around her, showing through her nightgown, revealing her slight legs. Her hair was different. New bangs skimmed her forehead. Little gold flowers dotted her ears. Neither her coral lipstick nor her wan smile hid the disappointment lingering at the corners of her mouth. She must have finally given up, turned off Steve Allen, and decided to change for bed when they knocked on the door. Shame blossomed in Ruby's chest.

"Ruby, honey." Her mother sighed, drawing her daughter into her arms. Ruby rested her cheek on her mother's shoulder, breathed in the lily of the valley perfume, felt worry and relief — worry over how she must smell, relief for her mother's stiff warmth.

"You must be hungry, Mom. We brought steaks."

Teddy pushed past them. "I'll light the coals."

Sally stepped back, examined her daughter. Ruby hastily smoothed her hair. She ran her tongue under her lips, around the inside of her mouth. She wanted a mirror, a comb, and a toothbrush.

Sally's smile sagged with reproach. "Your father knows where I keep the aspirin."

"In the cupboard, above the percolator," Teddy hollered on his way out the back door.

Her mother set the suitcase on the spare bed in Ruby's room.

"So, here I am, Mom."

Sally turned her back to Ruby, clicked open the suitcase, and began shaking out the clothing, separating it into three piles, dark, light, and white. Her arms dipped and retrieved, rising and falling, her naked arm flesh jiggling with the motion. Ruby leaned against the wall, waiting for her mother to ask a question. "I'm sorry to be late, Mom." She hated that she kept saying *Mom*, as if it made her a better daughter. As if she should have to be a better daughter. She was in college now. Making her own decisions. "You don't have to do that." In the silence that followed, she picked up the alarm clock from the nightstand and slowly wound it. The room — with its seashell lamp, swim trophies, and magazines on the desk, the red pencils in a Hellmann's jar, the stretched and puckered swimsuits hanging from the doorknob — was quaint, like an exhibit.

Not one thing here seemed to be part of Ruby's new life. Not her mother's narrow stooped shoulders or her bony fingers checking over a paisley blouse as if she could discover something about Ruby's new life in a missing white button. "Stop. I said I could do that."

Sally paused, and then dropped the blouse in the darks pile. "Your dad will be wanting steak sauce, I suppose." Each word seemed to be marching out of her mouth on tired feet.

Ruby switched from remorse to frustration in a single tick. "And you'll be making it, I suppose." Closing her eyes, she wound the clock tighter. "I have a boyfriend now. He buys me flowers." She kept turning the key. Turning the key until she felt the pop beneath the metal backing.

Before she went to the kitchen to mix up ketchup, garlic powder, diced onions, honey, vinegar, and dry mustard, Sally touched Ruby's shoulder. "I have learned to shift my expectations. You'll learn that some things in life you just have to put up with."

Ruby swallowed down two words: *Bev* and *never*.

Her mother's kiss was light and dry against Ruby's cheek. "Don't take it so hard. I still love you."

Through her bedroom window, Ruby watched her father squirt too much lighter fluid on the coals. When he struck the match, a blaze flashed momentarily brilliant. Soon the three of them would sit at the kitchen table and Ruby would reach for her mother's hand, tell her a different set of stories about college.

Alone as She Felt All Day

RUBY DREW THE BLINDS apart with her fingers, peered out at Ira leaning against the giant mimosa tree in the brick courtyard. Beautiful and funny and absolutely the wrong boy. His white shirt, the pink blossoms, and the feathery green leaves were all muted by the lead weight of the sky. Thunderstorms were likely. The blinds escaped her fingers and snapped back into place. Sighing, Ruby returned to her hard plastic chair. A mocking illustration of a pink uterus with elegant fallopian tubes, an egg floating lazily downstream, was taped to the wall in front of her. HEALTHY REPRODUCTIVE SYSTEM the diagram proclaimed. She shifted her gaze to the carpet, which was as gray as the sky.

Ira had insisted on joining her. He wanted a chance to play doting husband, to hold her hand and call her snookums, as if anyone would believe his act. As if this weren't serious. Since Marco was neither available nor aware of the situation, she preferred to find out alone. When she relived this scene, she wanted to have nobly taken the news solo. The nurse knocked once, then strode in, crisp and precise. One hand rested on her square, uniformed hip, the other clasped Ruby's chart. Her face was impassive.

"Your test came back positive." A heavy line of bangs created a horizon across her forehead. Her eyes bored into Ruby, waiting for a response before committing to any emotion. When Ruby held her face in her hands and asked if the nurse was certain the rabbit had died, the nurse's tone revealed neither support nor enthusiasm. "We don't use those terms anymore. But yes. Absolutely."

The ceiling seemed to drop down onto Ruby's head, giving her a crushing headache. Squeezing her eyes shut, as if that could somehow protect her from the news, she quit breathing, crossed and then re-crossed her legs, grabbed at the fabric of her suddenly too tight skirt and tugged it down her thighs. Orange juice mixed with the bitter taste of aspirin burned the back of her throat. All the symptoms of early pregnancy, symptoms she'd learned about in health class, symptoms she had misread as hangovers, announced themselves. She was exhausted and sick to her stomach.

"When was your last period?"

"I'm sorry?"

"Your last menstruation was when?" The nurse paused, her efficient pen poised expectantly over the forms. Her unfaltering gaze, the pristine whites of her eyes, nailed Ruby to her chair.

"June? Maybe May."

"You found nothing unusual about your absent cycle?"

She'd missed her period before. Living on Frosted Flakes and Manhattans with two cherries all summer long, she thought she was too skinny to bleed. The crests of her hipbones pleased her. They flared like conch shells beneath her skin, and she liked to imagine Marco pressing his ear to her, telling her he could hear the ocean.

"Judging from the hormone levels in your blood, you're into your second trimester. Would you like to call your husband?" It was a challenge, not an offer. Ruby had seen the woman take in her bare ring finger.

Ruby swallowed and shook her head no. She was salivating uncontrollably. She hated the way the nurse used the capped end of her pen to sweep her bangs aside.

The nurse continued speaking, her mouth opening and closing, stringing words together.

Ruby had begun to pace. She clutched her elbows in opposite hands to keep from shaking. She wanted the appointment to be over, to leave the nurse and the room without crying, without tearing the damn uterus off the wall.

"Your baby has a beating heart," the nurse offered, calm and clear and definite.

Now Ruby heard it. A tiny, tiny pulse, like the start of a headache. Yes, she understood all the implications.

"Do you have a cigarette?" Ruby asked, her voice faltering.

"Miss Hargrove, surely you must have suspected?" The nurse walked to the window and parted the blinds. She jabbed her pen toward Ira. "Would you like to bring the father in?"

The revolving door cast Ruby out into the courtyard with the mimosa tree and Ira. He took one look at her pale and stricken face, held a fresh cigarette to his glowing cherry, and then passed it off to her as she came to his side.

"Poor bunny."

She inhaled a long, thirsty drag, her hand shaking.

"Honey, come here." Ira held his arms wide to encircle her. Ruby stiffened. She felt stringy, dried up, her muscles tough as jerky, and she had to stay that way. Were she to soften, to accept any small kindness, there would be no pulling away from a disastrous plunge.

"Don't talk to me," she whispered. Each time she brought the cigarette to her lips, her hand shook a little less, and when it was sucked down to the butt, she was still.

"Look, we can find someone to take care of this."

"I'm too far gone."

"You want to call anybody? We could go back to the bar and you could call *him*." Ira gave a halfhearted operatic flair to the *him*. They'd been performing the *him* aria all summer at the Flamingo Pond. When the bar's phone rang, they'd belt out, *It's him,* and then fight over who should answer, each hoping for a particular boy on the other end of the line. Of course it never was Marco. "Is he still in Europe?"

"Last time I saw him he wouldn't even stay for breakfast." Her heart beat against her ribs just as it had the morning she watched Marco pull on his blue jeans, even out his shirttails, and button from the bottom up. She watched from bed, wrapped in sheets that smelled of sex, sour and metallic. "He just got up, and kissed my forehead." All their partings made her anxious. "Didn't even tell me he was leaving for Europe." It was the first time she'd admitted his omission to herself or to anyone else. Until now she'd tried to tell herself she just hadn't heard him say it, or it had slipped his mind.

The wind picked up bits of leaves, paper scraps, and fallen petals from the brick courtyard. She watched the debris rise and then collapse.

"What about your parents?"

"That's a joke. My dad's too busy being a prick and my mom's too busy letting him. It's all melodrama. I don't know what . . ." It started to rain. "Shit." The clouds broke open the way they do in Florida in August and within seconds they were drenched. Steam rose up from the ground in front of them. She smeared her bangs off her forehead. "Ira, see you at the Pond. I've got to walk."

"Wait. I've got nowhere to be." This was an event for him, a chance to be loyal.

She patted his wet shirt to show she didn't question his sincerity. "No, I'll be in later." She held her cheek out for him to kiss. "Thanks for coming."

Her feet slapped one in front of the other down the buckling sidewalk, past the pastel clapboard houses with weathervanes and widow's walks. Did women throw themselves from roofs? She imagined herself, hand shielding her eyes from the sun, a dress blowing about her legs, gazing out to sea for a sight of Marco's boat. And when he didn't return, she would have the sympathy of neighbors.

Where was the dignity in rejection? Slogging through the puddles she felt trapped by her own healthy, busy reproductive system.

The last time she'd seen Marco he'd arrived on a Friday night, late, and they'd spent two days in bed. She was studying for her English literature final, warning herself that he probably wouldn't call. That it was just as well he hadn't invited her to his parents' home for his graduation dinner, she had exams anyway. Then he'd knocked. The knot of his tie loosened, his breath sweet with vino santo, he leaned against her doorjamb, grinning so wide his gums showed slick and pink. His arms were loaded with supplies from his parents' Italian market: Chianti, dry salami, Romano cheese, bread, and her favorite, a large red tin of amaretti cookies.

"I'm starving," he said. "Are you?"

Opening the door just a few inches, she filled the space with her body, as if she had something to conceal.

He peeked over her shoulder. "You have a surprise in there for me?" He leaned in very, very close and said, "I've saved a surprise for you too."

"Have you?" she asked, cocking an eyebrow, suppressing a smile. If only she hadn't let him in. If only she'd made him wait. If she hadn't let him kiss her collarbone, press his knee between her legs, and whisper, leaning into her, "I've missed you."

"At least you knocked with your elbows." She took the cookie tin from his hands and pulled him in. "I was getting bored."

The sheet rested on her bent knees and covered them both completely, like a child's fort, turning the light beneath soft and opaque. Her skin, she knew, would be lovely as cream, and she hoped he noticed. With Marco leaning over her, poised to touch her, she felt she could breathe his exhalations, feel her own breath catch at the back of her throat when he pushed inside of her. She felt herself slipping, her chin and heart lifting toward him, his arm wrapped tight around her back. When Marco came, he moaned a combination plea and exaltation. She listened for her name, for love, but heard only syllables.

Her tiny dorm mattress, squeezed into a corner, left them no space. Their bodies wedged tightly together, he slept and she crammed Dickens, delicately turning the pages so she wouldn't disturb his arm tossed over her shoulder. Her prescription, which she'd meant to fill the day before, which she would absolutely fill on Monday, was in the bottom of her pocketbook. Surely, she'd reasoned, missing one, two pills at the very most, wouldn't make a difference. Between naps and sex, she fed him cookies, licking crumbs from his lips, tossing wrappers on the floor. Monday morning, when she wanted to go out for coffee and poached eggs, he buttoned his shirt. "I'll call you."

Even if she knew how to reach him now, what would she say? She imagined him on a Vespa, on a cobblestone lane, his collar blown open by the wind, his teeth flashing in the sunlight. How could he even hear her calling, see her waving at him from the sidewalk, saying, "Marco, I'm pregnant"? She could imagine herself neither in Europe nor pregnant. It was only over the telephone that she could imagine telling him, a long black cord snaking over a fluffy, down-covered bed, the Alps out the window, the phone clutched in his hand, his face horrified as he listened to her distant mousy voice bothering him in his hotel room all the way across the Atlantic.

She fought to light another cigarette in the rain. At this moment she needed to be outside her own life. She thought if she could pull far enough away, imagine her life was a movie, she might know what she was supposed to do. She pictured her own wet hair, gamine face free of makeup, drenched blouse clinging to her breasts, thin wrists, fingers striking the soggy match tip until all the red was worn away, tears mingling with rain. She was scared and furious and stupid. Poor little match girl. Water dripped into her shoes, and she could think only in fucking clichés? The rain showed no signs of letting up and she was still blocks from the hotel room she'd rented in June, planning to stay only until September, when she would return to school. Her father had hung up on her when she told him she wouldn't be home for the summer. He needed her in the house, as a buffer, someone to speak to her mother for him, as in *Tell Mrs. Put-Upon I'll be late*. If she called home with this news, her father would explode with loud disappointment. At the very least, couldn't someone as smart as Ruby have chosen some original path to screw everything up? Ultimately he'd take it out on her mother, who would absorb everything with quiet disappointment.

The neon tuna beacon of the Blue Fin Motel blinked at her from the roof. For forty-five dollars a month, her room came equipped with a hot plate, an icebox, and once-a-week fresh sheets. She kicked her pumps off at the door, abandoning them next to the bathing suit she'd dropped yesterday after her swim when she was still just Ruby, a cocktail waitress at the Pond, summering in the Keys, waiting for classes and another chance with Marco. Sitting on the edge of her unmade bed, surrounded by damp towels and flat pillows, an electric fan short one blade on the windowsill, she was overwhelmed by how pathetic her summer, and now her life, had become. Even if the nurse hadn't told her about the beating heart, she still would have been terrified by the alternative, pain and blood. Death. She watched herself unbutton her blouse in the bureau mirror. Her wet hair, clinging to her skin, looked greasy, as if she'd totally let herself go. Tears fell down her cheeks to her neck and admirably fuller breasts. Rain clattered on the metal roof. A fresh pack of cigarettes sat on the nightstand. She lit one, stared in the mirror at the pretty girl alone in the depressing room.

It was still raining when she woke up, though not as hard. She was chilled, and her mouth tasted of stale cigarettes. The bedspread did little to warm her. She lay there, staring at the phone, willing it to ring, though she knew if it did it would only be Ira, checking in. She couldn't stay trapped and dejected in this room all day. She couldn't become someone whose life was defined by accidents. She'd already let that occur by thinking Marco would have a plan for their summer, and here she was, alone in the Keys. Certainly she had choices.

In the bathroom, she vigorously brushed her teeth, then peeled her skirt down her hips. Red ridges were carved into her flesh from the zipper and the waistband. If she wanted to wear this skirt in the near future, she was going to have to take over, trick her own body. It was simple, really. She'd wear herself out, move furniture, throw herself down stairs. Miscarriages were common; her own mother had had two. She would start right now. She pulled on her swimsuit, ran the four blocks to the beach, and plunged in. The ocean, compared to the rain, was warm. She dove through waves and was quickly past the shore break, pushing herself, waiting for the moment when she could no longer touch bottom and was simply taking her daily swim, supported by the hammock of deep water. She concentrated on the mechanics of her own body, the pivot of her shoulder joints as her arms circled through air and then water. Straining forward, she felt muscles stretch across her abdomen and hips. She kicked hard, straight-legged, fighting against the choppy sea. As her heart beat with the exertion, she thought she could hear blood speeding through her veins. She could see it too; each time she turned her head to breathe deep, salty gasps, she could see her blood in the private red sky behind her eyelids. A tide of blood flowed through her body, and she willed just a little to flow out between her legs.

At the mile buoy, she turned in a slow circle, treading water. The beach, empty of umbrellas and beachcombers, was a sandy smudge. To the right, a jetty thrust out, one solid line of rock until it disappeared in water dark as the sky. The horizon had vanished.

How easily her problems would evaporate if she just stayed out here with everything so impossibly far away. Gone. Empty and gone. Everything stretched away from her; the sound of wind and water filled her ears, stopped her thoughts, covered the sound of her gasps as she struggled to avoid swallowing water, and then her mouth was full of it, salt stung the back of the throat and she panicked, turned her face straight upward. The buoy swayed heavily nearby, its bell clanging, loud and forsaken, with each swell.

Water the color of bourbon gushed from the tub spout. She ran it hot as she could bear, hoping to raise her core temperature, to make her body inhospitable. To that end, she poured herself a glass of vodka as well. Her legs and ass itched terribly from the heat as she hunched in the tub, forcing herself to take it. She ate maraschino cherries out of the jar she'd pilfered from work, dropping the stems into the bath, one after another. With a rusty Brillo pad she'd found under the sink, she scrubbed at her legs and arms, her abdomen, thinking heat would seep in easily through wide-open pores. Once, Marco had scrubbed her back in the shower. She'd pressed her hands flat against the tiles as he soaped her all over. They'd made love there, her hands pushing her against Marco's chest, the water pouring down into her open mouth. She ran her palms over her chest, cupped her breasts the way Marco had, only now they were tender; had they been this sore yesterday or was it knowledge that made them ache? Cherry stems and soapsuds floated around her in the bath. Her hands explored her belly. It had always been soft, a layer of baby fat just below her bellybutton. Soon the skin would be stretched taut, itching, leaving marks. Down her hips her hands stroked, and then between her legs, inside her. She felt her cervix with the tip of her finger, rubbery and tight as a fist. Never had she been so accommodating, so passive as she was with Marco. It hadn't always been so; at first she was self-assured, happy to have him fetch her a drink, light her cigarette, sneak into her dorm, beg her roommate to leave for half an hour. When Marco had become aloof, his time taken up with vague obligations, he unhinged her.

She finally stood, her legs wobbly, whether from the vodka, the heat, or the swim, it didn't matter. She gripped the towel rack to steady herself. Wisps of steam rose from her red and chapped body. If there had been a snowbank outside, she would have dived in. Instead, she turned the shower on cold and shivered beneath it for as long as she could stand, and then she made herself count slowly to ten.

She smoothed her sheets and blankets, jammed dirty clothes into a pillowcase, hung the towels and her swimsuit, lined up her shoes along the bottom of the closet. By six thirty, the time she had to leave for work, she was exhausted.

Her black bolero uniform fit — one good thing. Before she left she slipped a tampon into her purse, just in case.

Uncle Iggy's tubby back was the first thing she saw every night when she arrived at work. That and his cocktail-onion head parked at the bar near the waitress station, where all night long he popped olives and offered advice. Tonight was no different except for his baby blue party hat with festive cursive claiming IT'S A BOY!

"Kitty cat . . . She's here." Ira sported a pink IT'S A GIRL! hat at a jaunty angle on his forehead. He grinned behind the bar and held up a bottle of cold duck.

The door closed behind her but she made no move to enter. Uncle Iggy, his plump white hand clutching a Gibson, his hat crooked on his slippery head, was smiling shyly. "You're okay?" He swallowed a mouthful of salted peanuts. "I worry, you know." It was the first time since she'd found out that anyone had looked her straight in the eye and asked how she was. She swallowed hard, blinked.

A balloon bouquet hung at the corner of the bar with IT'S A

BOY! and IT'S A GIRL! balloons all in a crazy mix. "I didn't know what to do when I watched you schlep off in the rain. I thought you could use a new point of view, so . . . voilà!" Ira leaned over the bar, held out a handful of dimes. "Go put on the Lady Diana or something. Make us move while I pop the cork." He continued in a stage whisper. "I had to tell him." He twitched his head toward Uncle Iggy, who as far as she knew was nobody's uncle.

"You realize how completely fucked up this is?" Her voice shrill, she waved her freckled arm in a grand gesture, taking in the entire Pond. The kidney-shaped bar with glasses hanging in easy reach, the plastic flamingos perched around the edge of the scuffed black-and-white dance floor, the sticky pink vinyl booths, and now the glossy balloons. Uncle Iggy slid the hat from his head and crushed it in his hands. "I've known for exactly seven hours."

"Any excuse for a party?" Ira said, his voice tipping up at the end. "Look, I'm sorry, I just didn't want you moping around all night."

She grabbed the dimes, went to the jukebox, selected the Supremes and then Mel Tormé for Uncle Iggy. Ira flipped the switch for the mirror ball, and bits of light sputtered along the walls. The Pond was empty except for the three of them and a couple of bored, sunburned tourists who had stumbled in to get out of the rain. "Come on, kitten, take this." Ira held out a champagne flute.

"I deserve to mope."

"And you're so good with that lower-lip thing." He wrapped his arm around her shoulder and squeezed as if all she'd suffered was a pulled tendon. The full implications, what this meant to her real life—things like parents, and school, and Marco, things that kept crowding in on her—all that stuff obviously escaped him. But here at the Pond, Ira was her only friend; he and Uncle Iggy were the only people she knew.

She tilted her head back and swallowed the entire glass. "You know, my mother had two miscarriages."

He refilled her glass too fast. "A toast then." Bubbles, vigorous and delicate, foamed up and over the sides onto her fingers. "To miscarriage."

She gulped this glass down just as quickly as the first. Ira caught her, swiveled, shimmied, and snapped his fingers. He was long and lithe, made for dancing; she was limp and dizzy and bloated and tired and pregnant — expecting, with child, knocked up, a bun in the oven, preggers — there was a parade of words that could describe her state. Through two songs they passed the champagne bottle back and forth between them like a third partner. The tingling started in her feet and spread up her legs to her pelvis, across her belly and breasts, to her armpits. Her scalp prickled.

"There's a bloom in her cheeks," Uncle Iggy called out. Mel Tormé singing about April in Paris brought him to his feet, and he swept her into his arms. With his soft hand at her back and his amazingly nimble feet, he guided her around the floor.

"Why, Uncle Iggy." She smiled at his agility, rested her head on his shoulder. All summer he'd been looking out for her. Making sure she ate, walking her home when she'd had too much to drink.

"Promise me you won't try anything risky?"

"I can't," she said.

"What do you mean? Of course you can. It would be dangerous and wrong." He gripped her hand. His stomach pressing into hers made her wonder what it would be like to dance with him in a few months when they both had bellies.

"I mean I can't try anything. I'm too far along."

Uncle Iggy lived alone. As far as she knew, he did the same things every day. Read, walked, gardened, and came to the Pond to nurse three Gibsons.

"I want you to remember, I go home to a television."

"How's that supposed to make me feel better?" His was just the first in a long line of opinions that would come at her. Everyone would have one. When she finally told, and she would have to tell, her life wouldn't be her own. Ira was right. She needed this party.

Ira clanged the bell at the bar. "We've got customers."

A birthday celebration blew in and she clustered tables together along the edge of the dance floor. They were loud and sloppy-drunk, swaying in their seats, dancing in a clump to Chuck Berry. Any other night, she would have insinuated herself into the group, swayed her hips while balancing a tray full of cocktails, charming them with her customer service. But tonight, she felt graceless, both heavy and hollow, like a pumpkin, solid in your arms but light enough to float.

It was the second to last Friday of the summer. The Pond kept busy with heavily drinking holidayers desperate to connect before the season ended. Men sent drinks across the bar, lit cigarettes off the butts of the last, and rubbed up against each other on the dance floor. Ruby and her reproductive system were completely irrelevant to the scene. She kept imagining cramps, hoping for damp, rusty spots in her underpants. In the bathroom, she slid the tampon in just to see, and for most of the evening, she thought about it, felt it, invested it with all her hope. She nursed a Manhattan until Uncle Iggy filled the glass with orange juice. The birthday party kept drinking. He ordered her French fries. In between serving cocktails and complaining about her headache, she gobbled the fries down. He ordered her a second, greasy plate. When she took two aspirin from his palm, she thought of her mother's kitchen and the bottle of Bayer aspirin Sally kept above the percolator. Her mother might still be up if she decided to call.

She never acknowledged Uncle Iggy looking out for her. She just took the juice, fries, and aspirin. When she remembered to thank him, after the party left, chattering like a flock of birds, and only a couple of boys in Marlon Brando T-shirts leaned toward each other at the opposite end of the bar, Uncle Iggy had already gone home. Ira was folding the boys' tab into an origami crane to flutter down before them. Nobody wanted to go home alone.

"I," she said. "Give me a smoke?"

He flicked the package of Salem cigarettes toward her, never shifting his gaze from the boys.

She held on to the dime, standing in front of the pay phone for the length of the entire cigarette before placing her call. She imagined the abrupt jangle of the telephone in her mother's kitchen. Her mom curled up beneath the blankets with her back to the window, her father's old pipe propping it open. His side of the bed would be empty. He slept in a chair; better for his back, he claimed.

"Hello." It was her father's gruff voice. The operator spoke in an official voice. Ruby closed her eyes. The last time she'd talked to her father, she'd told him she wasn't coming home for the summer. "What?" He coughed one dry, deep cough, like a door slamming. "What'd you say?"

"Will you accept a collect call from Ruby?"

He cleared his throat and she felt hers constrict. The last time, he'd hissed about all he'd given up for her, who he'd given up for her.

"Sir, will you accept the charges?"

The last time, he'd said that because of her he was stuck in a shithole of a life and she couldn't even come home to her own goddamned mother. Ruby spoke over the operator's request. "Daddy, it's me." She pressed her free arm across her stomach. "Daddy, please." He didn't respond. "Get Mom."

"Sir?"

"Get Mom," she said, squeezing the phone in her hand.

"I'm sorry, miss. I'm going to have to disconnect you."

"Don't disconnect this phone." She found she was sobbing. "Get Mom! Daddy, please."

"Sir, will you accept the charges?"

"I'm pregnant."

"Sir?" Simultaneous with the words, his line clicked off.

Her forehead pressed against the wall, Ruby held on to the quiet phone. After a moment, the operator asked, "Miss? Is there anyone else I can connect you with?" Her voice had gone soft, conciliatory. Now someone else knew.

Ruby could hear Ira and the two boys laughing and charming the pants off one another at the bar. When she finally returned the receiver to its cradle, her dime clattered into the coin box.

Ruby slid a rag down the bar top, stopped beside Ira. He was singing and performing a little merengue step in front of the cash register, making change for the cigarette machine.

"Those two are delicious." He drew her attention to the two boys with big white smiles, the seams of their forearms, the flesh pressed against flesh.

"Which one do you like?" she whispered.

Ira gestured with his chin toward the blond. "I think I'm in love."

"I'll see what I can do for your cause." Before she stepped their way, she kissed Ira on the cheek. "Thanks for the party." The phone call was something she couldn't talk about just yet.

Ruby plucked a bottle of vodka from the well, poured shots for the boys and for herself. "Drinks?" She removed her bolero jacket and stood before them in her white blouse. "You have no idea about my day." She exaggerated the task of unclasping her bra through the cheap silky fabric, then slipped a hand inside the neckline, over her collarbone, easily sliding the strap over her elbow and wrist. She repeated the gesture with the other strap and slowly extricated her pink lace bra from her sleeve. "Much better." She sighed.

The dark-eyed boy held his lighter and an unlit cigarette. "Are you a magician's assistant?"

"What shall we drink to?" she asked, taking the cigarette and holding it in the flame. She blew the smoke out the side of her mouth, away from the longest eyelashes she had ever seen wasted on a man.

He paused, held up his glass, and said, "There are no little things."

"At least, not among present company," Ira said, coming over. On the cusp of blitzed, he clinked heartily with the blond's shot glass and swallowed his vodka down.

"Nothing counts, right?" Ruby closed her eyes, brought her glass to her lips, and flung her head back dramatically. She didn't care about anything. With Mr. Eyelashes watching, she held her head back longer than necessary and then stroked the empty shot glass down her neck and chest. When she finally lowered her head and opened her eyes, he would be staring at her.

His blond friend had been denied the forearm contact but Ira was leaning in, eagerly filling the vacuum.

Stepping backward along the bar, her dime still in her hand, she sashayed out onto the dance floor and slipped the coin into the jukebox.

Mr. Eyelashes followed and they danced to Percy Faith.

"So, are you ready for summer to end?" he asked, his lips brushing against her ear.

"Shh." She held her finger in front of his soft mouth. "Do you like girls or boys?"

He pressed against her, entwined his fingers with hers, and despite tender breasts, Ruby pressed back. "I'm flexible," he answered.

Even in the smoky bar she could smell his aftershave, toasty, like buttered popcorn and rum. He'd applied it for someone else, and now it was for her. She decided she needed him to kiss her before the song ended.

"I like the way you smell," she said.

He leaned down; his lips were thin and he pushed his tongue past her teeth. The surprising thing was how cold his mouth felt inside. "What about the way I taste?"

"Nothing I can't fix." She kissed him again, slowly warming his mouth with her tongue. "Now you taste like me."

They left the Pond hand in hand and walked through the alley toward her hotel. The air was thick enough to chew, the way it got after a storm. Rotting orange peels and wet cardboard cartons scented the night, made it seem lush, alive.

"It smells like cells are dividing all around us."

"Which are you, a magician's assistant or a scientist?" he asked.

She laughed, bitter and forced as a whip crack. The sound alarmed her. Worried she might frighten him away, she squeezed his hand and didn't let go. Once at her room, they wasted no time undressing, were quickly, suddenly naked together on her bed, groping and thrusting, two strangers pleasing themselves. She never once opened her eyes, and when they were finished, he fell asleep. Ruby stayed awake a long time, looking out the window at the cars in the parking lot. Four people wandered down the sidewalk singing "Jingle Bells." A bottle smashed and they laughed. A sliver of moon drifted out from behind the clouds, its light reflected off the wet pavement. She hoped sex would bring on cramps, though she knew that, along with everything else she had tried, this would not make her bleed. This was happening to her.

Much later in the night, he pulled her toward his warm body.

"You're cold," he whispered. Holding her in his arms, he kissed her softly. "Hey, it's okay. I promise, everything will be okay."

Free to a Good Home

ON THE WAY BACK from Chinatown, they stopped to share a carton of kung pao pork on an abandoned sofa. FREE TO A GOOD HOME claimed a torn cardboard sign. With an unflattering grunt, Ruby lowered herself down, then lifted her swollen feet onto the ugly tweed cushions. Marco, dropping peanuts from the chopsticks into his open mouth, circled the couch and kicked the curved wooden legs as if he were testing tires. Aside from a large cigarette burn and a certain wilted-cabbage awfulness, the couch was fine, and he saw no reason not to drag it home to their apartment. For months Ruby and Marco had been collecting abandoned furniture off the sidewalks of New York City. Ruby also picked up odds and ends at secondhand stores, things she found on her own while Marco worked at his new job, insurance adjuster, in an uncle's office. They filled their three rooms with battered mahogany dining chairs, a lime-green Formica table, and a utility-wire spool they used as a coffee table. The only new item they owned — a Humpty Dumpty lamp — Ruby's mother had purchased with nine Green Stamp books. Ruby called what they were doing nesting. When Marco called it temporary, she assumed he was referring to the furnishings.

He flipped the burned cushion and then stepped back, squinting at the sofa and at pregnant Ruby. He had long legs, wide shoulders, and a solid neck, yet he was surprisingly thin. In college Marco had wanted to play football but was unable to gain the twenty-two pounds the coach insisted on before he would put him out on the field. Now Marco thought his admirable physique would serve him well onstage, which was another reason he and Ruby were in New York, for him to pursue this new dream. Ruby squinted back at him. Even through the haze of her eyelashes, his face seemed hard, eyebrows like dark gashes on his forehead, high cheekbones, and a hatchet-straight nose, all of it unreadable. All but his deep red lips, slick with oil; they were curved, tender, and generous. She hoped their child got his lips.

"It's functional," he said.

"It's scratchy." Everything made Ruby itch. Her skin was stretched to capacity, taut and dry over her belly, tight over her expanded thighs. Even her ankles itched.

He gestured for her to move her feet and then plunked down beside her. "We'll wait." What he meant was, they'd wait for someone to help them get the sofa off the street. And of course help would walk by; Marco had that kind of luck. He'd always had that kind of luck — winning door prizes, finding five dollars in the gutter, suffering only sprains. Marco inhabited a generous universe. Now that they were living together, soon to marry, Ruby wondered if she could claim some of his luck as her own. After all, Marco had called her when he returned from his summer abroad. They'd decided, together with both sets of parents, that under the unfortunate circumstances, it would be best to move to New York and make a go of it. Her mother was relieved that the move put Ruby near her aunt and uncle — just in case. Ruby would not be alone. And surely constant proximity to Marco gave Ruby some license to his luck.

After twenty minutes, two teenage boys eagerly accepted three dollars and half a pack of Lucky Strikes to drag the sofa two blocks to their apartment. Ruby waddled behind. Her hips had grown so wide she supposed there really was no other way to describe her walk, though the first time Marco said it, he hurt her feelings. Twilight rushed at them along with the throng of office workers. Streetlights came on; hatted men, clutching briefcases and their girls' elbows, hurried for cabs or for the subway, hurried toward cocktail hour and dinner, toward life after work. The women wore suits with tight skirts and pumps that reminded Ruby of the shoes her aunt had sent from Bergdorf's when Ruby went away to college. She wondered about office life and belts. Would she ever wear a belt again? A young man in a brown suit, the same color as their new sofa, held a cab door for his date, his hand guiding the small of her back. He slid in beside her, tossed his cigarette into the gutter with the candy wrappers, a tattered page from the *Times*, and the last of the autumn leaves.

Soon it would snow. Drifts would entomb the tree trunks, and she and Marco would have the baby. She imagined holding an infant, looking out the window at the quiet street, the snow absorbing the sound of traffic, reflecting light, remaking the world, clean and new. Behind her on the stove, a yellow kettle would whistle, ready to warm the baby's bottle. When she thought of the months ahead, that was the fullest moment she could imagine, clear light, the whistle from the kettle, the baby real in her arms. The two of them, alone in the apartment. Today the November light fell pale and flat, as if the entire day was flu-ish. She scooped the last of the rice into her mouth, burped up spicy pork. Kung pao was Marco's favorite.

The sofa was preposterously large, and even among the menagerie of accumulated furniture in their living room, it was awkward. Again, Ruby spent the evening home alone. She arranged a chenille bedspread over the sofa and shoved it from one wall to another, heaving against its bulk with the backs of her thighs. Her belly was too big, and the sofa too unwieldy, to move it any other way. Marco came home late from auditions most nights, his shirt smelling of smoke, his breath sweet and medicinal, like mouthwash. If anyone knew the smell of a bar, it was Ruby. For now, it was enough that he came home at all. It was only late at night, when he returned and sat on the edge of their bed, removing his shoes in the dark, that she was brave enough to mention the future.

"Classifieds have plenty of secretarial jobs."

He held her ankle, his fingers firm against her skin.

"We can pay someone, or maybe my aunt could help out."

"Meep," he said. She never knew why or where the name came from, she was just Meep. Like a private joke he had with himself. Now when he said it, his voice was a cocktail of frustration and resentment. "Meep. It's not my time." He just wasn't ready. And neither was she. They could stay together, keep trying, if it was just the two of them. "I brought papers. From an agency. Someone I know knows someone who used them. They have good families." He loved her, he said. Yes, he did. He had made an appointment. This is what he hoped for.

His hand grew tight around her ankle, shifted from reassuring to insistent to forceful, his fingers sinking into her swollen flesh. She would say anything to bring him beneath the blankets beside her. The truth was, the only thing that terrified Ruby more than the idea of giving up the baby was the idea of giving up Marco. No matter what, she lost.

Now she had the sofa lodged in front of the window. She was acting out her mother's game, as if finding the exact sweet spot for the sofa was the key to everything working out. Sally had been re-arranging the furniture back at home for the past five years, lighting one cigarette off the butt of the last. Ruby wanted a cigarette too, but Marco had given the last of theirs to the boys who wrestled the sofa up the stairs. She tucked the bedspread beneath the cushions, just so. A weighty exhaustion swept up from the soles of her bare feet, overtaking her, as if someone, her mother, was pressing her down with hot, heavy hands, ironing her flat onto the furniture. This is how a doorstop must feel, dull and immovable.

She pulled their sun-baked curtains closed, the fabric so brittle in her hands her fingernail pushed through, as easily as paper. Ruby dragged her fingernail all the way down, one long satisfying slit. Pregnancy had made her nails strong. She gave herself frequent manicures, filing them into ovals and polishing them icy pink. She pushed her nail through again, another long slit, then another, and another, shredding the curtains. More than anything, she wanted to be free of this crappy apartment, free of her huge body, out with Marco, drinking a Manhattan in Manhattan.

When she woke in the dark with a fist clenching inside of her, she knew it was too soon. First she tried holding perfectly still, as if she could trick the pains into stopping, and for a time they did. But when the gripping started again, she sat up, lay back down, rolled over, and tucked a pillow between her thighs. She kept re-arranging herself on the sofa until the clenching fist turned into a hot vise. Maybe peeing would help. On the toilet, Ruby curled herself around the pains, and that was the first place she cried out. Her voice, a sharp yelp in the tiny bathroom, terrified her. Marco wasn't even home yet. She hadn't made any kind of a decision. She paced the apartment, went back to the sofa, drew her knees to her enormous belly until that too became unbearable. Where was Marco?

"Please," she panted as another pain gripped her low back. "I'm not ready. Stop."

Brakes hissed on the street below their window, a panel-truck door rattled open, and a stack of newspapers thumped onto the sidewalk. It was the thump that made her scream. The thump of morning. Marco still wasn't home, and when the next pain slammed into her, she felt a warm gush between her legs.

The nun wrapped a hot-water bottle in flannel and denied her co-deine. Her thick, practical fingers massaged Ruby's belly. The fun-dus, she called it. Apparently having the baby didn't change everything; Ruby's fundus bulged and surged with cramps as if it held a life of its own, as if she hadn't given birth two days ago. Marco had found Ruby on all fours, huffing and crying in the center of their apartment. His face went pale when he saw blood on her nightgown, and he kept repeating "I'm sorry," as if it made a difference. Down the stairs of their third-floor walkup, waiting for the cab and driving uptown: "I'm so sorry. I'm sorry." He brought her into St. Vincent's, his arm wrapped around her wide waist, his face ashen. "Where were you?" she whispered. The doctors induced twilight sleep, and Ruby felt herself peeling away, as if she were a felt cutout of a woman, no longer a part of the story.

"Your baby is perfect," Sister Joseph said. "Sometimes we have to worry about breathing and sucking with preemies, but your daughter is healthy. A little small, but healthy." She smoothed blankets, staring at Ruby while she spoke, hitting the words *preemies* and *daughter* with extra verve.

Ruby squeezed her eyes shut. "Why is your name Joseph?" She twisted her fingers in the frayed satin edge of her blanket. The sofa was the reason. The damn sofa and how it wouldn't fit right in the apartment. It had brought on labor three weeks early. Three weeks she needed to make Marco fall irrevocably in love with her and the idea of their baby. The sofa had put her in this hospital bed, unrecognizable, alone. Beneath her hospital gown, her own breasts — nearly blue with crisscrossing veins, engorged as if two extra heads had been stuck to her chest — shocked her. Sister Joseph wrung out hot diapers and laid them over Ruby's chest. She gave her pills to dry up her milk and instructed Ruby to clasp her hands on top of her head while she wound Ace bandages around and around, pressing Ruby's nipples flat beneath the truss.

"Your daughter startles easily. The smart ones do. They sense any change in their environment." She pinned the bandages together across Ruby's back. "I leaned over the bassinet, and her eyes flew open."

"How long will I have to wear this?"

"They're brown, your baby's eyes, like bark." Sister Joseph tied the hospital gown together and patted Ruby's shoulder. "Dark eyes are unique. Most babies have blue, you know." Before leaving, she mentioned that Ruby would be uncomfortable.

Uncomfortable did not begin to describe the heaviness and burning Ruby felt waiting in her bed for her milk to vanish. She stared at the worn floorboards of the charity ward, wincing each time she shifted. The green curtain drawn around her bed did little to keep out the sounds of the Puerto Rican girls on the ward with her. At first, the shrill newborn cries, interrupted by heart-stopping lulls as their babies sucked air into brand-new lungs, frightened Ruby. But as her stay lengthened, she found herself sitting up in bed, listening. The mothers spoke Spanish to their babies and one another, sealing Ruby's isolation. She did not see many men pass by the crack in her curtains — just three boys with flowers, daisies, daisies, and daisies. Yet all the girls, even those who might be alone in the world, resisted when the nuns came to take their *bebés* to the nursery at night. *¿Solamente diez minutos, por favor?*

Marco visited in the mornings, clean-shaven, his cuffs buttoned. The skin beneath his eyes was scuff marked, as if he hadn't slept well, and Ruby clung to that. He asked how she was and brought her mascara, a bottle of shampoo, a pack of cinna-mint gum, and cigarettes, which she wasn't allowed to smoke. Though he never said it, he was ready to finish things. Just seeing him sitting there, with his long legs stretched across the space between Ruby's bed and his chair, with square hands folded over his fly, she knew he'd signed the papers.

"Her eyes are the color of bark," Ruby offered.

"I know."

"You've seen her?" She pushed herself up in bed.

Marco nodded. His cheeks were smooth as marbles. She imagined him staring at himself in the bathroom mirror, watching the sweep of the razor along his chin. There were specific things about

Marco that she missed: his smell, wool and mint. By not seeing her daughter, she was protecting herself from future missings as yet unknown to her.

"I looked in," he said.

"Did you hold her?"

"Ruby." He closed his eyes. "They make you, before you sign the papers." His lips continued to move, steadfast, determined. "We've been over this."

"I thought now things would be different."

"You've got to decide." Marco stood and stepped to the side of her bed. "She won't be motherless." He lifted Ruby's bangs from her forehead, and then brushed his lips across her skin. "Have you called Sally?"

She felt his kiss, like a phantom limb, above her left eye. She wasn't ready to let her mother know she'd delivered. Buried beneath the weight of Ruby's dead sister, Sally had opinions about babies and responsibility.

Marco lingered, his hand on her hair. She leaned the curve of her head into his cupped palm and closed her eyes. More than anything, she wanted to sleep right then, to drift off beneath Marco's palm. The babies on the other side of the curtain were quiet. What must the mothers think of her and Marco?

"You're tired, Meep."

Hearing his whispered voice made the backs of her eyes and her breasts sting. She nodded, ever so slightly, so she wouldn't disturb his hand.

"You've been through . . . I know it must . . . it's . . ." His voice drifted off. He was right. There was no way to describe what was happening to them. When she opened her eyes, he was staring at the buttons that raised and lowered her bed. "Are you comfortable?"

How in the world could she even come close to comfortable?

"I saw a mouse yesterday," Marco said.

"In the apartment?"

"Ran out from the kitchen and under the sofa."

She pictured the exposed mouse scurrying across the floor.

"I thought I'd better check underneath. There's a nest, or a litter, whatever you call it."

"In the sofa?"

He nodded. "Don't worry. I bought poison."

"It's a nest?" She shook off Marco's hand.

"You know, pest spray, Raid."

She sat up. "Raid?"

"For the mice."

Her shoulders beginning to shake, Ruby flung back her covers. Her fundus cramped, and her Ace bandage was suddenly, amazingly soaked. Marco laid a hand on her shoulder. Tears and mucus dripped down Ruby's cheeks and into her open mouth. Marco shifted his weight, and when she didn't stop, he mumbled her name, sat down on the edge of her bed. Finally, he went to call a nurse.

"Please, give her something?"

Sister Joseph wrapped her arms around Ruby. "Leave her be." Marco stepped aside while Ruby keened. Sister Joseph stroked Ruby's hair away from her face.

At two in the morning Ruby called her mother. She had no answer when Sally asked her granddaughter's name. Sally promised to call Uncle Paul and Aunt Lilly to tell them about Baby Hargrove. Everyone was on the way. Ruby pictured Sally, driving herself to the Amtrak station, her hands at ten and two on the steering wheel, her foot pressed firmly on the gas pedal, heading away in her good pantsuit. Her route would take her right past the Avenue and Ruby's father, perched on his barstool.

The very next morning Aunt Lilly and Uncle Paul took the train in from New Jersey. They came with buntings, receiving blankets, and hand cream. Aunt Lilly sat next to the bed and removed her talcum-sprinkled gloves to hold Ruby's ragged fingers. She asked if she was still having contractions and told her they wouldn't last much longer, her uterus was shrinking. She asked Ruby if she could sleep, and she told Ruby about her beautiful baby. She told her about the baby's elegant lips. "I've never seen anything more perfect."

Uncle Paul paced around Ruby's bed, twirling an unlit cigarette in his hands. "I haven't seen the boy here."

"He's at an audition."

"An actor?" Uncle Paul practically spit the words out.

Ruby didn't have the energy to defend Marco to her family. Aunt Lilly rubbed hand cream into Ruby's cuticles, one nail at a time. Uncle Paul continued to pace, his eyebrows raised in surprise or mild shock. A baby's whimpering seeped in from the other side of the curtain, and Ruby imagined the Puerto Rican girls watching Uncle Paul's polished wingtips pacing beneath the curtain's hem.

"We have plenty of room," Uncle Paul told her. "As long as you and the pipsqueak will have us." She held her free hand out to him, making a V with her fingers, and he passed her the cigarette. Even unlit it tasted cool and vaguely sweet.

The next morning, Ruby was allowed to shower. She hesitated, not wanting to be gone when Marco arrived, but Sister Joseph insisted, draping a towel over Ruby's arm, giving her a small bar of soap, a razor, and a gentle push toward the shower room. "He'll wait," she said.

Ruby shuffled down the hall, her legs wide to negotiate the pad. She went the long way around, avoiding the nursery and justifying her route in the name of exercise. The bleached shower room stood empty, and Ruby was glad when the door clicked shut behind her. It was nothing more than a large, tiled closet, the same sickly green of the curtain drawn around her bed for four days now. Three showerheads lined one wall. A drain pierced the center of a sloping floor. Ruby ran hot water, hoping to warm the space. She slipped off the hospital gown, and when she bent to pull down her underpants, her sagging belly reminded her of withered grapefruit peel. Red stretch marks groped upward from the stubble of pubic hair. Carefully, she unwound her bandage, filling the room with a tang of sour milk, and sweat, and dried blood. She had a battered, animal body, torn and leaking.

Hot needles of water stung her shoulders and back. Ruby closed her eyes. It felt unbelievably good to be alone in a clean room. Warmth spread to her chest; a germ of energy traveled through her limbs as she gradually soaped her body, ending with her still firm calves. She slid the razor up her leg, over the curve of her knee, and along the skin of her thighs. She still had swimmer's legs though it had been a long time since she'd entered a pool. She wondered about a Y and the possibility of joining, swimming every morning before her new secretarial job. And then she realized she could, if she had the nerve, walk away completely free.

"*¿Con permiso?*" The door swung open. The girl's belly strained against her hospital gown, two wet spots spread across her chest. A mother. Ruby turned back to her legs.

The other mother kept her eyes lowered, away from Ruby's body. She sat on the bench and quickly undid her braid, her upper arms jiggling with the speed of her hands down the length of black hair.

"It feels so good to shower," Ruby said.

"*Sí.*"

Ruby scrubbed shampoo into her short hair. She wished she had makeup and Aqua Net. She wanted to look great when Marco showed up. With the water flowing over her, standing on her own smooth legs, she felt the returning pleasure of being in control. Her arms were still slim, and when she could start smoking again, the weight would melt off.

The other mother slapped her feet across the tile, her towel barely meeting beneath her arms, barely covering her dimpled flesh. When she stood beneath the water, she let loose a comfortable sigh, as if she'd never been more content. She soaped her armpits, and then lifted each breast to wash beneath. She filled her palm with shampoo and began finger-combing suds down the length of her hair. She was patient, took her time with each snarl. "At home, I shower like this never."

Ruby closed her eyes.

"No time with *cuatro* boys. I am always feeding them. Plus, we have only the tub."

"You have four kids?"

The mother smiled proudly. Her front tooth had gone gray, as if the root had died. She looked too young for four children. "*Mi marido* keeps telling me to come home but I begged Sister to give me *un día más* alone with my baby." She leaned back beneath the shower spray; her brown nipples, big as silver dollars, leaked milk. "How many niños?"

It was the first time a stranger had spoken to her about her child. Ruby watched her own fingers clasp the handle and turn the water off. She reached for her towel, lifted it from the hook, and began precisely drying herself.

"You have more children?"

Ruby shook her head. She continued rubbing the towel over every inch of her skin.

"I saw your daughter in the nursery. *Pequeñita.* So tiny in her bassinet."

"She came early." Ruby fumbled with the ties of the clean hospital gown.

"You have luck." The other mother reached for her towel in one easy swoop. Her dark hair flowed smooth as mink down her back. "*Una hija* will never leave you. Girls stick together." From beneath a mound of towels and hospital gowns, she removed a pack of Winstons and held it toward Ruby.

"Oh my God, yes." Ruby slid a cigarette from the pack while the other mother struck a match for both of them. They sank to the floor, their backs against the tile wall, legs extended toward the drain, and smoked. Ruby could not remember when a shower and a cigarette had felt so perfect. "Thank you," she said. "Gracias."

The other mother lifted her chin toward the ceiling, blowing smoke rings into the harsh hospital light. "It is nothing."

"Girls stick together" is what Ruby repeated to herself as she walked back up the hall toward her bed. She skimmed her hand along the wallpaper, over the laughing dog, the happy dish escaping with the spoon, the soaring cow, and the moon beaming bigheartedly in the night sky. Her hand left the wall and came to rest upon a window. Five babies slept in soft light. Swallowing down her thumping heart, her gaze racing from one baby to the next, she found her daughter in the second row. Baby Hargrove. Ruby could see the little body, wound tight in a pink blanket, curved like a kidney bean. She could see the downy head, the face turned toward the window, the lips; were they moving? Ruby pressed her palm against the cold glass. Sister Joseph stepped into the nursery, and seeing Ruby in the hall, she lifted the baby and brought her to the window. The baby's face was scrunched tight, her skin tone blotchy and uneven, red along the chin and across her nose. The baby's faint eyebrows were drawn together in a scowl. Ruby motioned for Sister Joseph to unwrap her daughter. As she did, the baby's tiny fist flew up and her mouth opened, though she did not cry. The baby had her thumb tucked inside her hand. Her fingers wrapped over the top for safekeeping. Ruby stayed in the hallway, shaking her head no when Sister Joseph motioned for her to come in. Ruby preferred to keep the window glass between them.

She was having difficulty holding the bottle just right when Marco pulled back her curtain. His smile looked planned. Marco could do that, behave strategically. Her baby slipped in the crook of her elbow, formula dribbling out of the corner of her mouth. "Don't cry," she whispered.

Marco let the curtain fall behind him. Color drained from his cheeks. He pulled his lips inside his mouth, clamped down, and stood there, pale and lipless, with the curtain skimming his back.

The baby felt warm against Ruby's chest. The dark hair at the crown of her head swayed with the rhythm of her heartbeat. Sister Joseph had explained to Ruby about the soft spot, how the scalp was strong and the spot would gradually fuse — nothing to be afraid of. Yet the fact it was only skin protecting her baby's brain from traumas of the outside world terrified Ruby. So much could go wrong.

"I got a part. In an orange juice commercial."

"Congratulations."

"That's where I've been, at the callbacks, getting headshots."

Ruby nodded.

"You look good," Marco offered.

"I showered."

He held on to the back of a chair, as if seeing her with the baby had caused his knees to go weak. Ruby sat up straight. She readjusted the bottle so the baby wouldn't swallow air. She had to look great, like she knew what she was doing, with her hair clean, her face fresh. Even though her decision scared her, she felt strong right then. This was a result she hadn't expected. Marco would have to choose.

"So, she's eating okay?"

"She lost three ounces, that happens. I'm supposed to push the formula."

"I'm supposed to drink the orange juice at a breakfast table."

"They want us to go home tomorrow. Wherever that ends up being."

He blew air out of his mouth, practically erupted with it, and the baby flinched. "I'm meant to smile and say, *Healthy start to a happy day.*" He held up a pretend glass of juice.

"That shouldn't be too hard."

"Except I'm fucking miserable."

"What did you do about the mice?"

"Ruby, you're making a mistake."

"How is walking away better?"

"Someone else can do right by her."

"I can too. I can." She pulled the baby closer, perhaps too close because the baby began to cry.

Marco said nothing.

Ruby rocked, forward and back, biting the inside of her cheek.

Marco stared at his hands. "*Happy start to a healthy day.* That's how it goes."

"I have to go to sleep tonight feeling okay about myself."

"I don't know what that would take for me."

"You'll get it right."

Marco brought Ruby's suitcase to the lobby of St. Vincent's. When she and her mother opened it at Aunt Lilly and Uncle Paul's, her clothes had been washed and neatly folded. Twenty-five crisp twenty-dollar bills and a two-word note lay on top. *Forgive me.*

Ruby found a studio apartment, a fourth-floor walkup with a bathtub that doubled as a kitchen table. Marco's money paid the deposit with enough left over for a babysitter and a skirt suit. Ruby did get a job as a secretary, in an insurance office. She sent her daughter, whom she named Nora, to live with a babysitter Monday mornings through Friday afternoons, when she and Nora took the train to Aunt Lilly's for the weekend. Monday mornings, Nora watched her mother dress from her high chair. Her large, serious eyes followed Ruby cinching a belt tight around her waist, stroking eyeliner over her lids before a small mirror propped on the kitchen windowsill. "Happy start to a happy day," Ruby said, wiping banana from between Nora's fingers with a cool cloth. "Don't get any on Mommy. Mommy's got a date." There was a businessmen's bar she liked to stop at on her way home; sometimes she ordered a shrimp cocktail for her dinner. She and Nora didn't have a TV so they never saw Marco's commercial. He didn't come to see them either, in their new apartment. Ruby knew he'd returned to Florida. He must have set all the furniture back on the sidewalk. The sofa, the spool; she couldn't imagine anyone wanting to live with that junk.

This Is So Not Me

I WAS CLIMBING the stairs to Walter's brownstone, Ezekiel swaddled up tight like they showed me three times before I left the maternity ward. You know, how they're supposed to feel better if their arms and legs are wadded in close like the Baby Jesus lying in the manger. Seems it would make me want to scream, but whatever. So I'm holding him next to my chest when all of the sudden I got this urge, what if I just dropped him right over the side of the banister. *Kerplunk,* like a chestnut. I could almost see my arms reaching over the edge and letting go and that baby blue blanket careening to the ground and me just turning on my heel. I don't have to tell you that it scared the crap out of me and I pressed my ass against the brick wall the rest of the way up.

I kept that story to myself. Walter was already observing me for postpartum depression and the last thing I needed was Mr. Worst-Case-Scenario breathing down my neck.

They've delayed us here at the American Airlines gate for ninety minutes now. The most they'll say is that there has been some mechanical difficulty. Rumor is there was a chipmunk onboard and they're checking the wiring for nibbles. That news about sent Walter over the edge and he went for a Courvoisier on top of the Valium he took before we left. When I held out my hand for just one little blue pill he gave me that *what kind of mad cow are you* look, like it would go straight out my nipples and make Zeke a moron. *Everything* I do boomerangs back to Zeke. Now Walter's wearing out the burnt orange carpet with his pacing and *ujjayi* breathing. I told him the combination of pharmaceuticals, alcohol, and yoga would keep him blissful through any in-flight disaster. I wanted to tell him it kept me blissful through the pregnancy, but he's so damned sanctimonious.

Already I regret this blouse. I decided that since I could get the buttons to meet over the vast continent that is now my chest, I would wear it. Walter said the plum-size gaps level with my nipples made me look "overly-willing" so I said good, what a great impression to make on his parents in Coeur d'Alene, Idaho, home of the Klan. The blouse clings like shrink-wrap and I can feel sweat collecting along my spine. Zeke is lying in the crook of my elbow, spacing out on the fluorescent lights, one of his two tricks, and my legs have gone numb from the rubberized tights I wear for varicose veins. The nursing blister on Zeke's top lip burst this morning and the skin flap flutters in and out with each suck of breath. I tried to bend down and bite it off, but with my stiff neck from sleeping weird, it's impossible. I used to sleep on my stomach and I was skying at the idea I could again once Zeke was born. But the first night I tried, it was like sleeping on two hard bladders, and my milk left nasty, ripe wet spots.

Some jerk over at the counter is laying into the flight attendant. I watched him stalk over, his hammy thighs rubbing together so hard I could actually hear him wearing out the inside seams on his Wranglers.

"What the fuck? It's a chipmunk, like Chip or Bill, a fucking cartoon. How much longer are you going to keep us here?" He pounded his fist on the light blue Formica; you know how American Airlines tries to make everything patriotic, but not? I thought either the counter or the flight attendant would crack. She stood there with her fake smile pasted on her dark lips. I noted her lip liner when I was getting our seat assignment near the bulkhead, because Walter said it's the most comfortable place when you're schlepping an infant across the country to Idaho. I don't know how he knows these things.

"Sir, I must ask you to step away from the counter. The service crew is working as quickly as possible. We estimate departure in the not-too-distant future."

"What does that mean?" He pushed off from the counter and ranted all the way into the bathroom. I bet his stream is fierce. I never noticed anyone's stream till Walter started pissing about his. Forgive the pun. He said when he hit forty-eight he lost his power.

"I hope he's nowhere near the bulkhead." Walter nodded toward the men's room. "He looks potentially violent."

I was too sick and tired of soothing and providing suck to deal with Walter's paranoia. My nipples were chapped, the sutures from my tear barely dissolved, and Walter was already putting his head in my lap and mewing like a hungry kitten.

"I could get violent," I said. "It'd give you something to talk to your parents about."

"Shh." His eyes flickered in Wrangler Man's direction.

He stormed back toward us and dropped like a saddlebag in the seat directly behind me. I heard him strike a match and then I smelled the smoke. I closed my eyes, breathed in deep, trying to get a cigarette snack.

"Let's move," Walter whispered and cocked his head to the side like he had a bad twitch.

"No."

"The secondhand smoke . . ." he insisted.

"There's no place else to sit. Besides, I can't feel my legs." He didn't know about the firsthand smoke I had every day at four thirty when he went out to get the paper. I kept the hard pack of

Pall Malls under the center cushion of his leather couch. I'd take it out onto the balcony with one of those long fireplace matches and lie on his teak deck chair. I'd say, "Don't watch Mommy," and light up. My starved lungs soaked up the nicotine like sponges. After, I brushed my teeth, chewed two Certs, and made myself a cup of green tea. I'd be at the desk when he returned, ghosting a term paper for some Jane—"Eating Disorders in Twentieth-Century Feminist Literature" or "Poetry, Sylvia Plath, and Motherhood." My nerves appeased for yet another evening of Walter's prodding me, saying, "That could be your dissertation, Shelby." *Yeah, if I gave a fat rat's ass.*

Walter cleared his throat in his most professorial way. "Excuse me, sir."

Nothing.

"Excuse me?" Walter leaned over me and tapped the shoulder of Wrangler Man.

"What?" he fired at us both.

"Sorry to bother you but this is a nonsmoking section." He pointed out the THANK YOU FOR NOT SMOKING sign. "And the smoke, it's not good for our baby."

Wrangler Man looked at Walter like he was a chigger, took a big draw off his smoke, and exhaled a thick gray cloud.

"Secondhand smoke worries us." Walter pointed across the corridor to the dozen or so seats inside a glass cube. The smoking lounge. "They have a spot for you people." *Ouch.*

Wrangler Man snorted. "I am not moving again until I get my ass on that plane." He dropped his butt on the carpet and crushed it with his boot.

"Thanks a lot," I said to him, craning my neck to get one last whiff. "And by the way, it's Chip and *Dale*. The Disney chipmunks. Not Bill; Dale." Walter rolled his eyes at me and placed a protective palm on Zeke's head.

"Ladies and gentlemen, good news. Our troubles have been eliminated and the ground crew has cleared us for boarding. Families traveling with small children and first-class passengers may pre-board at gate eighteen A." It was such a blithe and lilting voice, like she'd be serving up Pop-Tarts to a table full of freckled, pint-size gymnasts.

"Eliminated?" Walter said a little too loud, seeking an audience from the poached faces of our fellow passengers "What? Little chipmunk mafia with cement shoes were called in?" And believe it or not, that's what I think is kind of sweet about Walter, his incredibly bad jokes. I heaved up out of the chair and shifted Zeke to my shoulder. Walter collapsed the stroller and I lumbered behind. Wrangler Man had already barreled past us and was causing a scene at the lectern.

"Sir, we're pre-boarding. Row twelve will board in a few minutes."

"This row twelve will board right now."

We struggled down the jetway like overburdened pilgrims, begging pardon for our bulky carry-ons. On the plane, Wrangler Man pillaged the aisle seats as he passed, grabbing pillows, blankets, and a *Cosmo,* for the breast shots, I was certain.

We squeezed into our row, stowing the baby carrier, the diaper bag filled with Parents' Choice award–winning infant toys, bottles of frozen breast milk (in case I throw myself from the plane), and cotton diapers. Yes, we use a diaper service, and yes, we are carting crappy diapers across this great land of ours. Whose idea do you think that was?

Walter let me have the aisle so I could stretch my legs and get up to pace every so often if my veins throbbed. Between the armrests, the tights and blouse, my swollen feet, and the pads stuck in my bra—totally soggy now—I felt like a stuffed olive. I gained fifty pounds with this pregnancy. My upper arms flapped; even my head felt fat. My scalp itched and sweated. I would have panted like a dog if I thought it would cool me off.

"Did you remember to order the vegetarian meal?"

I didn't answer.

"Shelby, you did remember to order me the vegetarian meal?"

"I might have forgotten."

He expelled a soft, disappointed sigh and looked away from me, out the window onto the tarmac. "Okay, let me check the diaper bag for apples or something."

Squeezing past my legs, Walter bumped Zeke, who started his infant wail, thin and plaintive, which caused my milk to let down. At the hospital the nurse told me to think of crying as strengthening babies' lungs. But to me it still sounded like woe.

"The captain says as soon as everyone is seated, we can pull back from the gate." This was repeated over the PA system three times in gradually more hostile tones while Walter continued foraging and came up with one apple, a slightly bruised banana, and a stale half a bagel.

"Sit down." It was Wrangler Man.

"Yes, okay," Walter grumbled. "Does he have tickets to the World Wrestling Federation or something?"

"Shut your hole" came Wrangler Man's lovely retort.

"Walter." I winced as Zeke latched on to me like a roach clip. "Sometimes mathematicians shouldn't try to make jokes."

Just as the captain ordered a crosscheck of the doors we heard vigorous wails come down the jetway. A man dressed all in black, like Johnny Cash but for the white collar of a priest, stepped carefully through the door, his hair a fringe in front of his eyes, his cheek pressed into the dark head of the reddest-faced baby I have ever seen.

"Holy fucking Christ," Wrangler Man cried from his seat, and we watched everyone lean away, like the parting of the Red Sea, as the priest and baby passed. He made his way along the aisle, petting the baby's head and clucking awkwardly. A flight attendant helped him get seated, the door shut, and, finally, for better or worse, we pulled away from the umbilical cord of the jetway and tore through the permanent frosting of brown muck over Newark.

• • •

Zeke can't settle down with the other baby's screaming. He's snorting and snuffling, and my milk is getting in his eyes. Every time he reattaches I dig my nail into the thin skin on Walter's left hand. No age spots yet. Walter has his tray down and he's arranged the limp banana along with the apple and bagel into a pathetic still life.

Behind us the priest's baby continues its caterwauling with impressive lung capacity. I turn and see Wrangler Man slam on earphones and pound the buttons on his seat trying to get the flight attendant, the in-flight music station, anything to drown out the baby. Another flight attendant rushes past with a cute little bottle of Jack Daniel's in one hand and a baby bottle in the other. The baby screams and hiccups and then is silent.

Walter sighs heavily and I close my eyes. Walter told me the name of the hormone that releases into a woman's bloodstream when she *lactates* (his term). Oxytocin. I only wish it was bottled and sold because it puts me right to sleep.

Walter is twenty-five years older than I am. It isn't hard to imagine that I was his student. I was in his Excursions in Math seminar and, surprise, I had to take even the bonehead class twice because math for me is like eating twenty-five hard-boiled eggs in one sitting, which I tried on a dare in sixth grade. I could swallow only the first six and they came back up. I won't bore you with the details of how I ended up in this life with Zeke and Walter, heading to meet octogenarian in-laws in Coeur d'Alene. Basically I moved upstairs. Quit my downstairs boyfriend and moved upstairs with Walter. I'll just say it was another in the series of nondecisions that my parents say make up the arc of my life. At least Mom and Daddy can say I married a professor, even if he is a Democrat.

At first I had all the time I wanted to lie around and read the Brontë sisters. As a faculty wife I could take classes for free, and I did, once. Walter didn't put any demands on me. He just liked me to be home when he came in. I liked the straightforward sex. For added mystique, I had him whisper things about π and solving for x while we *fornicated*.

Then I was pregnant and all of the sudden he asked me to quit smoking and eat six ounces of soy protein at each square meal. He dragged me on long walks and encouraged me to squat whenever possible to loosen the ligaments in my hips. This was Walter's Big Chance. His first wife, who raised Scottish terriers, fled after ten years of watching him calculate and avoid her. With me carrying his progeny, he took over my life, and now with Zeke here, named for his great-uncle, attention hasn't waned at all. He highlights articles about how the baby should *latch on* with my entire areola pressed up against his soft palate and how nursing myelinates the nerves for rapid-fire brain activity. I want to know if Zeke will ever smile. Walter informs me the social smile comes at six weeks, but I can't take two more weeks of waiting. I coo in Zeke's face, tell him my best jokes, and I get nothing. Walter bought a digital camera so I could take a shot of the first smile and e-mail it to him at CUNY, but there the camera sits on the sideboard and I haven't learned to upload.

When I wake, I've got a string of drool attaching me to the puce tweed fabric Velcroed to my headrest for lice control or something. I run my hand along my face and feel a crease down my cheek from sleeping on the seam. Still, when Walter notices me stirring, he looks at me like he can't believe how lucky he is.

"I ate the salad and I saved the tuna casserole for you."

"I've got to pee," I say, standing and holding Zeke. Walter lowers my tray table. He puts the cold lunch leftovers on it and raises his tray. He shifts to get comfortable in his seat. He takes the blanket and lays it over his shoulder. He puts the pillow in his lap.

"Walter, I've got to *pee,*" I stage whisper. I'm swaying from one foot to the other, doing Kegels like crazy.

Finally he reaches out and takes Zeke. Walter's warm hands cradle Zeke's innocent neck and butt. He pulls the baby into his chest with devout attention and grace. I am moved and nauseated at the same time.

In the wan green light of the bathroom I try to wriggle out of my tights but I have to pee so bad I can't hold it and a warm stream courses down my leg. The faucet won't stay on in the thimble-size metal basin so I have to keep pushing it down to wet the towels and I barely have the space to bend over and wipe myself off. I'm turning from one side to the other like a dog chasing his own tail and I end up cramming the mountain of elastic into the tiny mouth of the trash can. I lean back against the door, close my eyes.

When I come out a baby starts to scream. It's not Zeke; it's the priest's crier.

Wrangler Man shoves past me into the bathroom and attempts to slam the flimsy door. It's a completely unsatisfying *shump.*

The in-flight movie has started, something about a can-do secretary who vacuums in her lingerie, and passengers are shooting the baby death-ray stares. The priest has dark circles of sweat under his arms and he's rocking forward and back in his thirty-two inches of allotted coach-class space, holding the baby like you would hold a porcupine to your shoulder. As I pass him, I see his priest collar is cockeyed, and he has curdled spit-up on his chest. The baby's face is again ruby-colored and sweaty. Its hair is black and thick as an otter's.

My body responds with the prick of let-down, again. I swear, my whole being has turned into a physical response. I ask him, "Can I try?"

"Thank you." His entire body goes limp as he passes the rigid baby to me.

I place the baby over my shoulder and begin to sway, rubbing his tiny spine. He must be about four months old because he can hold his head up fine, but he's small, the same size as Zeke. He screams louder so I sway faster and start to hum. The priest looks from the baby to me; creases like question marks form between his brows, and I feel I'm being tested. I look up the aisle. Walter has the headset on. He's probably reading and watching the movie and stimulating brain growth in Zeke.

"Finally, someone with equipment." Wrangler Man comes back from the bathroom, jimmies into his seat behind us, "Tired of fucking hearing that kid." He has three mini bottles of Jack Daniel's on his tray table and he's talking loud, even for him. He latches his thick fingers over the top of the seat, leans in confidentially. "What the hell are you doing with a baby anyway? Get someone in trouble?" He has a sour grin on his face. And then, with a wink to me, "I thought they only liked little boys."

The priest ignores him.

"Maybe he has gas?" I project over the baby's cries.

"At the orphanage, in Romania, I think they subsisted mostly on sugar water. Could be the formula? It's hard on him?"

"Whiskey on a rag worked on my kid brother." Wrangler Man snorts.

"Maybe it's his diaper?" the priest asks.

He hadn't seen me slip my finger under the elastic at the baby's thin thigh. "He's dry. What's his name?"

"Stanyos. His new family may change it."

"Get up. Let 'er sit." Wrangler Man nudges the priest's shoulders forward.

Father Matthew, as he turns out to be named, slips from his seat and I sit down. I stretch Stanyos over my legs, skin to skin, so my thighs press into his abdomen, hoping he'll burp. His cries fade to whimpers and the three of us hush, watching his perfect little body writhe like he can't get comfortable in his skin. Wrangler Man breathes down my neck.

"Stanyos?" he says. "That's a name begging for a playground brawl."

I can feel his breath, smell the cigarettes and whiskey.

"There's nothing to him. He's so damn loud." His voice is softer now, slower too, as if my rubbing the baby's back is working to ease his discomfort as well. "My kid brother cried all the time. Inconsolable. My mom paced a trail in the carpet."

Walter has begun to look for me. When he sees Father Matthew standing, me in the seat, and Wrangler Man leaning over, alarm flashes across his face. I know he is going to get up, to come see if he can, once again, rescue me.

I turn Stanyos gently toward me. His eyes are screwed tight and he is preparing to wail. His face presses into my belly and he goes crazy smelling my milk. He immediately begins rooting around my blouse, banging his head against me, his mouth working eagerly at the fabric.

And then it is simple. I undo the top three buttons, lower the flap of my nursing bra, and bring his mouth, wide as a hatchling's, to my breast. "It's okay," I whisper. Stanyos pulls greedily at me and I feel the sting of milk rushing from my body into his mouth.

Father Matthew averts his gaze.

"Whoa." Wrangler Man pulls back like he's been hit. "Man. Shit." I hear the crack in his voice, and so does Father Matthew because he asks him if he's okay.

"My kid brother's name was Steven." And his voice breaks completely. "Shit."

Father Matthew has his hand on Wrangler Man's shoulder. He murmurs of loss and comfort as he leans over my bowed head. My husband and son are in the aisle now too. Walter's lips are pressed into a thin line and I see the questions in his eyes. *It's okay,* I mouth. Zeke is sleeping in Walter's arms. The blister on his lip still flutters with each breath.

Behind me Wrangler Man hacks and spits into a cup. He slides open the porthole cover between our seats and I am surprised by the sun reflecting off the fat layer of clouds. I'd forgotten what time of day it was here on this plane, flying toward our families.

Stanyos swallows and swallows; his soft brown eyes glaze over like he's been waiting for this his whole life.

Manx

NORA REQUESTED FLUFFY and white. A kitten to name Candi, with an *i*. A kitten who would weave figure eights around and between her ankles while she poured milk on her Cheerios. Instead, her mom dropped a box over the schoolyard stray. An emaciated, dark tabby who spent his time hissing at students and licking out the inside of Jell-O pudding cups. Ruby brought him home for Nora on Good Friday.

Ruby bathed the cat in their kitchen sink, using the last of the Short and Sassy shampoo. When Nora ran into their apartment after school, the damp cat was perched on the windowsill, clicking his jaw at a bird in the magnolia tree. If the cat had had a tail, he'd have been swishing it back and forth, pumping his frustration out, but he was a Manx.

Her mom sat at the kitchen table smoking, bloody toilet paper wrapped around her wrist where the cat scratched her. "Happy Easter." She re-crossed her legs, dangled a tan sandal from her toe. "Are you thrilled?"

Nora stood in the center of the room watching the shoe bounce on her mother's foot and then she looked back to the cat. A bead of drool glinted at the corner of his jaw.

"It was starving, Nora." Ruby leaned forward to stub out her cigarette, then she mentioned that owing to the cat, their karma would probably improve, for providing shelter and everything, and besides, maybe all the cat required was a full bowl and consistent love. When Nora asked her what she meant by consistent love, her mom took a long swallow from her wine spritzer and jiggled her shoe some more. "Someone to be there every single time he meows at the back door."

Weekday afternoons Nora walked home alone from Beachwood Elementary to their apartment on lower Primrose Terrace, a neighborhood of stucco apartment buildings renting to older couples, struggling actors, and stewardesses. Usually Nora would make herself a snack—Ritz crackers and marshmallow fluff—then watch a talk show on TV, Merv, Mike, Phil, or Dinah. After today, someone would always be home waiting to greet Nora, and she pictured her cat curled up in her lap, licking cracker crumbs off her fingertips while she waited for her mom. She named her cat Phil Donahue, hoping he'd greet her the way Donahue ran to the women in his audience, eager to hear anything they had to say about seat belts, war, or divorce.

It's not that Nora didn't have friends, she did, but Jocelyn, whose big apartment was on the first floor, went to St. Agatha's school and she wasn't available to play in the afternoons. They were the only children in the building and so they were friends. The only reason Jocelyn's family lived on lower Primrose at all was that her dad was the manager. He was also an official at St. Agatha's, and Donald wore a suit, either dark green or brown, every day of the week. When Nora delivered the rent check once a month, Donald would call her into his telephone study with the leather desk blotter, the dark wooden crucifix, and the rye-toast smell hanging in the air. She knew he knew she and her mother didn't attend church, which was why Jocelyn wasn't allowed to play at Nora's. But every month, as she waited in his tiny study while Donald wrote out a receipt in letters so small and pointy they looked like crabs crawling across the page, he made the same joke about her mother. *How's Diamond . . . er . . . Emerald . . . Sapphire . . .* until he settled on *Ruby.* Then he pulled a coin from behind Nora's ear.

Sometimes her mom sent her downstairs with a note requesting an extension, and Donald would run his tongue around the inside of his cheeks, clear his throat as if phlegmy displeasure were lodged there. Nora never knew if the envelope she carried contained a note or a check and she held her breath every time he slit it open with his silver letter opener. Either way, Donald, with his dark eyebrows that nearly met in the middle of his forehead, and the rash of capillaries spread across his nose, made Nora's mouth go dry.

Once, Nora walked into Jocelyn's kitchen to find Donald gripping Jocelyn's mother's arm. She heard him yell-whisper *erratic home life* and *multiple partners.* When he and Margaret noticed Nora, Donald clamped his mouth shut, and Margaret's pale English complexion flushed pink. The kitchen went quickly still. Nora averted her eyes from Donald's hand on Margaret's arm to the window and the 25 MPH sign out front. Sunlight streamed in, washing the spotless counter in sweet yellow light and bouncing off a china sugar bowl. "It smells clean in here" was all Nora could think to say.

Ruby told Nora that Donald's disgruntled attitude had nothing to do with the rent extensions. Donald's disenchantment revolved around his wife's habit of wearing pantyhose twenty-four hours a day, as reported by Nora who three times had spent the night in the big apartment.

Nora and her mom lived in the building on lower Primrose because it was an improvement from their last place and they were working their way up the hill to the green lawns and swing sets and cute white bungalows. Their building did have a sliver of lawn in front, but Jocelyn and Nora ignored it, mostly staying in the carport — rolling around belly-down on skateboards, or putting on plays in Margaret's clothes. Now that Nora had a real live pet to include, she thought their games might evolve. Ruby provided her with an old scarf to fashion into a leash for Phil Donahue, but when she tied it on, he nearly yanked his oniony head through his new flea collar.

"Keep that beast away," Jocelyn yelled. She stopped running circles around her mother and a large aqua mound on the floor of the carport and pointed accusingly at Phil Donahue. "His claws will ruin my new pool." She sang out the last two words as if she were a game-show host.

Margaret looked up from unfurling the blue plastic heap and smiled at Nora. "Have you a new pet, lamb?" Margaret baked scones and saved Jocelyn's hand-me-down Cotswold-wool sweaters for Nora. Nora knew she was an opportunity for Margaret to tend to those less fortunate and thus an avenue to God.

"My mom says he needs consistent love," she said to Margaret.

"You must come 'round for a dip later."

"Where's his tail?" Jocelyn stood with her hands on her hips.

Nora scooped up her hissing cat and stared at all the amazing blue. She breathed in the new-plastic smell and scratched the stump where Phil Donahue's tail should have been.

"He's a Manx, love." Margaret's British accent made anything seem charming.

Nora was secretly mastering the accent by whispering a list of words before bed each night, like a prayer: *tomato, trespass, brilliant, wee, biscuit, charming, love.*

On the first day of Easter vacation, Ruby insisted Nora come along to the vet since she was the one who'd wanted a damn cat in the first place. "The Catholics' pool will be there when we get back," she said.

They had to coast down the hill to the Mobile station with its red Pegasus soaring above Sunset Boulevard.

"We made it here on fumes," Ruby told the attendant. She also told him she was taking her daughter's new cat to the vet, and that's what the commotion coming from the cardboard box on the back seat was all about. The man peered around Ruby's blond head, Nora waved, and his eyes drifted back to her mother's slender neck and the front of her blue dress. Ruby was always doing things like this, making Nora go places she didn't want to, driving like a fiend, telling her story to anyone who would listen.

The examination room had a drain in the center of the floor, for hosing down, Nora supposed, yet it still smelled of ammonia, pee, and animal fright. The walls were decorated with posters of hip dysplasia, plaque-ridden canine teeth, and opaque eyeballs. Not one picture of a happy pet. This lack concerned Nora but her mother didn't notice because she was staring at Dr. Shapiro as he shuffled through a stack of forms, uncapped a pen with his square white teeth, and held the cap in his mouth, leaving his moist pink tongue exposed. Nora clutched Phil Donahue's box on her lap until his claws pierced the cardboard and dug into her thigh. When she yelped, her mom furrowed her brow, a habit she was trying to break by wearing Frownies to bed every night. Then, just as quickly, she stopped and turned back to Dr. Shapiro's glossy black mustache, freshly shaved cheeks, and cleft chin. A butt chin, Nora thought.

Dr. Shapiro set down his clipboard. His cheerful blue eyes, happy as polka dots, fixed on her mom, and Ruby lowered her lashes. "How old is Phil?" he asked.

"Phil Donahue," Nora corrected.

"We're not certain," her mom said, keeping her chin down and gazing up from beneath her brows. "The Easter Bunny brought him early for my daughter."

Dr. Shapiro examined Nora, her face, her height, trying to determine if she was too old for the Easter Bunny. Nora said nothing. It was one of Ruby's not-to-be-broken rules: Never tell a man your age (and Nora was especially not supposed to tell when Ruby was in the room).

"Shall we have a look?" He opened Phil Donahue's box. "Psst. Kitty . . ."

Phil Donahue hissed and swatted at Dr. Shapiro's long fingers, and the muscles in Ruby's neck stiffened. Nora smiled. She wasn't quite certain why, but she didn't want this to go well for her mom. She wanted to get it over with. She wanted to be swimming. Phil Donahue leaped from the box, and Dr. Shapiro grabbed for his hind legs. The cat writhed and spit, but Dr. Shapiro held on while Nora cajoled in her best Margaret voice, "Hello, love. It's all right, darling." After a moment Ruby reached over and pinched the fur at Phil Donahue's neck so hard she pulled his cheeks back, showing all his teeth. Nora was about to object, worried that Ruby was hurting the cat, but her mom saw her expression. "He's fine," she declared, lifting Phil Donahue by the scruff and arranging him in the crook of her elbow, his skinny body pressed against her chest. The unspoken threat—watch yourself—was clear to Nora from her mother's controlled tone and gaze that lingered too long, like a pinch.

Dr. Shapiro shone a light into the cat's yellow eyes, squeezed tight to the size of slivered almonds. He examined his ears, his gums, and the pads of his feet. He guessed Phil Donahue to be about a year old. Nora flinched when he administered three vaccinations. And all the while, Ruby stroked the cat's head. When Dr. Shapiro noticed the scratch up the inside of Ruby's wrist, he quit doctoring Phil Donahue and tenderly guided Ruby's hand beneath the light. "I don't like the way this looks."

"It's only a scratch," she said, but she let him hold her hand while she stared at his bald spot as if it were a halo.

All but forgotten, Phil Donahue sat beneath a chair, licking himself as if nothing had happened. While her mom blossomed under the veterinarian's concerned eye, Nora stared at a poster of a cat's heart. Spaghetti-length worms wriggled in and around the chambers in a complicated tangle of bodies.

"Thank you, Dr. Shapiro," Ruby said as he ran his finger along the angry red line.

"Please, call me Guy."

Dr. Shapiro pressed a tube of antibiotic ointment into Nora's hands, told her to be sure she "anointed" her mom's wrist three times every day. He told Ruby if it didn't get better she might need to have it looked at again. He also said they should plan on coming back soon, as Phil Donahue should be neutered. He whispered the last word, as if the cat could understand. Nora's gaze never left the poster and Dr. Shapiro nodded toward the diagram of the cat's heart. "Strays get those worms," he said with a lilt to his voice.

Even Nora had the good sense to know parasites and flirtation were a bad combination.

"Bring Phil Donahue back and we'll fix him up." His gaze finally left Ruby and found his patient. "And, Nora, make sure you keep fresh water in his bowl."

"Oh, she will." Ruby stroked the top of Nora's head. Dr. Shapiro couldn't see how she lightly tugged Nora's hair with her next sentence. "Nora wants to be a vet."

Dr. Shapiro's eyes lit up. Both he and Ruby stared at Nora with proud smiles, as if they'd all leaped forward ten years and were dropping Nora off at her new dorm. It wasn't the first time her mom had made her over in someone else's image. Nora dropped to her knees to retrieve her cat. Still nonchalant, he ignored her fingers wriggling on the floor. She reached toward him and he let her pet his head. He even rubbed his cheek against her palm, growing affectionate. Nora and Phil Donahue were united in their dislike for the vet.

Dr. Shapiro saw them to the front door of his office, his hand floating an inch above the small of Ruby's back. Ruby asked him if he liked jazz and suggested that perhaps he'd like to hear an amazing piano player this Saturday night at the club where she moonlighted from her teaching job. He said that sounded fine, wonderful. Ruby gave her horn a single toot as she drove out of the parking lot.

On the way home they stopped at Safeway for two Dreamsicles and a dozen cans of Kitty Queen cat food. Ruby chucked Phil

Donahue beneath the chin, saying, "One good turn deserves an-other."

Donald's Pontiac was gone when they arrived home. Nora dashed to the carport, taking both ice cream bars. Since Ruby had a date this weekend she didn't want one anyway. She wanted to look fantastic in her black cocktail dress. "Go now," she agreed. "His holy tight-ass isn't home."

"Nora, hello." Margaret answered her knock in a gingham housedress and pantyhose. "Jocelyn's in the kitchen."

Margaret always wore pantyhose. Nora had seen her pull a fresh pair from between sachets in her lingerie drawer on one of the nights Nora had been allowed to sleep over. Margaret, who changed her clothes in the closet, would step out in fresh hose, chenille slippers, and her nightie, the limp pair, still bearing the shape of Margaret's legs, hanging from her wrist. She'd make a black and tan for Donald and then watch TV from the other end of the flowered sofa while he stifled belches. At bedtime Margaret slipped into her side of Jocelyn's bed while Nora slept on the floor in a pile of lilac-scented quilts. Donald had his own room, though most times he slept in front of the TV. Nora didn't think much about it, just assumed that British people used cream on their cereal, said *telly* and *bum,* and kept separate bedrooms.

"Can't swim today," Jocelyn announced. She licked a glob of lemon curd off a teaspoon. "Donald says it's too close to the Resurrection. Too holy for swimming. Mummy says we must listen."

When Nora tried *Mummy* at home, like "Mummy, I've got to use the loo," Ruby looked up from her lesson planning with a sour smile and told her she wasn't *goddamned Julie Andrews.* As if Nora needed reminding.

"My cat has worms."

"Will he be okay?" Margaret asked from the sink.

"We hope so." Nora nodded. "The worms are inside his heart."

. . .

Though Phil Donahue wasn't the cat of her dreams, he did swat around the Sugar Pops Nora tossed him, torturing them until with a final pounce he'd lick off the sweet coating. He liked them so much Nora took to mixing some with his cat food. She kept his water bowl full as Dr. Guy had directed, but Phil Donahue preferred to drink from the bathtub. He'd balance on the edge and dip his tongue toward Nora's hand, cupped just below the surface. She liked feeling his tongue under the water, rough and soft. When he finished, he'd pad out of the room, stepping high, shaking each paw.

At night, when her mom was correcting papers and watching *Laugh-In,* Nora let him out to do his business. Nightgowned and barefoot, she would stand in the dry grass and wait for him. There were no streetlights on lower Primrose. The stars flecked across the velveteen night sky were incredibly bright and as dense as the freckles across her mom's shoulders. Nora often didn't know Phil Donahue was back until he surprised her, turning figure eights around her ankles.

Saturday night, before the date with Dr. Guy, Ruby and Nora stretched out on their twin beds, sharing a bucket of chicken. Ruby lounged in a lacy black bra and sheer black hose; a triangle of pubic hair showed dark below her bellybutton, a wine spritzer rested on her stomach. She dangled a cigarette from her fingers. Nora's 7Up was tinged pink with the treat of one splash of wine. Phil Donahue nibbled shreds of thigh meat off Nora's palm.

"Nora-bean." Her mom had the soft, confident voice she got after a glass of wine. "Pick out my dress."

Gathered in her mom's closet like a knot of beautiful women, her mother's dresses mysteriously held their shapes on the hangers, like Margaret's pantyhose, all curves. Nora stood on a chair and shuttled through, chose the black chiffon, arranged it across the empty bed. Her mom then motioned for Nora to take off her own nightgown, and she slipped a red spaghetti-strapped mini dress over Nora's shoulders, saying, "Let's see this on a beautiful girl." Nora loved everything about the dress, the cool fabric pouring over her, the rhinestones clumped in the bodice where breasts would someday appear. Mostly she loved her mom calling her beautiful.

"Makeup?" Ruby asked, setting the makeup-mirror bulbs to candlelight. She brushed iridescent pink eye shadow on Nora's lids. Mimicked how she wanted Nora to close her eyes, hold her lips while she brushed on mascara first and then lip-gloss. "This skin is the best thing your father left you," she said softly, her breath warm on Nora's cheeks. She didn't often bring up Nora's father. She mentioned him now as casually as if she were describing weather. Other times Nora might have seized on the words *father left you* but not then. Right then all she wanted was her mom's creamy complexion and for her mom to skip the date with Dr. Guy, to stay home so Nora could have her all to herself. Ruby slicked her signature shade of lipstick, Frosted Rumor, over her lips, turned up the volume on the stereo, then petted Phil Donahue, who was stretched across Nora's bed lazily watching the two of them through half-closed eyes as if he didn't care what they did.

"We love veterinarians, don't we?" her mom asked him. His fur rippled and he tilted his head into her hand. Little beads of drool formed at the side of his mouth. "You're a love-glutton." She shimmied her behind with her glass held high above her head, singing loudly and out of tune with her favorite song, "Ruby Tuesday."

The two of them danced in the speck of space between the beds. The next song, "Have You Seen Your Mother, Baby, Standing in the Shadow," was faster and Nora bumped hips with her mom. Phil Donahue watched, purring and kneading away at Nora's bed, remembering when he was a kitten.

When the song ended, Ruby stepped into her dress. "Zip me, Beanie." She smelled of cinnamon and roses. She bent into the closet for shoes, and immediately she started screaming, "Goddamn it. Fucking asshole cat." She sniffed high-heeled shoe after high-heeled shoe and hurled each one over her shoulder. "Your fucking cat sprayed them all." Shoes flew from the closet in an unending assault. Even in the best of moods Ruby wouldn't tolerate ruined clothing, shoes, or accessories. "Shit. We should have neutered the son of a bitch right away." She flung a black pump hard at Phil Donahue, who dove under the bed.

"Don't! Mommy! Remember, consistent love . . . consistent love."

Ruby bent down, frantically patted the carpet, and finally yanked the cat out by his hind legs. Her face was red, and her breath came in bursts. She stalked to the back door holding Phil Donahue by the scruff of his neck and hurled him out.

Nora howled.

In trying to grab the cat, Ruby had smeared a long pink gash of lipstick onto her cheek. "Find the least stinky pair," she hissed.

They knelt on the floor smelling shoes and finally settled on a pair of black mules. With her mother in a rage Nora knew better than to cry for Phil Donahue. Instead she slumped on the couch, twisting the red satin in her hands, the front of the dress drooping from the weight of the rhinestones.

When the babysitter arrived, Ruby offered Nora her cheek for a goodbye kiss. "Your cat will be fine," she insisted. Then she continued, talking more to herself than to Nora, "Thank God he's a veterinarian, hopefully desensitized to cat piss."

As soon as Ruby left, Mrs. Childers and Nora called for Phil Donahue. Nora held her sitter's hand as they walked past Jocelyn's window. Inside, pots of white Easter lilies glowed like candles on either side of the sofa. The outline of Donald's round head shone darkly in a pool of watery blue light from the TV. Margaret and Jocelyn must already be in bed. Nora wanted to knock, to ask about Phil Donahue and let them see how upset she was, but Mrs. Childers said absolutely not, why turn a situation from bad to worse by letting others see her traipse through the neighborhood in a cocktail dress, as if there weren't enough to talk about already.

Mrs. Childers made them turn around when her ankles started hurting.

In the morning, Mrs. Childers snored softly on the couch. Nora pressed her forehead against the window, scanning the street. Puddles from the sprinklers shone slivery bright on the sidewalk. Despite Phil Donahue's absence, the sky was clear.

Mrs. Childers poached eggs, and since there was no bread for toast, she served Nora a stack of Ritz crackers with a forbearing sigh. She held her palms up for Nora to place her own hands atop while she examined Nora's fingernails, bringing them up to her watery blue eyes. Yes, she said, Nora most definitely suffered from an iron deficiency. She should eat raisins. Then she told Nora to scoot, to go watch cartoons. When Ruby finally called, at ten, Nora told her mom about raisins and her deficiency and demanded they offer a reward for Phil Donahue.

"You're healthy as a Shetland pony. Phil will survive one night outside. Besides, Dr. Guy says not to worry." Nora knew her mother was smiling when she said *Dr. Guy*. Her voice hit all the right notes. "The cat is punishing me for booting him. Cats can hold a grudge, you know."

"His name is Phil Donahue."

"Go swim at Jocelyn's. I'll be home for lunch."

Nora searched under cars, up the magnolia tree, and behind the Dumpster. Nothing.

"Don't fret, lamb," Margaret said. Her chair sat just beyond the carport in a patch of sun. Next to it, she'd placed a card table with a rose-printed tablecloth, a pitcher of iced tea, and a china platter of crust-free cucumber sandwiches. Donald had stayed behind on church business and they were sneaking a Sunday-morning swim. "Phil Donahue will return," Margaret said. She'd removed her church clothes and wore her robe with the sash loosened so sunlight hit the V of pale flesh and the small gold cross at her neck.

She held her cherished stack of British *Vogue*s on her lap. "A cat would be loopy to run away from you." When she said it, Nora found she could almost relax.

"Come on." Jocelyn pulled at her arm. She wore a new paisley swimsuit the Easter Bunny had left inside a giant pink plastic egg, which now bobbed on the surface of the pool. They swam around the circle of aqua plastic as fast as they could, trying to make a whirlpool, calling for Phil Donahue every time they surfaced for air. When Jocelyn yelled, "Switch," the two girls turned to face the flow of water. Jocelyn's feet were so close to Nora's face she could feel the current ripple past her ears.

They ate cucumber sandwiches while hanging over the pool's edge. Margaret's scissors flashed as she snipped fashion photos from her magazines, a smile floating on her lips as if this was her idea of a delicious morning. She'd unwound her bun and occasionally asked them what they thought of a particular outfit. Nora, Margaret exclaimed, had a great fashion sense. It would have been Nora's idea of a delicious morning too if Phil Donahue were home. She envisioned him strolling up, nonchalant, with the sun shining off his Kitty Queen–glossy fur. The two of them would regally ignore her mother for days. She finished her cucumber sandwich and flung herself backward into the water.

"She shouldn't have hurt him," she said to herself and the sky.

Margaret lowered her magazine. "What, love?" Her round brown eyes looked at Nora with so much Catholic sympathy that Nora found she couldn't help herself.

"My mom beat my cat with her shoe." Nora's eyes stung and she didn't mean to cry, but there was Margaret, her forehead creased with concern, reaching a hand toward Nora's wet head. She couldn't stop herself, she sobbed, sucking in air and water until she was coughing, nearly choking. Margaret held a big yellow towel open to her, and when Nora wouldn't get out, Margaret climbed into the pool, the water lapping over the edge, her robe

hanging on the chair. She hugged Nora to her soggy white pad-
ded bra, and Nora loved feeling her own shoulders heave beneath
Margaret's hand.

Jocelyn watched them, sidling closer to her mother. She patted Nora's back a few perfunctory times. The crying must have
seemed endless to Jocelyn because finally she jumped from the
pool and ran dripping into her apartment. Nora heard slamming
drawers before Jocelyn returned, her arms heaped with pantyhose.

"Josie, don't."

Jocelyn ignored her. "Seaweed," she said, tossing them into the
pool, "for Mermaid Island." The legs fluttered, quivering beneath
the surface as if they were alive—a sea garden for Jocelyn and
Nora to splash through. She shrieked and dove, winding the shimmering hose around her arms and the pink plastic egg, stealing
her mother back.

"You'll ruin them." Margaret's hands left Nora. She shambled
around the pool, grabbing at pantyhose and Jocelyn's legs, slippery
as white eels. "Stop it this instant," she said, huffing. Soggy brown
tentacles clung to her arms as she slapped at the water. "They're
costly."

Nora pressed her back against the side, waiting for one of them
to notice she wasn't part of the game. She'd pretty much exhausted
that particular burst of sorrow over Phil Donahue, though she
managed a few more sobs. When Jocelyn and her mother kept up
their game, the chastising giving way, eventually, to laughter, Nora
blurted, "My mother didn't come home last night."

Margaret halted. Instead of sympathetic clucking and a return
to Nora's side, she sealed her lips tight. Right away Nora knew she'd
said something wrong. She thought she might cry some more, but
she was all dried up.

"Is your mother home now?"

Nora half shrugged, half nodded, uncertain which answer
would work best. A hummingbird paused over the pool. Its wings

thrumming, it hung there, suspended for a long moment, before switching directions and darting away. "She had a date." Nora didn't mention Mrs. Childers.

When Margaret stood, water streamed off her body. Her pale stomach rolled over the top of her pantyhose. From what Nora saw, she didn't have the silver stretch marks her mom lamented over in front of the mirror. "We've had enough," Margaret declared, climbing from the pool.

"Why?" Jocelyn objected.

"Do as I say." Margaret wrapped Jocelyn in a thick towel and tossed one to Nora as well. "Spit-spot."

Jocelyn scowled. Margaret scooped the pantyhose from the pool, draped them over her chair. Nora wondered what Donald would think when he saw the harem of pantyhose exposed in his carport.

"You'll have to come in and wait until your mother gets home." Margaret tsked and marched smartly toward the apartment door. She was mumbling to herself about Ruby and about Nora, who had switched from an opportunity to a responsibility.

When Nora bent to pick up her shorts, she saw Margaret's scissors lying on the carport floor, and she didn't mean to, but she found herself edging them along the concrete toward the pool and then jabbing the tips into the plastic, nothing more than a wee nick. She needed something new to think about, all that leaking water, while she waited for Phil Donahue and her mom.

Ruby and Dr. Shapiro rang Jocelyn's cheerful doorbell. Nora saw that they were holding hands. Her mom's cheek grazed his shoulder as if she were petting him with her face.

"Is Nora here?" Ruby wore a breezy smile.

Margaret kept Jocelyn behind her, as if she needed protection.

"She's been here all morning, I've fed her lunch and washed her hair."

"One less thing to do." Her mom laughed and held her hand out to Nora.

"May I speak with you in the kitchen?" Margaret asked.

Jocelyn and Nora stayed on the front porch with Dr. Shapiro. They made a small, awkward clump, like people waiting for a diagnosis.

"Who are you?" Jocelyn asked.

"The vet." He stuck out his hand. "Call me Dr. Guy." He kept his other hand in his pocket, jiggling coins. The tails of his shirt hung over his khakis in a sloppy, jaunty fashion. He rocked in his loafers, then smiled wide and easy, as if he had nothing better to do than chat with a couple of kids on a stranger's front porch. Nora didn't trust him with his butt chin.

"Her cat ran away."

"Yes, strays do that," he said. "I wouldn't worry too much. Maybe he needed a night on the town." He play-socked Nora's shoulder. "Do you dance as well as your mom?"

She rubbed her arm as if he'd hurt her. What kind of vet was he? She hated her mom for making her unworthy of Margaret's attention.

"I thought you were the boyfriend," Jocelyn said.

Nora cringed. It was another of her mom's not-to-be-broken rules: Let the man call himself boyfriend. Nora had heard her advise friends over the telephone: *Don't scare them off. Aloof. Aloof. Aloof.*

Right then her mom stepped out. Her lips were thin and tight as Margaret's. "Let's go," she said too quietly, as if she were counting to ten in her mind. It's what she was supposed to remember to do when she was angry with Nora. What she should have done last night with Phil Donahue. She did it now, refraining from saying anything else because she had an audience, but Nora saw her frown lines deepen. Halfway to their apartment she said, "Margaret thinks I need church." Then she forced one loud *ha*, sharp as a pinprick.

"From what I know of you, I think Margaret is absolutely right." Guy laughed. He didn't know not to tease her mom when she got like this. "Come on, it's a joke."

Her mom called her into the bathroom to talk. She smelled the armpits of her dress and tossed it in the dry-cleaning pile. With one hand she unhooked her bra and dropped it into the sink, then she began scrubbing the lace with a bar of soap. "Why did you tell them you were home alone?" Ruby and her pale nipples stared accusingly at Nora from the mirror, as if she had two sets of eyes.

Ruby tried to mimic Margaret's accent. "'She's a wee vulnerable child.'" It was a horrible attempt. "Margaret thinks I don't have your best interests at heart. She thinks you're in danger."

Margaret had pulled on her dish gloves to wash Nora's hair. She'd raked her rubberized fingers over Nora's scalp, scrubbing twice before she combed cream rinse through, furiously yanking at the snarls. Never before had Nora washed her hair twice. She was beyond clean. She was sanitized.

"Catholics are ruthlessly judgmental." Ruby squinted at Nora, swished the bra back and forth beneath the running faucet.

Nora almost told her mom about the pool, now draining from the bottom, its sides slowly folding in like a morning glory. She was afraid her mom would laugh her approval rather than make her go confess.

"Why aren't you talking to me?"

"I miss Phil Donahue."

On Tuesday night they were invited to dinner at Hamburger Hamlet with Dr. Guy. Right away things didn't go well. First, he called to say he couldn't pick them up because he had a veterinary emergency. Her mom scratched the air with two fingers when she repeated it so Nora knew she didn't believe him. Then they waited for him in the parking lot for twenty-three minutes by her mom's Timex.

"It happens." He shrugged when he arrived. "I just put forty-seven stitches in a rottweiler."

"What happened?" Nora asked.

"Hit by a car."

"I hope Phil Donahue is okay." Nora jammed her brows together with concern and her mom reached over to smooth them out. She was constantly warning Nora about her bad habits.

"Felines are smarter than canines," her mom said. She sniffed Dr. Guy's shoulder. "You don't smell like dog."

"And that's a good thing, right?"

Ruby led the three of them into the restaurant, past families seated in booths, swaying her hips in her green capri pants. Dr. Guy pressed his steady hand on her and reminded her she wasn't delivering cocktails. She claimed she had the same walk for the freezer aisle at the grocery store, and he said he was surprised there wasn't a thaw. That made her happy. She suggested sharing a shrimp Louie, but he wanted a roast beef sandwich. She pouted, said a turkey club would be fine. Halfway through his placing their order, she interrupted, changed her mind to the Louie after all. They looked like any other family on a Tuesday night: the mom smoking and looking out the window, the dad lecturing about multiplication facts, bike safety, or cat-care tips. Nora played the kid, unscrewing the lid on the saltshaker. The food came and Dr. Guy made little moaning sounds with each bite. At first her mom nudged him and grinned like it was a private joke. When he didn't stop, Nora could tell it got on her mom's nerves. Ruby finally crushed her cigarette into her salad before she was even halfway done.

"That's disgusting," he said.

Nora kept her eyes cast down.

"I had no idea vets were so sensitive." Ruby unfolded a napkin over her plate so it looked as if they had a cat-size corpse on their table.

"Well. Okay," he said in the parking lot. "Thanks." He removed a toothpick from his mouth to kiss her mom's cheek. Then he slipped it right back in.

"Thanks for removing it first," her mom said. She leaned toward him and bit the toothpick as if they were playing tug of war. He relinquished it.

"I'll call you," he said, backing toward his car. "Sorry. I've got to check on the rotty. Good luck finding Phil Donahue." He waved to Nora.

On the way home her mom banged the steering wheel with her fist.

Ruby mimeographed REWARD FOR LOST CAT signs and borrowed a stapler from her school. The next afternoon, they walked the neighborhood, not saying much, just walking and stapling. They passed Donald, sweating in Bermuda shorts and a plaid shirt buttoned up to his neck, as he patched the pool in his carport. "Looking for the Manx?" The way he asked frightened Nora because his eyes and voice didn't go together. One gleamed and the other pitied.

"What happened?" Ruby pointed at the pool.

"A slow leak. Have a private moment?" he asked Ruby.

Nora hung back, fearful. Nothing he said would be good news.

"Saw your Manx," she heard him say. Ruby looked over her shoulder at Nora, her eyes wide with sympathy or hope.

"She was trotting down the sidewalk when a car" — he slapped his hands together hard — "braked." Ruby flinched. Donald looked at Nora, who dropped to a squat, pretending interest in a pill bug, and then he turned back to Ruby. His voice grew oddly loud and fake. "A family got out of the car, a mum and a dad and a boy. The three of them fussed over her, called the Manx, and she jumped in their car."

Nora was doubly relieved — Phil Donahue was fine, and Donald hadn't linked her to the pool carcass at his feet.

"He," Ruby said. "Phil Donahue was a he."

"Of course," Donald said.

Ruby crossed her arms over her chest, then moved her hands to her shoulders, as if she were trying to cover as much of herself as possible.

"I suspect *he* moved in with a family. You know, consistency makes a happy home." Donald lifted his hand and Nora thought he would pull a coin from behind her mother's ear. She stood and walked toward them, then pressed against her mother's side. Donald jerked his thumb toward the 25 MPH sign. "Drove a bit too fast." Sunlight glinted off his thick watch, and Ruby's hand fluttered up, covering the O of her mouth. Nora rubbed her toe against the mound of plastic. "Sorry, Nora." He pulled a tube of glue from his pocket. "Looks like we've both had a bit of bad luck."

Her mom banged her fist against her thigh. It was the second time that week she'd banged her fist. She led Nora down the sidewalk. "Sanctimonious bastard. *Moved in with a family!*"

"Phil Donahue is gone?" Nora hurried to keep up with her.

Her mom turned sharply on her heel, gripped Nora's shoulders, and searched her face. "What do you consider us?"

The question seemed so strange. Did she mean *us* without Phil Donahue?

Her mom's voice tightened and her hands trembled. Whatever her mom wanted to know, it was costing her a lot. "When you think of me, what do you think?"

"Mommy?" Nora closed her eyes and swallowed, trying to push back her feelings. Her mother was scaring her.

"Yes, and you're my daughter."

Nora wanted so much to give what was needed. Ruby stared at her hard, then looked over Nora's shoulder, toward Donald, hunched in his carport. She looked as if she were deciding something important.

"The way he said *family,* talking about Phil. As if we aren't." She knelt in front of Nora, stroking bangs away from her eyes. "You have to know your cat didn't prefer another family."

Nora felt a lump in her throat.

Ruby hesitated. "Phil Donahue was hit by a car. Beanie, honey, given the choice, Phil dead or Phil picking a new family, we have to choose dead."

Nora cried and her mom did too, right there on the sidewalk. "I am so sorry."

Ruby hugged her close, and in the waning light, their shadows lengthened behind them. Neighbors they didn't know pulled into driveways, arriving home from work. A dog yapped, waiting to be let out for a walk. The ice cream man's tune played in the hills above them.

Nora missed Phil Donahue so much. But she missed more than just her cat. She missed everything, the pool and Margaret and Jocelyn. She missed the whole idea of a pet. And even with Ruby right in front of her, holding her, she missed her mom.

"I hate this street," she said.

Her mom sighed. "So do I."

Take Your Daughter to Work

THE NEW DENT in the passenger door had jammed it shut. Since her mother decided to use the insurance money from the accident to pay off her Ohrbach's charge card, they would both be climbing in on the driver's side from now on.

"Four doors were so conventional." Ruby slid in easily after Nora, filling the car with her scent: cigarettes, coffee, and Jean Naté After Bath Splash.

Today Nora was excused from school. Her mother, who had been reading *Ms.* magazine, had decided that since she was definitely raising a liberated daughter, it was important for Nora to see her in action at Hollenbeck High, where she claimed to be breaking down boundaries as the youngest, hippest teacher in East LA. Nora squeezed her hands together to stop herself from jouncing in her seat and irritating her mother. She was nervous about visiting Hollenbeck High and delighted about missing a day at her new school, where her fifth-grade teacher, Mr. Marshall, was making good on his promise to turn his students into *real men.* Instead of playing red rover or steal the bacon, Nora's class spent their PE time marching in formation around the blacktop while Mr. Marshall shrilled his whistle. As much as she hated marching, Nora hadn't mentioned the drills to her mother for fear Ruby would forbid her to participate as an antiwar statement. Nora was having a hard enough time fitting in without being sidelined with the asthmatic kids.

Rush hour on the Santa Monica Freeway—the early-morning sun bouncing off so many windshields made Nora squint. Despite pervasive smog and auto exhaust, a huge and alarming hedge of dusty pink oleander flourished in the median strip. Nora had heard that at a cookout, an entire family had died from eating hot dogs roasted on oleander sticks. Highly poisonous. Yesterday at her school they served hot dogs at lunch and then everyone had to stay indoors for recess due to the air quality. You just never knew what could happen.

Ruby tapped her short fingernails on the steering wheel. "I hope there's no smog alert today."

"Mr. Marshall says only grubs stay inside for bad air." From the glove box, Nora removed the last strawberry Pop-Tart and peeled open her breakfast. She would have to remind her mother to stop at the store on the way home.

"Remind me to talk to your principal about Mr. ROTC." Ruby pointed to her purse on the floor. "Dig me out a cigarette, Beanie." In deference to Nora's lungs she dangled it out the window and blew the smoke from the side of her mouth. "This morning I especially need you to keep quiet while I teach. I have a plan, something new I'm trying in homeroom."

Ruby often complained about her homeroom. Nora overheard her talking to her friend Maxine about it nearly every night, a wine spritzer in one hand, the phone in the other. It was Ruby's answer to the not-drinking-alone problem. Homeroom was a waste of time, she fretted. How could she connect with her burgeoning girls—shellacked by Aqua Net, trapped by girdles and the sexist stereotypes of their small-minded community? "Holy shit, it's the seventies!" she practically shouted into the phone last night. "You're so right. My girls should aim higher than having babies for the church! I should aim higher than being Frank Lessing's dalliance!"

As soon as Ruby flicked her cigarette butt out the car window, she told Nora to grab another one.

"They cause cancer," Nora said.

Ruby held her two peace fingers aloft until Nora finally slid a fresh cigarette into the V. "You can draw or something," Ruby said.

"I brought books." Nora had *Are You There God? It's Me, Margaret* and *A Tree Grows in Brooklyn* tucked into her knapsack, along with a hairbrush, chewing gum, a package of oyster crackers her mom brought home from a dinner date at the Santa Monica pier, a collapsible cup, a small tin of aspirin, a Stayfree maxi-pad, and a clean pair of underpants. She'd added the last three items to her inventory after the weeklong Family Life class she'd endured with the other fifth-grade girls. Nora didn't want to be caught unprepared.

"I wish my students read as well as you do, Beanie. Never forget . . ." Her voice trailed off as she craned her neck, seeking to merge toward the off ramp. "Damn it—let me in." She leaned over and took a bite of the Pop-Tart. "*You* are smart. Oh my God. Turn it up." Crumbs flew from her lips. "A Taste of Honey" by the Tijuana Brass filled the car, the turn signal clicking steady with the beat as they rolled off the freeway. "I love this song."

Homeroom girls arrived in clusters—stiff haired, torpedo chested, and tight skirted—after the tardy bell. Nora stayed behind the teacher desk while Ruby greeted the girls at the door. Her mother nodded and touched girls' shoulders, delicate creases appearing at the corners of her bright eyes. Even her voice was different here, warm and open, so unlike her most recent at-home moods, either lackluster monotone or spring-loaded tension.

"Marisol, you brought your notebook. Wonderful. Good morning, Carmen. Anna, how was the test?" The girls smiled and answered her questions. "Lucy, come on. You know that skirt is totally wrong at school. Fabulous out in the world, but tug it down." Hollenbeck High had a dress code that required girls in question-able-length skirts to kneel in front of the class. If the fabric didn't meet the floor, they were sent home to change. At home, Ruby ranted against the rule and called it sexist. "Elena? To what do I owe the pleasure?"

Elena, a slender girl with teased hair and Life Savers–candy-green eyes, strolled in. She looked past Ruby then snapped her gum.

"Lose the gum, and just so you know, once a month isn't enough."

Elena made a big show of stretching the gum and wrapping it in a long string around her index finger, then she slid a pack of cigarettes from her pocketbook and stuck the gum to the cellophane.

A slight smile played at the corners of Ruby's mouth. "You won't pass my class," she said, tension leaking back into her voice.

"What a tragedy." Even Elena's eyebrows were haughty.

Girls laughed, smoothed hair, tugged at blouses with tiny pearl buttons, and watched one another. Around their necks, heavy boys' rings and crucifixes dangled from chains. Their beige foundation makeup ended abruptly at their throats, revealing darker skin. Their lips were iced with pale pink lipstick. Everything about them was put together, all of them except for one girl, her dress shapeless as a Brownie uniform, her face bare of makeup. She stumbled in the aisle on the way to her seat.

"Are you okay?" asked the girl Elena, her voice slinky and frayed, like ripped satin. "Maybe it was your shoelaces?" she added, her chic black heels peeking into the aisle, condemning the girl and her blue Keds.

"*Puta*," the girl said.

"Skunk."

"Hey! We're all in this struggle together," Ruby said. When she turned to take Nora's hand, Elena whispered another insult, and Nora looked down at the scuffed toes of her own Buster Browns.

Ruby's hand felt damp, and Nora let her own hand go limp clasped inside her mother's. She was stuck between pride and worry over what her mother might say. Stuck between belonging to her mother and wanting to belong with the girls who only half listened, whose brains were filled with mysterious and far more important thoughts. Ruby explained about Gloria Steinem and equal rights and *Ms.* magazine and the bright future while girls filed their nails and stared out the window. When Ruby finally introduced Nora, she slid her hand from her mother's and wiped it on her skirt.

"What's her name?"

"Can I braid her hair?"

"She's cute."

"How old is she?"

The way the girls fussed over her wasn't all that different from her mother's boyfriends' fawning, with their stuffed animals and Tootsie Pops for her, wine and flowers for her mother. "Knock with your elbows," her mother always told the men, encouraging gifts. The ones that hung around for a while, like Frank Lessing, brought books when they realized Nora would disappear with them into her bedroom.

"She's so smart." The girls pointed to Nora's books, talked about her as if she weren't standing right in front of them.

"She's beautiful," Elena said. "Do you have a boyfriend yet?"

"She's ten," Ruby answered.

Nora pretended to pull up her knee socks, hiding her pleasure and disappointment. She was thrilled Elena spoke to her, but she wanted to be older, thirteen. More than anything, she wanted to be part of this club.

Her mother pointed to an empty seat across from Elena and behind Celia, the girl who had tripped. In the roomful of teased hair, Celia's long braid, pouring down the middle of her back like oil, seemed out of place, as if Celia had been deprived of important girl-knowledge, as if she'd been forced to live without girlfriends or television or *Teen* magazine — which Nora sometimes bought with her mother's cigarette change when Ruby sent her to the corner store.

"These are journals." The tap of her mother's heels against the wood floor as she handed out composition books lent authority to her words. "These are private. Write anything you wish. I'll count the number of pages you've filled but I won't read a word unless you mark a star at the top of the page."

"What's the point?" Elena asked.

"The point is — these are for you. The point is — I've had the antenna broken off my car four times this year." Ruby paused and looked over the girls' heads toward the back of the classroom with its map of the United States and the WAR IS NOT HEALTHY FOR CHILDREN AND OTHER LIVING THINGS poster she kept retaping to the wall. "My antenna — filed into a shiv, a weapon for some crazy rumble." There was snickering in the room and Ruby nodded her head. "Okay, laugh, but I like music in my car. I can't afford to keep replacing my antenna. Every day people tell you who you are: enemy, girlfriend, sister, daughter. These journals are a place for you to figure it out. On your own terms." Her mother paced. Her blond hair and pale skin made her stand out in the classroom, but watching and listening, Nora felt that Ruby was more like these girls than not. Ruby was more like these girls than Nora was. She was young and pretty, with her short hairdo, her cinch-waisted dress floating just above her kneecaps, her high heels emphasizing her shapely calves.

Elena glared at Ruby. She was snapping her gum again. "You act like this is *West Side Story* and we're all Maria."

"Not true. I'm leaving it up to you to tell me who you are."

"What about your *hija*?" Elena gestured toward Nora with a slight lift of her eyebrow.

"Great idea." Ruby nodded and set a composition book on Nora's desk.

"Who are you?" Elena whispered to Nora, loud enough for Ruby to hear.

Nora's smile shifted toward uncertain and stuck there; she felt pinned down, like a butterfly specimen. She never thought about who she was. She was a fifth-grader. She was Ruby's daughter. She was trying to make friends. Ruby was a mother and a teacher, often a girlfriend. Sometimes on weekend mornings, stirring up frozen orange juice with the spoon thunking against the plastic pitcher, her mother would ask Nora if she was happy. "We're happy, right?" Ruby would say. "Even if it's just us girls?"

Her mother allowed fifteen minutes for writing. Girls took up pencils. Elena leaned back in her seat, tapping her eraser on the blank page. Celia drummed her fingers on the desktop, her nails chewed to raw skin. "You'll only read if there's a star?" she asked. Ruby said yes, that was so. Then Celia cramped her raggedy fingers around the nub of her pencil and began.

Amid these grown girls, with their scented deodorants, pantyhose scratching each time they shifted in their seats, Nora didn't know whether to slouch or sit tall, to become as small as she felt or to strive against it. Soon she would matter in a way she didn't quite matter yet. She was on the cusp of something private and fulfilling. She imagined the girls around her wrote about love, about the searching, sleepy look in men's eyes after a kiss. She'd seen that look in movies, and in Frank Lessing's eyes late one night when she got up to pee and surprised him in the bathroom. Staring out from his reflection in the mirror, his bristled cheeks dripping water, Frank's sleepy eyes seemed to have forgotten who Nora was and why she was in the apartment. He quit humming and asked her how she liked the new TV. She thanked him again, then he dried his face and left to go home to his wife. Once the front door shut, Nora's mother called her into her bedroom and asked if Frank had said anything. When Nora said not really, Ruby told her to get back in bed.

Ruby had given Nora a picture book about puberty called

What's Happening to Me? Along with discussing pimples and sprouting hair and the mechanics of sperm and egg, it described sex as being exhilarating, like jumping rope all afternoon and then eating a double-scoop marble fudge ice cream cone with exhausted and tingling legs.

Nora focused on her composition book. Starting with deodorant, she wrote a list of things she needed: a training bra, feminine hygiene spray. She'd detected an unpleasant odor in her armpits, which she learned in Family Life class was a first sign of puberty. She also learned that odors could happen in other places on her body and it was important to feel fresh. Next she wrote about Lana, who sat next to her in Mr. Marshall's fifth-grade class and whom Nora was trying to develop as a friend. After three elementary schools, Nora had friend-making skills — a practiced smile, a just friendly enough *Hi,* the ability to compliment — but the fifth-grade girls at her new school already had best friends. She added to her list: headband, Dr Pepper Lip Smacker, a fringe skirt. Lana's best friend was Kathi W. They wore fringe skirts and everyone treated them like royalty. At recess Nora lingered near their bench, imitating the way Kathi W. stood, with her knees hyperextended and her chest thrust forward, looking like a bent straw. So far, all Nora had managed to do was finesse herself a role as their gopher, delivering notes to the popular boys.

Then, because Nora felt like she had to write something in the journal for her mother, she put a star at the top of the next page and told Ruby how much she loved her visit to Hollenbeck High. She thanked her mom for taking care of the Frigidaire someone dumped behind their apartment building, between the Dumpster and an abandoned sofa. Nora spent her afternoons reading on that sofa as if it was her very own living room. When News Channel Four reported a boy had suffocated inside an abandoned refrigerator, her mother lectured her about climbing inside, as if Nora had no sense. Then she hounded their landlord to haul the Frigidaire away. Finally, Ruby unhinged the door herself and dropped it in the dirt.

"Two more minutes," her mother announced.

Nora stopped writing. Every *i* on her page was dotted with a perfect tiny circle, as if bubbles floated up from her words. She glanced around to see if anyone was looking at her. In front of Nora, Celia sighed and leaned back in her chair. Her journal was also covered with words, the cursive tiny and precise, each *f* a flourish of curlicues. The entire page was covered with one word, written over and over. *Fuck.*

At home, with a game show on the TV, Nora and her mom settled at opposite ends of the sofa. In their apartment the TV was always on, beating back the quiet. Nora rearranged herself, coughed, ate a Ritz cracker, glanced at Monty Hall, who was talking to a man dressed in a giant diaper, and waited for her mom to find Celia's journal.

"Sit still already." Ruby balanced a wine spritzer against her chest and held a cigarette between her fingers as she flipped through the journals, counting up the pages. When she came across Nora's journal she set it on the sofa between them.

Nora didn't touch it. "You can read it. If you want."

"Holy shit. Will you look at Elena's?" Ruby held up a journal. Elena had drawn a star at the top of every single blank page in the book, inviting Ruby to read exactly nothing. "It's her screw-you gift to me." Ruby shook her head, and then she wrote, *I'm here if you ever want to talk.* Followed by a red zero.

"Why'd you give her a zero?"

"Listen, Beanie" — she held her drink in front of her mouth — "even though in your life it doesn't seem like it yet, there are plenty of men to go around. Beautiful women don't have to hate each other. We don't have to compete. Elena wrote nothing, she gets no credit." She sucked ice into her mouth and crunched down hard, like she was chewing rocks. "Holy shit. I could be her friend . . . her mother even, her really young mother." She tossed Elena's journal aside.

Nora was uncertain what her mother meant about *men to go around* and what any of it had to do with the blank journal. Was she talking about married Frank Lessing or Nora's absent dad? As far back as she could remember Ruby had always been focused on getting Nora a dad. Ruby was either dewy in love, angry about an argument, or sad after a breakup. Nora wedged her feet beneath her mother's legs. "Why don't you read everything?"

"I want them to trust me, to feel safe enough to write anything at all."

Ruby stayed true to her word until she sat up and plunked her drink down hard on the coffee table. She'd found it. Celia's journal was star free but Ruby flipped back and forth through the pages anyway, biting her lip.

"Did Celia say anything to you?"

Nora pretended to think. "She chews her nails."

Her mother watched a Nice 'n Easy hair dye commercial then stubbed out her cigarette. *The closer he gets . . . the better you look,* the voice from the TV said. Finally Ruby commented, "Celia has no friends," as if nail biting and friendlessness were linked. She totaled up the pages and circled an eight and two pluses on the cover. Something about that eight hugged by a circle of red ink made Nora happy. It was as if her mother's decision to honor the girls' secrets meant that Nora's future secrets would be safe too — safety by association. She shifted her position on the sofa again, this time resting her head against her mother's bony shoulder. Ruby set her work aside and wrapped her arms around Nora. They turned up the TV and watched Monty Hall pay a woman twenty bucks for the can opener in her purse. Ruby told Nora to switch to the news, where they followed a story about the hiring of the first-ever women FBI agents.

"Shh." Ruby held her finger to her lips and then continued to talk right around it. "You are going to have so many choices."

Spring came so early that by April the volunteer flowers — daffodils, cornflowers, dandelions — out by Nora's sofa were already withered. For months she'd been sneaking the girls' updated journals outside, and as a result, she was panicked and enthralled by all that could happen in a teenage life. You just never knew.

Unlike her mother, Nora read all the pages — heady and alarming stories of dates gone bad, overcrowded apartments, broken wrists, calls to God, formal dances, withdrawal method, probation, and VD — whether there was a star or not. After her *fuck* entry, Celia starred all her pages. Her brothers had beaten a boy she spoke to at church. Elena had cut off the end of her braid during science period. Celia found her locker filled with kitty litter. She didn't trust any of the girls at school. She wanted heels. Her father would not allow her to wear store-bought clothes. She had to wear the shapeless dresses her grandmother sewed for her. Her mother had no say because her mother was dead. Boys and wine were the only things that made Celia happy, so she started sneaking out her bedroom window. Happiness was worth risks, she wrote in one entry.

Nora thought about that for a long time. The statement seemed essential and romantic.

When Celia was caught with a boy, her father, a welder, blackened her eye, then installed bars on her window to keep her in and to keep thieves out. She was miserable, and her brother supplied her with reds. She mentioned suicide. It was so huge, Celia's isolation, that Ruby had created a contract in the journal. *Next time I want to swallow reds, I will call Miss Hargrove.* In return, Ruby promised discretion. They both signed it, Celia in her flowery cursive, *Celia Delgado.*

Elena had written exactly four entries, all marked with stars.

She wrote about a boy, Hugo, who was twenty and deluged her with warm kisses. Hugo tattooed her name on his arm twice . . . once was not enough for him, Elena wrote. Next she wrote about sitting by herself in the last row at Our Lady of Solitude, staring at the back of Hugo's mother's head, afraid to look inside the casket. Then she wrote to say her family was sending her away indefinitely to visit an aunt in Juárez. Ruby responded to that entry. *I am so sorry. If there is anything I can do to help, anything at all, let me know. You have choices.* She'd signed her note *Ms. Hargrove* and then she'd crossed that out and written *Ruby,* along with their address. The fourth entry said only goodbye and thank you.

The journal idea was working. Nora felt glad her mother wanted to aid and comfort the girls. It made her mother seem stronger somehow, as if there was enough of her to go around. Sometimes, late at night, her mother sat alone in their living room, on the brink of something Nora did not understand. The first time Nora felt her mother awake in the apartment, she tiptoed to the threshold of the living room but found the sofa empty. The red glow from her mother's cigarette was the only point of light in the dim room and once Nora's eyes grew accustomed to the dark, she found her mother sitting on the floor in front of the door mirror, blowing smoke rings at her reflection. "It's quiet," Nora worried out loud. Her voice butted up against a soft thing rising in her throat. "It's a lonesome night," her mother murmured back and Nora swallowed hard. Lonesomeness often threatened to descend upon her mother, and when it did, Ruby sometimes couldn't get out of bed. How could she feel lonesome when Nora was right here, right beside her? A smoke ring hovered between her mother and the mirror but it was her mother who seemed like she might fade away. Nora curled up on the floor next to her that night, one arm hitched over Ruby's thigh. How could a person feel safe when she never knew anything about anything?

On her couch outside, Nora traced the blue ink with her pinkie

— Ms. Hargrove, Ruby. Her mother wanted to be a safe place in her girls' harrowing lives. That had to be good. She stretched out long, wondered what it would be like to be sent away like Elena, to be locked in like Celia, to weep in the dark like her mother. She stared up into the orange-tinged haze that forever clung to Los Angeles. It was all tragic and beautiful. The journals she clutched to her chest grew heavy as the Yellow Pages. She felt tired and imagined dropping them in the dirt. Dead flowers, strange alien light, the faint thrum of traffic helicopters scuttling up and down the freeways bordering her neighborhood, reporting on delays, accidents, and air quality. Then she imagined a sudden rise and swoop, being lifted by the whirring helicopter blades. She imagined looking down upon a never-ending line of brake lights below her, red like the pills Celia's brother gave her, like the blood in the diagrams from the Family Life filmstrip, like the wine spritzers her mother drank at night with the phone in her other hand. She imagined sweeping down and gathering motherless Celia from her imprisonment, ducking to climb back aboard. Celia's long hair would fly up dangerously close to the propeller, and Nora would help to gather it together at Celia's neck. They would hunt the Greyhound bus that carried Elena with her Life Savers–candy–green eyes and the dead boy in her heart. Hugging herself, Nora thought she would like to save Celia but she would like to be Elena, with her amazing tragedy, her name written twice on a dead boy's arm. Would anyone ever love Nora enough to tattoo her name onto his skin?

"The closer he gets, the better you look," her mother narrated in a throaty, lilting voice. She was posing before the last-look mirror she'd nailed to the back of the door for giving herself final once-overs before greeting anyone or heading out.

Nora, who had just returned the journals to Ruby's desk, gazed into the mirror from behind her mother. Her bangs and front teeth were crooked. Beneath her rainbow T-shirt she saw the small soft beginnings of her adult life. There were so many frightening questions she could not ask. The room with its beige walls, heavy tweed rental drapes, and ham-colored sofa felt terribly close. Stiff-looped carpeting caused the soles of her bare feet to itch horribly. Her mother had all the windows shut, and the sun glaring in showed streaks from her attempts at cleaning with newspaper and vinegar. A small oscillating fan whirred on the coffee table, stirring the hot air. Their tiny apartment could not contain all that Nora yearned to know. She wanted to sit her mother down and ask but she had no idea where to begin. Her heart felt gummy and slow in her chest. What she needed to know, what she wanted to ask . . . was happiness worth risks? Does it hurt this much to be in love?

". . . the better you look. Beanie, would I look better as a red-head?" Ruby raked her fingers through her hair. "Hey." She squinted at Nora. "What's wrong with you?"

Nora shook her head and was shocked by the weight, as if a bowling ball had rolled across the floor of her skull.

"You weren't outside? I told you not to go outside." Ruby placed a cool hand on Nora's forehead. There was a stage-two smog alert. "Look, I need you to feel better."

Nora followed her mother's quick movements into the kitchen. Ruby was making spaghetti sauce. Maxine was on her way over. "We're coloring my hair." Plus, she had a date later. She pulled an ice cube tray from the freezer, yanked up the metal bar, and released the ice onto the counter. The sound was deafening. "Go lie down."

Her mother filled a towel with ice, a glass with water, and brought in two aspirin. She commanded Nora to keep her eyes closed and stay still. "This will pass quickly, you'll see."

Nora slept on and off, a dark and empty sleep without dreams. She might have heard Maxine arrive, the door slam. Perhaps she heard the whoosh of the blow dryer or the rise and fall of conversation. She tried her best to not throw up. Someone set a plate of buttered spaghetti and a glass of ginger ale on the coffee table. There was delighted laughter and Nora saw her mother through half-closed eyes. Ruby's hair was fierce red. "What do you think, Beanie?"

"Did you call poison control?" Maxine was standing over Nora.

"What could they do?"

"They say milk helps."

Nora wondered, *Were they talking about the dye or the smog alert?*

"This damn city." She felt her mother's lips against her forehead, inhaled the thick chemical/floral scent of the dye. Her eyes and mouth watered. The muscles at the back of her throat contracted and Nora retched, nothing but foam and soggy noodles, like wet, stringy brains.

"Poor little thing."

"Holy shit." Ruby ran into the kitchen to get paper towels, then knelt at the foot of the couch, sopping things up.

"Who are you?" Nora whispered, which made both women laugh.

"See, she's rebounding," Ruby said.

And then Nora was. She sipped ginger ale, and, to make Maxine feel helpful, she drank some milk before Maxine left. Her mother turned on *Room 222*, the show Nora liked about a student teacher at a big Los Angeles high school, and tucked a blanket around her knees.

When Frank Lessing arrived to take Ruby out for just one drink, he patted Nora's leg and asked again about the TV.

"We love it, okay?" Ruby said. Then she turned to Nora and her voice softened. "Don't answer the door and only answer our special ring. You remember?"

"Ring twice, hang up, call back."

"Stay inside."

"Will you bring home ice cream?"

Her mother kissed her forehead. "You'd better be asleep when
we get back."

"What flavor?" Frank Lessing winked at her. His shirt was so
white it hurt Nora's eyes.

At first she mistook the knocking for a sound in her dream,
her mother pacing the wooden floor of her classroom. By the
time Nora crossed the carpet to the door, the whimpering voice
sounded desperate. "Ms. Hargrove." The doorknob felt comforting
against Nora's hot palm. She bent down and touched her forehead
to it — so cool; she paused and closed her eyes. "Ms. Hargrove," the
voice said again and Nora was confused. Her mother told her not
to open the door but this person knew them.

"Who is it?"

"Is your mother home?" Nora thought she recognized the silky,
gritty voice. She opened the door and there was Elena, leaning
against the doorjamb, her palm pressed to her forehead. She at-
tempted to smile, but to Nora it looked like a grimace.

She opened the door wider and Elena stumbled in. She wore
a simple black dress and flat shoes. Her hair was flat too, and her
face was bare of makeup. Her green eyes were clouded, and her
gaze darted around Nora's living room.

"My mother isn't home." Nora hung back by the open door,
gripping her elbows in front of her chest. Her arm burned where
the boy would have Elena's name inked onto his flesh, twice.

"You're home alone?"

"I'm sick," Nora answered, as if that had anything to do with it.

Elena slumped onto the sofa, her knees squeezed together.
"What's the matter with you?"

"Smog poisoning."

She huffed like she didn't believe Nora, only the huff turned
into a groan and she tipped over onto her side.

Nora shut the door. "What happened to you?" She was part frozen, part ready to spring into action. "What do you need?" She tried to imagine what her mother would do if she were home. She would move around. She would get things.

Elena squeezed her eyes tight and Nora ran to the kitchen. A moment later she was back with aspirin, an ice pack, a bowl with two meatballs, and ginger ale. Strands of dark hair clung to Elena's forehead where she was perspiring, other bits curled in tiny ringlets. Her face was very pale and she was sweating on her top lip as well, perfect little dots. Her hand shook as she brought the glass to her lips to swallow the aspirin. "Do you know." Elena paused. "When will she be back?"

Nora shook her head but she said soon. "They went for one drink." When she reached out to take the glass away, Elena grabbed on to her wrist and squeezed. Nora didn't say that one drink could take a long time. Something was terribly wrong. Elena was supposed to be on a Greyhound. How long ago had she written that entry? Nora thought of Celia and the reds. She didn't even know what reds were but maybe they could make you this sick. Elena reached down and touched between her own legs. When she brought her hand up, she cried out, and Nora stepped back, her hand covering her mouth. "Should I call for help?"

"No, no, no, no. Don't. My parents can't know."

Nora ran from the room and returned with her knapsack. She dug out the maxi-pad and gave it to Elena, who gripped it in her hand, leaving a dark red smear.

"A towel," she said, and Nora ran from the room again.

Elena lifted her hips and slid the towel beneath. She was lying flat now. Her eyes closed; she was terribly pale.

"Promise you won't leave me alone. Even if I fall asleep," she insisted. "Promise."

Nora sat stiff straight on the floor, near to Elena's head, far from the other part. She slipped a small pillow under Elena's head then stared at the door, mouthing the words *Come home, come home, come home.* Just in case, she wanted the telephone beside her, yet she was afraid to get up. The long black cord snaked from the kitchen into Ruby's dark bedroom. Once Elena slept, Nora would turn on all the lights in the apartment and retrieve it. From health class she knew where to feel for a pulse. Nora wrapped her fingers around Elena's slim wrist and began to count while on the TV Johnny Carson told jokes. The audience laughter nearly drowned out Elena's coarse and shallow breathing. Nora lost count twice before she gave up and took small comfort in the faint beat.

"Dr. Beautiful?" Elena whispered. "Do you have a boyfriend yet?" She offered her smile-grimace one more time.

"You should rest."

It was the station sign-off on the TV screen, an American flag flapping in a stiff breeze, when the doorknob finally turned.

"... not what I meant. I do, I like it, very, very much," Frank was saying, and Ruby responded, "Shh. Nora's asleep."

As soon as Nora saw them she ran at her mother. "Why did you leave me alone?" she wailed.

Ruby stepped back, away from Nora's fists. "You're up?" There was a laugh behind the question, which disappeared when she looked into Nora's worried face.

"Who's that?" Frank said.

"She's bleeding." Nora sank down onto the floor and began to shake.

"Elena?" Ruby knelt at the couch, ran her hands down Elena's arms, checked the tender skin of her wrists. She looked at Nora over her shoulder. "What do you mean, bleeding? Did she tell you anything?"

Nora rocked on her knees, afraid to ask if Elena was dead.

In her spring-loaded voice Ruby told Nora to make coffee. "Black and strong." She repeated Elena's name, louder each time, while she hooked her hands beneath the girl's armpits to pull her upright. When Elena inched upward Ruby caught sight of the sofa. "Holy shit. Get towels. Forget the coffee. Get water."

Frank was already dialing.

"Can you make her better?"

"She's hemorrhaging. Quick, elevate her legs." Ruby pushed Elena's upper body back down, then stepped to the other end of the sofa to heave her legs farther onto the cushions. Elena's black dress fell to her hips. Her bare legs emerging from the pink of her underpants looked rubbery and gray, completely wrong. "Shove pillows under her hips. She needs blood to her brain and heart."

Frank spoke numbers rapidly into the phone, their address, and then "Oh God," when he looked at Elena. "She's been butchered."

Her mother stood, her hands clutching her new red hair. Her voice was steady, intent.

"They're on the way." Frank opened the front door and stuck his head into the hall, looking in each direction.

"Nora, get a blanket. Get two."

When Nora hesitated, Ruby said more sharply, "Now. I need you. Elena needs you. We have to keep her warm."

She ran to her mother's room and pulled off the chenille bedspread and a blanket then brought them back. Ruby shoved one beneath Elena's hips, and Nora covered the girl. Ruby slipped the pillow from beneath Elena's head.

"What are you doing?" Frank asked.

"We need to keep blood flowing to her brain. Until they get here, this is all we can do." She raised one of Elena's eyelids with her thumb. The muscles along Ruby's jaw tensed and relaxed as she watched Elena's eye. "It will all be okay, honey. Hold on."

"She knew exactly what to do," Frank said later that night. He lugged the soaked cushions and blankets out to the Dumpster. Nora followed, opening doors, afraid to be alone.

"She'll be fine?" she asked.

"If your mother has anything to say about it." The Dumpster lid clanged down, and Frank turned to face her. Nora stared up at him, her lips parted, her eyebrows raised. She didn't know what to do with her arms, so she switched them from hanging at her sides to crossing over her chest.

"Please don't worry. Your mother is amazing. She was a life-guard, huh? What hasn't your mother done?" He patted his thigh as if Nora were a puppy, but she went to him anyway, let him put his arm around her shoulders. "The paramedics said so too. Remember? When they started the IVs?"

Nora barely remembered. The whole day and night was confusing. What she most remembered was her mom telling Elena to hold on; her mom's new fierce red hair; her signature in Elena's journal; her steady voice; her strong arms; Elena's gray legs; and the smell of all that blood, like buried nails, sharp and old.

"That poor kid. What a choice," Frank said. He shook his head and started to say something more, but stopped. Instead, he led Nora to her sofa. "There's no rush to be involved with boys," he said, draping his arm around her shoulder. They sat quietly together in the warm night air. His shirt was smooth against her cheek; his body felt solid, reliable. It felt like something she could get used to. When Nora breathed in, she smelled her mom's Jean Naté.

Before Ruby followed the stretcher into the ambulance, she made Frank promise to stay with Nora until she returned. She gripped his elbow and made him promise, twice. "I know it's a big deal," she'd said. Frank nodded and told her to go, that he'd figure something out.

"You must be tired," he said to Nora.

She shook her head, but she was lying.

"It's okay. I won't go anywhere. I promised, remember?"

From the distant freeway came the muted wail of another siren, not sharp-edged like Elena's ambulance, which had howled before it even pulled away, before the door closed on her stooped-over mother, who held on to Elena with one hand and flashed their *I love you* sign to Nora with the other.

"Your mom would want you to get some sleep."

Nora struggled to keep her eyes open. Dots of light — apartments lit up inside tall glass buildings, planes and helicopters crisscrossing overhead, tiny distant stars — pricked the rust-colored night sky. In Los Angeles it was never completely dark.

A Whole Weekend of My Life

THE DIAMONDS WERE huge. And they were mine.

"They're the size of birth control pills," my mother commented dryly.

In front of the mirror, I poked the thin gold wires through my earlobes, and bits of fractured light swirled around my face as if from a disco ball. My father had sent them special delivery. I had to sign for them.

Our living room windows were thrown open wide, and the Santa Ana winds felt like they were blowing in off the tip of a match. José Feliciano doing "Light My Fire" played low on the stereo. My mother was curled up on the couch in her baby-doll pajamas with her drink du jour, tequila and orange soda. She held the cold glass to her neck and picked up her book, a Sidney Sheldon novel I'd devoured the Saturday before, locked in my bedroom, the tops of my thighs tingling and sweaty.

On my way out, when I leaned over to kiss the top of her head, my mother licked her finger and placed it on the page. "Do you have a ride home?" Her eyebrows arched like Catwoman's, perfect and predatory. This was not an offer but a veiled threat. I couldn't go to the dance if I hadn't made arrangements.

"Yolanda's dad." I hoped he wouldn't pick us up in his squad car.

"That's what you're wearing?"

Her dress hung from my shoulders. It was a little long but I liked the V in front and the rise of skin it revealed. The palm-frond print made my eyes look almost green. Lately I'd taken to calling myself Jade in my diary and to wearing its slim silver key on a chain around my neck. I drew my shoulders back, and shut the door behind me.

At John Burroughs Junior High, the gym doors stood open to the wind. Fall-colored crepe-paper decorations rustled like real leaves. People gathered in drifts. Anxious boys feigned boredom beneath the hoops. Mr. Ridge surveyed the dance floor from behind the punch bowl, his arms hanging stiff as baseball bats at his side. Our art teacher, Ms. Pearl, fluttered around the door in her gauzy skirt, welcoming students to the Harvest Dance.

"Wow, that green is — positively electric," she said. She pressed her lips into a tight smile.

My halter dress was entirely wrong. When I took it from the hook on the back of my mother's bedroom door, I'd pictured her in it, wet from a shower, reading on our postage-stamp porch with her coffee, looking fresh and pretty in the morning sun. Exotic was my hope as I slipped it on. But the girls at the dance were zipped into pastel velvet dresses with Peter Pan collars and they wore ballet flats, the efforts of their curling irons wilting against damp necks. Yolanda wore a long-sleeved peach dress, lace collar stark against her caramel skin. She was dancing to Three Dog Night's "Joy to the World" with Anthony Mendoza, the boy all the girls wanted to like them back.

Doug Jordan with the nickel-size nostrils pulled me from the line of timid observers. He danced the funky chicken with his hands nested in his armpits, elbows flapping and feet stomping. I smiled to be nice when he gripped my hand, and then, after our dance, while I waited to be asked again, I smelled my fingers, just to know.

Pretty much that's how it went at the eighth-grade dance on the night before I was to board a plane and fly to meet my father for the very first time. Yolanda and Anthony clutching each other, and me standing by myself at the opening chords of each song until Doug Jordan bloomed in front of me, his damp hand extended.

At ten thirty he led me out to the bike racks. The fog had finally seeped in, moist and fat after the crackling heat of the Santa Anas. I breathed in the changed air, felt the coolness against my skin, while we talked about the digestive-system test and shoplifting. He told me he'd stolen a flashlight from Woolworth's and used it to creep around the bushes of his house and spy on his family.

"They look so different from outside," he said. "Like people I don't even know."

Me, I regularly stole from World Imports, hooking earrings into the rubber band around my ponytail. I'd smile and always say thanks as I drifted toward the door.

"Never sneak out," I advised.

Doug Jordan stepped closer to me. His Stan Smiths pressed against my toes. I pretended it was normal, standing this close to a boy, but my armpits prickled to attention. I was fourteen and counting. I'd kissed exactly two boys; one named Raymond, who smelled of animal crackers, a babyish smell for a teenager, and whose sliver-lips vanished when he smiled. In exchange for the kiss I made him promise to quit following me to the Dumpster at our old apartment building, but we moved before he had a chance to prove he would stand by his word.

Trembling in my mother's dress, I arranged my face and waited for Doug Jordan to lean in. He reached for my diamond-tipped earlobe, pinched it softly, as if he were touching some private part of me.

"Did you steal these?" He leaned closer to my upturned face. His nostrils were cavernous from that angle.

"My dad gave them to me. They're real." I almost never talked about my father, but the words felt solid in my mouth, hard as my diamonds.

Then Doug kissed me, his fingers still pinching my earlobe. His salty tongue, the texture of sautéed mushrooms, flicked all around my mouth. I closed my eyes, searched for any agitation in my body, and felt nothing besides slight revulsion. After, he slung his arm over my shoulder as if he had done it a thousand times, as if his arm and my shoulder had a history.

"We should see a movie tomorrow?"

"I'm going to a jewelry convention in Chicago."

He nodded one backward nod, first up and then down, as if it didn't really matter. Then he slid his hand down my arm to cup my elbow and I let him pull me even closer. The warmth of his hip against mine, the Fifth Dimension song "Up, Up and Away" spilling out the gym doors behind us, the streetlights illuminating individual drops of moisture as the fog drifted past seemed like gifts for me. As I stood there with a boy's arm claiming me, knowing where I was going tomorrow, it felt as if the doors of my future were thrown wide open.

"When you come back," he said.

"Maybe." My mom had rules, and one was to always leave a man wondering.

Mr. Hernandez did pick us up in his squad car. He came around and put his heavy hand on Yolanda's head when she climbed in, guiding her like a perp. The sour laundry smell of captured men lingered in the back. I imagined criminals slumped on this same cold vinyl seat.

"Finally, the Santa Anas are finished," Mr. Hernandez said.

I rolled down the window, bathed my face in the fog. A sign — IT'S HERE! PUMPKIN ICE CREAM — glowed orange from the Baskin-Robbins on our corner. Yolanda pointed to a dark smudge on her neck, the bud of a hickey. I nodded yes, I could see it, and she began to softly cry. Her dad would freak when he discovered it. I brushed my hand over my own neck, wondering about my father, how he might feel if a boy left his mark on my body.

At the United gate, a trio of slim stewardesses in navy uniforms strode past, wheeling efficient bags behind them. I waited alone by the window facing the plane and the calm day outside while my mom went for more coffee. She'd already gulped two cups and dressed by the time I'd awoken. I found her drumming her fingers on the arm of a chair in the living room as if she hadn't slept. She wanted to know what I'd packed, insisted I wash my hair and part it on the side, and asked the departure time twice. She rifled through my school bag for the tickets, and then picked at the stitches around the Funky patch I'd sewn on the front. When I asked what she was doing, she practically cried out, "You can't take this piece-of-shit bag," and dumped her purse onto the kitchen counter — cigarettes, Bic lighter, keys, tampons, Doublemint gum, checkbook, mascara, and Tabu perfume clattered on the Formica.

Whenever my mother started dumping things out, I got nervous. "Here," she said, then zipped my tickets, a tube of lipstick, a twenty-dollar bill, the gum, change for a phone call, and a hairbrush inside the bag. I pictured myself walking off the plane with her fringed suede purse on my shoulder. As much as I wanted to go, as often as I'd imagined my father's life and how I might fit in, holding her purse, I missed her already.

On the tarmac below me, two men with large black headphones and tangerine jumpsuits tossed baggage from a conveyor belt into the belly of the plane. I watched for my suitcase with the rainbow shoelace tied around the handle as if I couldn't recognize it by its shabbiness, by the diaper pin holding the zipper together. The suitcase was the same age as me. I'd known the story since I was old enough to ask. When he left, Marco brought all of my mother's clothing, folded neat as you please, in that Samsonite. My father left it with a nurse in the hospital lobby when I was born. It wasn't specifically me, my mom insisted, it was the *idea* of me that scared him away.

Was the idea of me different now? I'd written him, care of his mother, on my fourteenth birthday, just a note.

Hi! How are you? I'm fourteen now and I was wondering if maybe, could we someday meet? I am fine and I live in Los Angeles. Write back if you want!

    Love, Nora (Hargrove)

My mom had asked if I was sure I wanted to go down that path and I shrugged like it was no big deal either way. Remember, *that bastard left us.* He answered with diamond earrings and, later, airline tickets — Miss Nora Hargrove, LAX to O'Hare, seat 28D — as if he'd been waiting fourteen years to hear from me. I'd tucked the tickets inside my diary and marked the date on my calendar. My mom said he always knew where we were. She kept his mother up to date on our addresses in case any of the Gianettis wanted to go Dutch on my upbringing. I don't know what I was supposed to do with that information, if I was supposed to feel sorry for me or sorry for her.

My mom returned to the gate with both hands wrapped around a large Styrofoam cup. She sighed like it was already the end of a long day and sank into the plastic seat behind me.

"Did Mr. Hernandez pick you up in the police car?"

I nodded.

"Fathers can be a real pain in the ass." She held her coffee just below her lips, the steam rising and opening her pores, a coffee facial. I sat next to her, reached for a sip of it, but she shook her head. "I'm having a Ray Charles."

"You're not supposed to drink out here."

"For Christ's sake, it's in a coffee cup."

She squeezed my hand, chattered on about what she would do

while I was away: have a long spa weekend with manicures, pedi-cures, luxurious baths. Really she'd just be in our same bathroom with the lime-green plastic shower curtain our landlord bought and left on our doorstep with a bow around it. Landlords were al-ways leaving things for my mother: new plungers, doormats, their home and office telephone numbers in case *anything* needed look-ing at.

Her coffee was nearly gone. Once my plane took off she'd drive home alone. I'd been in the car plenty of times with her loose from a cocktail, me stiff and upright on the edge of the seat, watching both the road and her hands tapping the wheel, ready to grab it in a heartbeat, though so far that hadn't happened. "How do you know Ray Charles even drinks those?" I snapped because now the morning was all about her.

She ignored me, went on about a juice fast and some article she'd read by Linus Pauling about direct sources of vitamin C linked to youth and healthy skin. Maybe she would buy a juicer. "I'll be so gorgeous when you get back, you won't recognize me." She leaned back in her seat, sipped coffee, and closed her eyes, all the time holding on to my hand. "You haven't told me a thing about the dance."

I thought about Doug's proprietary arm. Doug spying through the windows at his own family, the view up his spacious nostrils when he leaned down to kiss me, the salt of his tongue.

"I kissed a boy," I told her, trying out the words.

Her eyes half opened. "Do you like him?"

"He likes me."

"That's not enough, Beanie. Lots of boys are going to like you."

Though nothing in my life so far pointed to the accuracy of her prediction, I felt a quickening when she said it, a hopeful glim-mer.

We stood when they called out for unaccompanied minors, and my mom hugged me close. "I'll save you some avocado facemask."

I started to pull away but she held on and I hugged her again, not wanting to be the first to let go, not wanting to leave her disappointed at the gate. They made the announcement again, and she pressed her lips to my ear, so close I smelled her mix of coffee, cigarettes, and perfume, so close I felt them moving. "Be careful. He can be charming." Then I was walking away with the other passengers.

"I'll see you in a couple days," my mom sang after me. "He's really tall."

When the plane began its final descent through the clouds, approaching skyscrapers, treetops of rust, green, and gold, I still hadn't decided whether to rush out to the gate or leave him wondering while passengers filed out. Waiting felt contrived, like something my mother would do.

When the plane eased into its slot, we passengers leaped up before the seat-belt light clicked off. Then I was thanking the pilot and moving toward the gate. I slung my mother's purse over my shoulder, scanned the crowds for someone tall striding down the beige walkway. People happily called out to one another, arms circled waists, hands reached for luggage handles, but no one seemed to be looking for a fourteen-year-old girl. I tried not to look anxious as I sat waiting in a plastic chair, but the arrival gate continued to empty, and my palms grew moist.

I chewed my gum completely flavorless. He was fifteen minutes late and it seemed like an hour. I thought about having him paged. "Marco Gianetti, please meet your daughter at United gate twenty-two." Would it sound too desperate? The loudspeaker announced new flights and destinations. Flight 484 bound for Tahiti boarded at gate eighteen. Ten more minutes, I decided, before I called my mother. I could already hear her: *I told you he was a colossal waste of time . . .* That's what I was thinking when I saw his back and knew, immediately, that he was my father. He stood in the middle of the next gate. His white shirt stuck to him as if he'd been sweating, and you could see where his undershirt sleeves stopped at his biceps through the thin cotton. His pants were gray, serious, crumpled. The cuffs skimmed a pair of shiny alligator cowboy boots. A stuffed panda bear hung limp at his side.

If he hadn't come, I could have continued believing everything my mother told me. I could have boarded a flight home and nothing would have changed. *That bastard left us.* Only, he had come. He'd brought me a panda bear.

My father walked toward the window, placed his hand flat against the glass, looked down at his boots. Right then I stood and moved closer. I was afraid his next step would be to turn away without me; afraid I might recognize relief on his face.

"Marco?"

He turned. I could tell by the way he held his mouth—lips parted, perhaps releasing a sigh—and by his half-closed dark brown eyes, but mostly I knew he'd been drinking by the way he slowly dragged his flat palm down the window, leaving behind a smeared trail.

"I've been waiting . . ." my voice squeezed out. So far, my parents had two things in common, drinking and me.

"For you." He held the panda across the foot of space between us.

Its button eyes reflected the fluorescent lights as Marco waggled its head back and forth in front of me and then nudged it into my arms. It smelled of cigarette smoke, and I imagined it slumped next to him on a stool in the airport bar. Maybe he'd confided in the bartender about how anxious he was, meeting his daughter for the first time. Maybe the bartender offered one on the house, congratulating him, wishing him luck and making him late. "Thank you."

"Do you have any bags?" His voice was buoyant, hovering just around my shoulders, as if he trusted that everything between us was going to work out just fine.

"I was afraid to go get it. You know, that I would miss you." I wanted him to take out a cigarette or something so I could stare at his face while he was occupied with lighting a match, but he didn't. His hair was the exact walnut brown as mine, and longish. It was slicked back to skim his collar and had a bit of gray at the sides, like he'd been sugared. He was handsome. I could imagine my mother in love with him. Marco and Ruby. Ruby and Marco. When Ruby decided to keep me, this was what she had given up. I was walking close to him now, and his smell — beer, peanuts, and something else, something I couldn't name, not like Doug Jordan's at the dance, something his alone — seemed exotic.

"Sorry to be late." Marco leaned forward and brushed his lips across my forehead, then placed his hand upon my shoulder.

When he said it, when he touched me, something swarmed inside me, quick and light as bees. We weaved down the corridor, past fellow travelers, with his apologetic hand on my forgiving shoulder, past the red vinyl booths in the restaurant where we might make plans over French fries before my flight out on Monday afternoon. Past bathrooms, pay phones, past the bar where he must have meant to stop for just one beer to settle his nerves. He steered me into the gift shop, for gum, he said. He reached for a pack big enough to share and set it down on the counter. I never took my eyes off his hand with the perfect half-moons at the base of each nail. A father seemed like such a big thing, I needed to start with one small piece of him. He fished change from his pocket and held it out to the clerk. She smiled at him the way women do at handsome men, like she'd be willing to unwrap a stick of gum, slide it into his mouth, and tuck the wrapper into her purse to throw away later.

Behind her, a shelf crammed with panda bears, price tags dangling from their paws, ran the length of an entire wall, a gap where mine must have sat. I worried my fingers through my panda's fur, staring first at the stuffed-animal shelf, then at all the shelves lined with coffee cups, corkscrews, dolls, T-shirts, shot glasses, magazines, and chocolates. What made him think I'd want a three-foot panda? I was fourteen. He must have known what I was thinking because at the last minute he grabbed a snow globe crowded with skyscrapers and the elevated-train track. Before he held it out to me he gave it three quick shakes, confusing the Chicago scene with fake snow.

"Your second souvenir," he said. I slipped it inside my mother's purse.

He'd rented a black sedan, a Lincoln Town Car, to get back and forth from the airport to the hotel and the jewelry convention. He asked if I wanted to drive but I told him I didn't even have a learner's permit. A pine-green cardboard tree hung from the rearview mirror, and the car smelled like someone's clean bathroom. He seemed at ease driving around Chicago, one elbow hanging out the window.

I arranged myself on the seat next to him, crossing my legs, folding my hands over the purse, trying to look comfortable, trying to think of something to say. I wanted this to be easy as any father-and-daughter outing. He told me we were staying at the Drake.

"That's where Phil Donahue puts up the guests for his show." I watched every afternoon while I did math homework and ate Ritz crackers. When he didn't say anything I kept right on talking. "I had a cat named Phil Donahue. He got run over. A long time ago." I paused because thinking of Phil Donahue still made me a little sad and I didn't want to be sad in a car with my father for the first time. I wasn't exactly sure what I should be, but it wasn't sad.

My father looked at me with his brown eyes and said, "Too bad."

"Isn't it funny that the real Phil Donahue married the woman from *That Girl*? I mean, he is so serious and she seemed like she was just having fun starring in commercials and running around with a matching hat and gloves?" He asked me to pick a radio

station and I was relieved to have something to do. I found Paul
Anka singing "Having My Baby." It was becoming one of those
times where everything can embarrass you. I went past that station.

"Turn back to that," he said and for the rest of the song he
tapped along with his thick gold wedding band. I hoped it was just
nerves and that my father wasn't a Paul Anka fan.

"You must be hungry. Early dinner okay with you?"

When we pulled up to the valet at the Palm, I opened my door
before the man had a chance to come around and let me out.

My dad held the restaurant door open for me. I stood next to
him while he talked to the maître d'. The times my mom and I
went to fancy restaurants, birthdays or paydays or just for our
mental health, my mom never had a reservation, partly because
she wasn't good at planning ahead, partly because, as she said, *I
thrive on challenge.* Usually she'd flirt, touching the maître d' on
his wrist. Once, when a table couldn't be found, she'd walked her
fingers up the guy's arm all the way to his elbow, saying, *I won't
take it personally,* but I could tell by the way she flounced out that
she did. In the parking lot, she clamped down on her cigarette and
called him an asshole.

My father slid his hand deep into his pocket. I watched the
graceful exchange of the folded bill from my father's hand to the
maître d' and realized that my father was a man who made things
happen.

We were led us through the restaurant with its burgundy carpet, polished wood walls, and thick white tablecloths. Our corner
table felt romantic, operatic. My dad asked what I liked to eat.

"Stew?"

He ordered without even opening the menu, steaks, medium
well for me, rare for him, creamed spinach, new potatoes, and a
bottle of Chianti.

He swallowed down one glass and poured another. "I'm a little
nervous. Are you?"

When I nodded, he poured some wine into my water glass and said, "Don't tell your mother."

Ruby let me sip from her wine spritzers, but this was different. My dad poured from an elegant bottle. It was offered in a thoughtful manner, like *maybe this is just the ticket for you and me right now*. We clinked glasses and he said, "To a fresh start," then closed his eyes to swallow. I did too. The wine was warm and slipped easily down my throat.

My dad impressed me by cutting his entire steak before he started eating. He paused to sip wine after each bite. I organized my meal too, alternating steak and vegetable bites, while he described his six jewelry stores spread out in strip malls across southern Florida. I imagined working with him, arranging pearl and diamond necklaces in black velvet display cases, winding the watches in the timepiece case. He explained the 4 Cs of diamond quality—cut, color, carat, and clarity. Mine were princess cut, SI$_2$, rated J for color, which, he emphasized by stabbing his fork in the air, was very good. "They look perfect on a pretty girl like you."

I loved being in Chicago. I loved this meal. Most of all, I loved falling in love with my father.

He pushed his plate away and continued talking, about his family now, his German wife, Gretchen, and his twins, my eight-year-old half sisters, Louise and Charlotte. Both a couple of pistols, he told me, grinning. He said I'd really like them. The family had two basset hounds, Captain and Tennille, and lived in a ranch house in Fort Lauderdale.

He's married. He may have kids; be prepared. Ruby's voice filled my head as he went on about his girls, how they liked to ride around the yard on his lawn mower cutting crazy designs into the grass. It all sounded so . . . nuclear. I imagined him leaning back at a breakfast table, cowboy boots slung up on a kitchen chair, sipping black coffee and trying to read the Florida paper, which had been delivered to his door. Charlotte's arms flung around his neck; Louise, blond and braided, ransacking his paper for the comics page.

When he asked about my life, I rearranged the food on my plate. I sometimes did that at home when Ruby and I were having leftovers, chili or ham-and-lima-bean casserole. She knew what I was trying to pull and delivered her making-ends-meet rant. When I was little, I'd hidden a hot dog inside an empty milk carton in the trash. She washed it off, reheated it, and then sat at the table while I choked the thing down. Now, when I'm mad at her, she still brings it up. *Don't forget to tell them about the hot dog*, she says, *when you notify the child protection authorities.*

He asked only the basics. Did I like school?

"Yes."

What was my favorite subject?

"Biology and language arts."

Did I have a boyfriend?

"Yes." I hoped he wouldn't ask for a name. If he did, I would say Doug Jordan. It could be true if I wanted it. I couldn't really picture Doug Jordan here. He seemed more of a hot-dog type. I hoped I didn't. Here in Chicago, in black velour pants and SI₂ J-color princess-cut diamonds, I was inventing a pretty daughter for Marco and his life.

"What about a stepdad?" Marco asked. He twirled the wine around in the bottom of his glass.

"No," I said. Though I thought about Frank, who gave us a TV and almost moved in before he'd changed his mind, said he didn't want to leave one family and jump into another, and ended up relocating to Denver.

"That all sounds good." He nodded. "Sounds like you've got a full life in California."

I didn't know what he was trying to say. My life wasn't full. It had plenty of room for lawn mowers, half sisters, and a dad. It seemed like things were being offered and then retracted. Here at the table it was suddenly too unpredictable, too tipsy. At least with my mother, I always knew what to expect. "I've got to use the restroom." I walked slowly away, trying to look relaxed, certain he was watching my back. I found the phone in the hall next to the ladies' room. She accepted the charges. "Everything is fine," I said, pressing my ear against the phone and her voice.

"How does he look? Did he ask about me?"

"We're at a restaurant and then I guess we're going to the hotel."

"You don't sound okay."

"He's got twin daughters. They live in a ranch house."

I heard a man laugh in the background, heard my mom's muffled "Shhh! My baby's on the phone." And then more clearly, "Did he take you somewhere nice at least?"

I flicked the coin return open and shut. "I should go."

"Did you tell him about your grades and how we camped last summer?"

"He said it sounds like we have a full life." The ceiling was smudged gray directly above me from people smoking while they talked. This must be the type of conversation someone would light a cigarette for.

Her hand went over the mouthpiece again. "Stop," she said. And then to me, "My friend Leland is painting my toenails."

When I turned toward the mouth of the hall, there was my dad, watching me. I felt caught, like a fly under a glass, as if I'd betrayed him somehow by reporting to my mother and as if I'd betrayed my mother by coming to Chicago.

"Call me tomorrow. I love you . . ." And her voice rose up at the end the way it always did, like a question, as if her love required an answer.

"She says hi," I said. I had to turn sideways so he could squeeze past me and continue down the hall to the bathroom.

He plunged his hands deep into his pockets. "Tell her hi from me."

Saxophone or trumpet moaned from the radio as we roamed around Chicago. My dad's chin rested almost on his chest; one hand hung from the bottom of the steering wheel.

"You don't mind if we take a drive?"

I didn't say anything because I could tell he wasn't really asking. He steered along a boulevard, past brightly lit high-rise condos and department-store windows full of furs and overcoats. Gradually, buildings thinned out and we were cruising through neighborhoods. Streetlights flickered on, the engine hummed, and the wine glowed in my stomach like a night-light.

Streets were named after the trees that lined the sidewalks, Oak, Maple, and Aspen. They dropped crisp leaves in the fading light because that's what trees are meant to do in October. Soon their bare branches would stand out against a pale, wintry sky. People would make soup and haul out the Halloween decorations. They'd pull on heavy coats, while in Los Angeles palms and magnolias were always green and you could wear your swimsuit in November. I guessed that's what it was like in Fort Lauderdale too. Another thing my parents had in common: winter-free lives.

I could have relaxed if it weren't for my father seeming like he was just about to say something. He kept clearing his throat, glancing over at me every time he pulled up to a stop sign. I would have liked to reach my hand toward his on the seat, to let him know that I was ready to hear what he was trying to say, only I wasn't. I steered the conversation toward something I already knew.

"We have a dog. A cockapoo—part poodle, part cocker spaniel. A stray. The vet gave us pills to crush into his food because he smells bad. When I take him for walks he goes running in open doors, barking and wagging his tail like he's some long-lost pet yelling out, 'I'm home. Thank God, I'm back.' Ruby calls him shameless."

"You just need to train him."

"I'm afraid he'll find his old house."

He pulled to the side of the street, pressed a button to roll down both our windows. The air was cool and smelled faintly of wood smoke and lasagna. I wrapped my arms around my chest, so he left the engine on with the heat blasting my legs and a cold wind chilling my face. My body felt confused, hot and cold, sitting in this dark car with a stranger.

"I want you to know what happened." His voice was serious and sincere. He seemed to need to muster up courage because he stared out the window before he spoke again. I saw everything he saw. A lit porch hugging the length of the house, the red handle of a spade sticking up from the dirt, a forgotten sweatshirt draped over a bush. Dark shapes inside, moving toward a dining room and dinner.

"It wasn't the right time. I was young."

I held my hands under the heater vent, then pressed them into my cold cheeks. He looked at me like I should understand. I told him I did. It was the idea of me that was too much.

"You weren't planned," my dad said.

I pictured him eating his dinner so carefully. I guessed I'd cured him of not planning. As far as I could tell, this man would never not plan again. Even though it was the last thing I wanted to happen, my throat closed up and tears stung my eyes.

He noticed. His face went pale and he started petting my head. "Now, none of that. Come on."

Do not cry. Do not cry, I was telling myself over and over, so I almost didn't hear the next thing he said.

"You weren't even an idea. It was your mother I didn't love." He ran his thumb across my cheek.

He was nearly pleading with me. This was the piece my mother never told me. It wasn't me at all. I stroked my hand along the fringe of her purse, as if I were untangling hair. My eyes overflowed and I never felt sorrier or more relieved.

"I've been wanting to tell you that for a long time." He pulled out a pack of gum, unwrapped two sticks, and held one out to me. "I'm trying to quit smoking. Don't ever start. It's a nasty habit."

We sat chewing, staring at the house. He popped his gum.

"This is really good gum," I said.

In the hotel elevator, my dad told me to go ahead and press the button, as if I were the same age as his twins. The bellman left all our bags in one room and my dad asked me to choose a bed. We were sharing. I pointed to the one with the sand dune painting over it. He tossed the panda and my mom's purse on top and went into the bathroom.

The bedside lights worked in a surprising number of combinations, dim or bright, both on or just one, lots of possibilities for a family sharing a room. I sat on the end of my bed, listening for the toilet to flush, but instead he started talking and it took me a minute to realize he was on the phone. A phone in the bathroom was a whole new level of luxury. When Ruby bathed, she dragged the phone in from the living room with the cord snaking around the coffee table and across the hall. My dad spoke about his flight, dinner, what time he would head over to the jewelry show in morning. I hardly breathed, listening for my name.

"Sweet dreams, sugarfoot," he said; his voice sounded eager, bright. This must be the voice he saved for his daughters. Ruby had different voices, for teachers, girlfriends, men. Her man voice—tipped up to show interest, and breathless to show enthusiasm—made me gag. I was glad she spoke plainly to me. When my father talked to me again, I wanted to hear this daughter voice.

I took out my nightgown and brought it under the covers to wriggle out of my clothes. I was peeling my socks off when he stepped out with his shirt unbuttoned partway. He sighed as he sank down on his bed, then began to pull his boots off. "Nora?" He dropped one boot onto the floor with a thud. "If the phone rings in the morning, let me get it."

"What?" I wasn't paying any attention to his voice.

He slumped forward to pull his other boot off. "It would just be my family." He dropped the second boot, then raked his fingers through his hair.

Again I hardly breathed.

"They don't know." He held his finger to his lips when he said it, like we were in on this together.

Something about his finger made me sit up in bed. "I'm a secret?" My heart clunked in my chest, like it had just hit the absolute hard bottom of my story.

"I haven't had the opportunity to tell Gretchen yet."

With my full life in California, there were so many other places I could be. At home with my mom and the avocado facemask. Yolanda was probably grounded because of her hickey. I could be at the movies with Doug Jordan, his hand claiming mine. But I was here, a whole weekend of my life, doing this thing I'd imagined forever.

"The girls are still too young to understand." He stepped back into the bathroom, ran the water. "Okay?" He tried to sound charming but it came out brusque.

Though he wasn't looking at me, I nodded, up and then down, as if the secret didn't mean our weekend had a definite end.

"Here's your water." He set a glass on my nightstand. "And now I'll turn off your light." He leaned over to pinch my toe. He said, "Sweet dreams, Nora," as if he'd said it every single night of my life.

Plum Tree

NORA CUPPED THE pot in her hand and stepped out to her backyard. Her best friend, Zellie, was waiting, digging through her backpack. "I don't have any papers," Zellie said. Instead she held up a Tampax and ran her tongue along the edge of the wrapper. "We'll have to use this." She ejected the tampon onto the struggling lawn, where it lay like a white firecracker.

Nora had scraped together just enough from her mom's stash to make a slim joint, the words *slender reg* along the side. The pot was hidden under Ruby's bed on a silver tray that in better times had displayed a tea set. When Ruby bought the tray at a neighbor's yard sale, its scalloped edges were already tarnished, and she never bothered with polish.

"My mom claims this pot is the same kind Hitler smoked before he committed suicide." Nora wondered if the pot actually had a family tree or if her mother was just trying to scare her off, or if Hitler even smoked pot. "It was one of my mom's voice-over moments. You know, when moms try to tell you stuff without telling you stuff. As if . . ." She sat in the dirt, leaning against the plum tree behind her bedroom.

"Here's to Hitler's suicide," Zellie said, sucking her voice down her throat with the smoke. Nora's mom croaked like that when she smoked pot. Sometimes she croaked out entire sentences, like

"What should we make for dinner tonight?" or "There's a *Thin Man* movie on at ten." Then they'd roll the TV into her mother's bedroom. Nora was named for Nora Charles, and she imagined reclining in a satin dressing gown with a dry martini and a sublime husband like Nick. Nora Hargrove would stroll across the bedroom imitating Nora Charles, her mother's cigarette held elegantly between two fingers. "A little more hip," her mother would say, or "God, I'd kill for your legs."

Zellie twisted a plum from the branch above her. "The only thing worth stealing from my mom is a diuretic pill." When Nora shrugged, Zellie continued. "You know, pee pills, for water retention. She's practically turned herself into a piece of beef jerky trying to pee away twenty pounds." Perfect and pert Zellie, with her straight blond hair, major tube-top collection, and the ability to say the exactly right hilarious thing, had nothing to pee away.

"I'd like one of those pills." Nora held her hand open and Zellie dropped a plum into her palm. This was the first house Nora ever lived in that had a fruit tree.

"Maybe I'll learn to preserve," her mom had said to their new landlord. He'd lit her cigarette and she re-inhaled the curl of smoke escaping from her mouth. French, she called it. He told her he'd come every winter to prune and spray for mold.

The tree was nestled at the back of the yard, where the two fence sides sharply met. If Nora had gone to geometry often enough she'd remember what kind of angle it was, acute or oblique or something worse. She'd hated her geometry teacher. Supposedly he was hypoglycemic. He nibbled sandwiches through all of his classes. His wife made them, and his suits. During quizzes Nora stared at the crust and bits of bologna sitting on a cloth napkin on his desk. She read the labels sewn into the suit jackets he hung on the back of his chair. HAND SEWN BY MRS. LESTER. If he didn't remove his jacket, no one would ever know the work she'd put into that suit. Now Nora took courses in which she knew she'd excel, typing instead of geometry. She quickly mastered the home

keys and aced all the self-tests. *Now is the time for all good men
. . .* That's how she slipped off the college track in school. She still
hadn't told her mother about her schedule change. Ruby had sympathy for screwups, but Nora thought this change was just a decision. Sometimes Ruby made snap decisions — like dyeing her hair
red, or adopting strays, or moving to Santa Cruz, or, one time, as if
she'd done it a thousand times before, passing Nora her little stone
pipe. "What the hell," she'd said, releasing a long, steady stream
of what smelled like burned honey. "We're home, you're safe. I'd
rather you try it here than somewhere else." Nora wanted to make
decisions like that, change big parts of her life in a heartbeat.

The plum tree's branches dipped over either side of the fence,
the plums dangling into the alley, tempting anyone who passed
by. Two years in a row Nora had watched the blossoms give way
to green lumps, tight as eyes squeezed shut, and then, with the
warmer days, when she came outside to get stoned or escape her
mother's moods, she noticed they'd begun to soften and purple up.
Someone had taken the time to plant this tree.

When Nora shelved books at the library to work off detention
for cutting classes, she'd come across a book on fruit trees. First
she thumbed through the pictures, then she found the chapter on
plums, and she'd slumped down in the stacks and read the names:
beauty, damson, elephant heart, Golden Nectar, Nubiana. Judging from the description — large, amber-fleshed pulp, deep purple
skin, sweet and firm, perfect for baking — she had a Nubiana tree
in her yard. There was even a recipe for a tart, and Nora thought
that this summer she might bake one. To plant a plum tree you
must dig a hole three times the size of the root ball, mound up a
pile of soil and compost in the center, and then spread the roots as
gingerly as a child's hair. She imagined a gardener tamping down
the soil around the trunk with the toes of her shoes, tucking it
in. For such a colossal effort, you'd better know you were sticking
around. A fruit tree meant total commitment.

Nora and Zellie passed the misshapen joint, biting hard plums between hits. The tart flesh made Nora salivate. When they couldn't hold the joint without burning their fingers, Zellie spit on it and dropped it in the film can with their emergency supply of roaches.

"What now?" Zellie asked.

It was the dead zone of the school year, a week left until summer, reports already turned in, finals taken. Yesterday the entire school participated in a rollicking locker purge. Teachers paced the corridors while students chucked torn pictures from *Rolling Stone*, empty lip-gloss applicators, old tests, and shriveled orange peels into strategically placed trash cans. Those who attended school today would be enduring cobwebby videos of *Masterpiece Theatre*, watching the institutional timepieces click: half a notch back, full minute forward. Nora had spent many hours staring at the clocks' stuttering hands, as if even the clocks had to work hard to gather enough momentum to make it through Junior Composition.

She stood, her left hand pressing against the trunk for support. Overhead, the sky was swept clear of clouds, and the afternoon stretched out before her, full of absolutely nothing. A light feeling crept up from the arches of her feet, along her thighs, and up her spine until she felt herself upright as a sunflower. "Head rush." She wiped the dirt from her ass. Plum pulp smeared the seat of her pants. "Shit. I promised I'd rake these up." She kicked at more fallen fruit around the base of the tree.

"Let's just hang until the party," Zellie said. Yesterday during PE, when Nora and Zellie were smoking, slouched against the cyclone fence in the senior parking lot and checking their reflections in car windows, a boy they hardly knew told them about a kegger on Ocean View Drive.

On Fridays Nora's mother could be counted on to hit happy hour after she finished teaching. Zellie and Nora had the house to themselves. Zellie flipped through the channels for an old movie.

Nora settled onto the wide sofa cushions where she and her mother used to sit together in front of the TV, first eating dinner and watching Dan Rather and then doing schoolwork to *Taxi.* Her mother had a crush on Judd Hirsch, and she liked Tony Danza.

"Something for everyone," Nora whispered to herself now. That was before Nora started cutting classes. Before she met Zellie. Before she mixed vodka and crème de menthe in pint milk cartons and brought them to school to share before fifth period. Before she joined her friends screaming insults out car windows at pigeon-toed, D-cupped Tara Danforth. Before she'd made out with a boy and let him slide his hands up and down inside her clothing. Before she was fitted for a diaphragm because all the girls she knew had one.

Her mother tried to get information out of her, calling Nora in to sit on the toilet while she soaked in the tub, a shell-shaped inflatable pillow behind her neck, a hot washcloth spread over her cheeks and chin, opening her pores. Nora didn't want to hear that her mother had done the same things—that she and her mother were similar in any way. "Beanie, take advantage of my experience," she would say, staring right at Nora's face. Nora couldn't stand when her mother was earnest and dumb. She wanted to make her own new and unique mistakes. She was nothing like Ruby.

After *Planet of the Apes,* and a rerun of *Hogan's Heroes,* Nora peeled Zellie off the couch. "You're such a slug." They walked through her neighborhood to the beach and The Boardwalk, just to kill time. Long arms of late-afternoon sunlight pierced through a fog bank that hung just offshore. A breeze fluffed the girls' hair around their shoulders and carried the smell of baked kelp up the cliffs to where they stood.

"Do you think Randall looks like Charlton Heston?" They both knew what Zellie was doing, shoehorning the potential glory of Randall into their conversation.

"You mean the noble astronaut George Taylor?" Nora climbed onto the guardrail, hooked her feet beneath the bottom rung. "Nah, more like the apes."

"No way." Zellie picked at her split ends as if she didn't care.

"Okay, Tom Petty."

"He's doggly!" She shoved Nora's shoulder, causing a lurch and a grab for the railing.

Nora yelp-laughed. "Relax. He's hot and he's into you. Trust me. I can interpret the way a guy stares." Though guys didn't stare at her. It was always at her mother. Fervent men in cars, at gas stations, in checkout lines, and her friends' dads — even her mother's ninth-grade-class school bus driver. Her mom used to sit in the third seat behind him just so they could "make eyes" in his rearview mirror. Now whenever Ruby smelled Old Spice cologne, she brought up Leroy, the bus driver, like he was some amazing treasure from her past instead of a creepy older guy. Nora once asked her if anything had come of the flirting, and her mother tipped up her voice and raised her eyebrows expectantly: "No?" Then she paused. The quiet between them was like a gaping window waiting to catch a breeze on a hot day, only she was waiting for Nora to share something about her life. When Nora didn't, Ruby finally said, "When you're ready, I'm here. Whatever you need: advice, birth control, a shoulder."

"I told Randall about the party." Zellie continued to pick at her hair. "I hope you don't care."

Nora shrugged as if she didn't, although with Randall at the party, she'd be either relegated to third wheel or on her own.

The sun was gone now and The Boardwalk lights flickered on. Shrieks from the roller coaster reached all the way to the cliffs. The screams were always louder in the fog. Shrill at the first drop and then quickly fading, as if the riders plummeted straight down a rabbit hole. Nora could sometimes hear them in the dark of her room. She followed the route in her mind, and like the passengers whose hips slid from side to side on the rattling train, Nora would sway in her twin bed, her heart pounding.

She had to lie down to lace up the front of her jeans, which were meant to look like sailor pants. Zellie was digging a straightened paper clip around the bowl of Ruby's pipe and up the draft hole. She smeared residue along the length of a cigarette and then lit it. "Wear the batik skirt, it makes your ass look good." Zellie passed the cigarette, then rifled through the pile of clothing on the floor. "Can I wear the raspberry angora?"

"It'll be tight."

"Exactly!"

Nora slipped the skirt on and turned sideways in the mirror, ran her hands over her hips. She'd seen her mother do this exact thing, stand in front of a mirror saying, "This is relaxed," letting her stomach pooch out, then sucking it in tight and saying, "and this is held in." Nora sucked her stomach in. She shouldn't have eaten so much today.

"I look fat."

"Yeah, right." Zellie slipped out of her shirt and pulled the sweater over her head. It was tight and it would never look that good on Nora. After tonight, Nora would give it to her. They stood before the mirror together, Zellie taller and blond. Nora liked the way her own hair curled and her small waist, but she would kill for nice boobs. If she and Zellie were blended together, they would be so foxy. She squeezed back into her jeans and relaced the front with a rainbow-colored shoestring. Both girls bent over and yanked brushes through their hair, then flipped their heads back and forth a couple times. Nora stroked a lip-gloss wand over her mouth.

"Your house tonight, right?" Zellie was already dialing home. "Mom ... Fine ... I'm sleeping at Nora's ... I said fine ... I dunno, the movies ... how early?" She took a drag off the cigarette and blew the smoke out the side of her mouth. "What? . . . Bounce? . . . I know what it is . . . Okay. Bye." She hung up and stared at Nora. "My mother needs Bounce." And they burst out laughing. "My mother has been doing laundry for sixteen years."

"Bounce," Nora said in her springiest voice and she laughed and felt at ease because now the evening had a theme, a private joke. If she felt uncomfortable, all she had to do was turn to Zellie and whisper, "Bounce."

Nora left a note for Ruby.

At the movies. Zellie is sleeping over.
    Love, N.

They plucked more plums to eat on the way. The fog never did come in and the first stars made pinpricks of light in the clear dark sky. The girls passed clapboard homes and cottages. Wavering blue light and the smell of cooking onions seeped out windows toward the street along with bits of the evening news, the clatter of dishes, "I'm in the kitchen," someone practicing piano — the loose connections of family in the hours between dinner and bed. Nora had the feeling of swimming past all that life on the inside.

"I'd want to live there," Zellie said, pointing to a dark house. "Everybody's out doing their own thing."

"There's mine." Nora pointed. Tiny lights illuminated shrubs on both sides of a straight path to a porch, like guide lights on a runway. A tabby cat perched on the rail, lazily flicking its tail, watching them through slit eyes. There was something solid, inviting, about the house that made Nora shiver. The porch light glowed off the doorknob, as if the house could hardly wait for someone to wrap a hand around it. "Wouldn't you love to come home to that?"

"You are so weird." Zellie pointed to the window boxes. "Those are plastic flowers."

"Maybe they went to Europe and they didn't want the plants to die."

"Europe's not so great." Zellie lobbed a plum pit into the hedges. Zellie tossed off statements like that all the time. As if her family vacations, family meetings, family meals, family code words, family outings were nothing compared to the freedom, the laissez-faire child-rearing Ruby claimed bloomed from her complete trust in Nora.

There were no plastic flowers at the party house. These parents had left for just a few days. Nora followed close behind Zellie. She hoped Randall wouldn't show up and whisk Zellie off, at least not until Nora found someone to talk to. It was awkward being alone in the center of so many people. Three clans populated the front porch: the smokers, the talkers, and the kissers. Nora knew she was a member of the first and she patted the pack of Winston Lights jammed into her waistband. She recognized people from school but no one she knew well enough for her to say hi first, so she drifted past, her hand ready in case anyone greeted her. The Stones' "When the Whip Comes Down" bellowed from washing-machine-size speakers just inside the living room. Music vibrated up from the floor into her stomach and throat as if she were nauseated. A black leather couch, its chrome arms glinting, held three too many people. As Nora and Zellie walked by, a boy thrust a corn dog toward Nora. She waved it away and then yelled over the music, "No, thanks. I'm a vegetarian." It sounded ridiculous. She was a vegetarian because she liked the way it sounded when she told her mother and her mother's friends, as if she believed in something besides men and fun.

Someone clicked off the overhead light and draped sheer scarves over floor lamps as Nora and Zellie weaved through knots of dancers toward the keg in the kitchen. White tiles covered the walls and ceiling; there were enormous stainless steel appliances, everything was sleek and hard, bright and loud, and the room reeked of pot and fast food. Der Wienerschnitzel wrappers littered the counters. A girl with black bangs unwrapped corn dogs she took from a greasy brown bag and loaded them onto cookie sheets. She said, "Voilà, *et* voilà," again and again while wrappers spilled to the floor.

"Hey, ladies. Can I buy you a drink?" A boy with a foam mustache held the keg nozzle toward them. He sucked at his upper lip and revealed a wispy blond mustache underneath, then gestured toward the corn dogs. "You should have seen the guy at Wienerschnitzel. They had to get the manager to unlock the freezer." He handed them each a cup. "Pretty righteous . . ."

Zellie smiled and Nora asked where the parents were.

"Mexico." He smiled with protruding lips, either imitating Mick Jagger or still protecting his lips from long-gone braces.

Another boy was taking jars out of the refrigerator and dumping them into one bowl — mayonnaise, relish, three different kinds of mustard, ketchup, and Major Grey's Chutney. "For our feast," he said to the corn-dog girl. This party had been under way for some time.

At the kitchen table, people slammed back shots of Jose Cuervo and sucked on grapefruit sections. A boy with hairy knuckles and a golden retriever smile held an eggcup full of tequila out to Nora. She leaned against the doorjamb and drank it down like it was a job, like taking out the trash. She'd tasted her mother's tequila and orange soda. Ruby and her girlfriends drank them summer afternoons, greased up with coconut oil, sunbathing nude in the backyard with an Indian bedspread flung over the clothesline as a gesture toward privacy. Nora kept her eyes closed to hide the tears that sprang up with the alcohol burning down her throat. The same boy pressed a grapefruit section to her lips. She smiled around it, bit down on the flesh. When she opened her eyes, Zellie and the boy had grapefruit smiles as well, and heat lit up her insides. They tossed the peels onto the kitchen floor with the wrappers and corn-dog sticks. He grabbed their hands, pulling them into the living room. Someone's sweaty back rubbed up and down Nora's arm. She let herself half dance, half be bounced by the crowd. "Bounce!" She yelled it twice before Zellie heard her and laughed. The boy heard too and he started bouncing and all three of them did and then it spread across the room like a wave and everybody bounced to Mick Jagger singing "Lies." They danced through three more songs before Randall popped up, wrapped his arms around Zellie, and she was gone.

Hairy Knuckles, whom Nora recognized from somewhere, brought his lips to her ear. "Beer?" he yelled and she nodded. He filled their cups in the kitchen and returned to her with a handful of tiny pickles and a corn dog, the stick between his teeth like the stem of a red rose. They leaned against a speaker, watching the dancers, watching their beer jiggle along with the bass line. Nora ate pickles from his cupped hand, and when he held out the dog, she took a bite, swallowed it down with beer. It tasted bad, like wet rye bread and sugar, but when he held it out again, she took a second bite.

A joint came by and he put the lit end in his mouth. He blew evenly and a turbo stream of pot smoke came off the back. Nora leaned close, held her lips in a tight O, and breathed it in until she couldn't hold any more. Then they switched and she felt the heat of the cherry just above her tongue as she blew into Hairy Knuckles's mouth. It was mean, thinking of him as Hairy Knuckles. She was glad not to have to stand alone now that Zellie had found Randall. She stared at him, pleasant brown eyes, thick eyebrows, and no pimples. His front teeth overlapped at a jaunty angle, like someone tipping a hat.

You okay? he mouthed, and she shook her head no, because just then, she felt incredibly dizzy. He led her outside, where the cold air felt fresh and clean on her face and she could breathe deeply. They stood beside a night-blooming jasmine. He plucked a flower and held it beneath her nose.

"I'm Nick."

"You are not," she said, trying to focus on the white blossom.

"Okay?" He cocked his head to the side like he was trying to figure something out. "Who am I then?"

She burst out laughing. "I'm Nora."

He smiled cautiously. Clearly he'd never seen *The Thin Man*. "I know." He said he remembered her from school, though he had graduated last June.

"Do you go to college?"

"Community." He asked if she'd ever been to another party here. She shook her head no and saw two white blossoms and two sets of brown eyes bobbing before her face. The jasmine smell was sweet and strong.

He threaded his arm through Nora's. "Let's walk."

She asked if he had a dog named Asta and he still didn't get it, but he listened to her laugh and didn't seem to mind that she had her own joke. They shared a cigarette, and her head swam.

"I think I'm pretty drunk." She leaned against his shoulder.

He smiled with his eyes as if he had all the time and shoulder space she would ever need. "Hey, don't worry," he said. "I've got you covered."

Nora thought, *Hairy Knuckles is so nice.*

She stumbled on a crack in the sidewalk and he caught her by the wrist, and then wrapped his arms around her so she fit right into his damp armpit like a jigsaw-puzzle piece. He kissed her neck, said maybe they should rest in his car, and then they were right next to it and he was helping her into the back seat and shutting the door. They eased back onto the seat, facing each other. He kissed her again with slack lips, and Nora felt as if she could tumble right inside his mouth.

I am kissing Nick. Nick Knuckles. Nick Knuck. And she kept saying that over and over in her mind while they kissed and she felt the ridge of his crooked teeth against her gums. She thought about a time in the future when they'd be eating lunch together and she could tell him how she'd called him Nick Knuck. She would tease the hair on his fingers when she said it. Perhaps even plant a row of kisses across all five.

Nick's tongue gently explored her mouth. She tasted grapefruit in front of other flavors, corn dog, smoke, tequila, and something else, something lush and warm. She wondered and worried over her taste, thought of her diaphragm, left at home between her mattress and box spring, and how she wanted to have a lot to tell Zellie later. Nick pressed against her and she felt herself pressing right back, facing him in the dark, her legs tangled with his, his hand reaching beneath her sweater; he tried to jiggle down beneath her waistband. She sucked her stomach in and felt, at one and the same time, regret and relief that she'd worn the tight jeans.

"I didn't expect this," he said softly.

She wasn't sure what Nick meant — the luck of meeting her, or the inconvenience of her pants. A seat belt dug into her back and she was acutely aware of where she was — alone with a boy in a car.

He kissed her again, more deeply, and his hand worked its way down toward her ass. The jasmine smelled sweet, and Nick's weight felt good. Over his shoulder, the windows fogged, and Nora believed they had done that together. No one passing by would see them inside. She had wanted this to happen to her, though things weren't exactly as she had imagined — they both still had their shoes on. But the air in the car was warm and thick as blankets. Nora untwined her arms from his neck and unknotted her pants. She loosened the rainbow shoestring and peeled her jeans down. As she revealed them, her hips and legs glowed in the amber light. Her thighs looked supple, firm. Nick never took his eyes off her, determined and grateful. Even in the time it took to get the jeans off, she didn't change her mind.

It was after. Back at the party, with wrappers now strewn across the living room carpet and the music blaring. It was when Nick looped his finger through the shoestring in her pants, pulling her toward him, that she changed her mind. She'd seen gestures like that, a slap on the ass, a tweaked nipple, a man pinching a cigarette from between her mother's lips and putting it to his own. Those gestures, like Nick's finger wrapped in her shoestring, were flip, cavalier, possessive. Her mother flourished under them. When Nick held his beer to her lips and said, "Drink up, baby," she felt something rise inside her that she didn't want to swallow away. He smiled at her with his crooked teeth, only they didn't look jaunty anymore. They looked as if they were crowding toward an exit.

"Who's this Asta you were talking about? Isn't he the dog on *The Jetsons*?" Nick asked.

She shook her head. "That's Astro."

"Right." He showed his teeth again.

"I'll be right back." On the porch, everyone belonged to the kissing clan now. Nora wanted a cigarette then realized they must be in Nick's car. She started toward it, down the stairs. They should have stayed in the car, just the two of them. Perhaps there, behind the fogged windows, she wouldn't feel so vacant.

"Nora?" Randall and Zellie smiled down at her over the porch railing. Two round, pale faces hovering from the planet Couple.

"Hey." She looked up at them. "I think I'm going home."

"What a good girl you are." Randall said it like it was a compliment. He had his arm around Zellie, their shoulders and hips touching.

"I'm going to stay with Randall. Cover for me?" Zellie asked.

Nora nodded. "Don't forget the Bounce."

Her mom's Rambler was parked straight, an indication Ruby hadn't been drinking. Nora took a deep breath and opened the door.

"How was the movie?" Ruby called from her bed, her tired voice barely audible over the drone of the TV.

Nora pretended not to have heard. She hadn't even thought about what movie she was supposed to have seen and now she tried to remember what was playing.

"Come talk to me."

"I have to pee." In the bathroom she wadded up toilet paper and stuck it in her underpants. She felt raw, pulpy. She pushed back thoughts about her clean and cornstarched diaphragm, useless in her room.

Her mother, cross-legged in the center of her bed, her faded kimono cinched loose around her waist, stabbed at the adding machine in the center of the silver tray. Her grade book lay open next to her, and a trail of white paper snaked over the quilt and onto the floor. Nora braced herself for questions about the pot.

"Did you and Zellie argue? I thought she was spending the night."

"She changed her mind." Nora stayed in the doorway, far from her mother's prying gaze. On the TV a team of lions chased a herd of gazelles across a landscape of dry grass. "What are you watching?"

"I was watching Johnny Carson." She kept a finger placed along a column of numbers, someone's grades, and stared steadily at Nora, whose breath slowed, became deliberate and loud.

A lioness, tawny, all muscle and bone, leaped from a boulder onto a lone gazelle's back. If anyone could intuit what Nora had done, it was Ruby. That she'd done it, she was glad. She thought she was glad. She had something to tell Zellie. She could cross it off her list. That was all good. "What are you staring at?" Nora finally asked.

Ruby held the grade book out to her. "I'm on Mark Cavanaugh."

When she was little, Nora helped her mother grade twice a year. They would stay in for an entire weekend and have potpies and candy bars while Ruby corrected stacks of papers and then read out the scores. Nora keyed them into the calculator and wrote the final tally like a prediction of someone's future. That's how she used to feel about her own grades, that they meant something.

"Nora, are you okay?"

"Why wouldn't I be?"

Ruby sighed, fished through her nightstand for a cigarette. "Tylenol helps." The match flared bright and blue. Through the cloud of exhaled smoke, her mother still watched. Nora realized she must reek of tequila. She took a plum from the glass bowl on her mother's dresser. Outside, beyond the bedroom windows, faint screams rose from the roller coaster.

"Are you happy?"

It was such a weird thing for a mother to ask.

Rate My Life

THE INDUSTRIAL MIXER gleamed in the clean light, its paddle raised in friendly greeting. Reliable measuring cups, mixing bowls, and cake stands lined the shelves. Croissants in various stages of development — frozen hard as pale stones, thawed to tender puffy crescents that reminded Nora of babies' arms, and baked to a worn penny shine — rested on the solid bakers' racks. She transferred trays from freezer to proofing case to oven to racks, everything happening in the right order. Her mix tape — Pink Floyd, Billie Holiday — set on loop, her hair pulled into a tight ponytail, apron snug around her waist, Nora sang and worked, periodically slipping her hand into her pocket to touch the mysterious note. *Your shoulders. They're sexy and amazing.*

Before leaving the apartment, Nora had leaned down to kiss Thad's shoulder and smelled gin, cigarettes, and a whiff of the acrid bike grease that never washed from beneath his fingernails.

"Tylenol?" He emitted a pasty old-man click with his tongue. "Refrigerator water?" It was one of the differences between them: he liked his water chilled, she liked hers room temperature. He liked sleeping with the window shut, she liked it open a crack, to let in the salty air. Apparently he also liked sitting up late and drinking and smoking cigarettes with her mother, while she liked going to bed early and leaving before sunrise for work and then classes.

Nora tiptoed through the dark living room to accommodate Thad's request, still in her socks so as not to wake her mother. It seemed strange, Nora sleeping in the double bed beside a man with a hangover, while her mother curled up alone on the narrow couch. When had this happened, this switching of roles? Thad cupped the Tylenols in his palm and gave them a shake, like a pair of dice, before popping them into his mouth. "Come back to bed, chicken." His voice was raw from smoking or husky with desire. Either way, Nora again did not feel a quickening near her spine, the plummeting-elevator sensation she used to feel when Thad called her chicken. Stroking her arm, he offered a low-luster smile, cuffed her wrist in his callused hand. "That's some mother you've got." She twisted free, and then, in case she'd been too brusque, hooked his pale hair behind his ear.

Nora slid the last tray in the oven, set the timer, and pushed through the swinging doors from the kitchen to the empty bakery café. Streetlamps and the just-breaking day cast frail ashen light into the room. Chairs upended on café tables sent leggy shadows across the floor and up the walls. She paused in the room's calm center. When she was little, the television, always on, erased this kind of quiet. Last night, she'd lied to her mother, told Ruby she'd been denied her request for the day off. The truth was, Nora hadn't asked. What she didn't want to miss was exactly this: the unruffled mornings at the bakery, the relay between the walk-in, ovens, and industrial sink, the smell — butter and sugar baking — that conjured for Nora seasons and traditions, snow and bulky sweaters, cold milk and flag football, a pair of golden retrievers, leaves to rake and a checkerboard. It was a smell she imagined belonged on the Kennedy compound or in the pretend world of an L.L. Bean catalog.

Waiting for the buzzer, she thumbed through an old *Cosmo* she'd found on the rack out front and stopped when she came upon a Rate My Life quiz. She raced through *gender, marital status, siblings* (none), *age* (twenty), *best friends* (one); hesitated at *weight*, finally choosing "slightly over." *Ever been in prison* (no). *Are you employed* (yes, hence the slightly overweight: working at a bakery, it was hard to resist). *Financially independent* (partly. Thad didn't ask her to help with the rent, but she was paying her own way through college; her mother had given her one semester's tuition, eleven hundred dollars, and told Nora the rest was up to her. Nora was glad of it, as Ruby had already laid claim to too much of her life). *Are you addicted to caffeine, alcohol, cigarettes, junk food, illicit drugs* (she could check off only one, caffeine, and felt both pride and regret. Perhaps her life would be more interesting with addictions). *Are there one or more people who currently find you romantically appealing* — near her heart she felt a flutter, then a jolt when the timer went off. Nora ripped out the quiz and slipped it into her pocket with her note.

At nine, the baking done, she clocked out and headed to UCSB. Her satire class was held on Mondays, Wednesdays, and Fridays in a cavernous lecture hall, two hundred seats sloping toward a podium. Nora, living off campus with Thad, didn't know anyone. So last Friday she'd been surprised when a boy slipped her a note. He wore dark-framed glasses that magnified his eyes, and one peacock feather earring that made his large eyes seem almost violet. "I wouldn't lie," he'd said.

Your shoulders. They're sexy and amazing. All weekend she had held her back straighter, walked regally, felt as if she had a small red bird perched upon each shoulder. Nora had transferred the note from pocket to pocket, even taking it with her to Sunday brunch at Maple, where her mother and Thad each ordered gin fizzes, plural.

"Come on, Nora. How often does your amazing mother come for a visit? Have a drink with Dad and me."

"Thad," Nora corrected.

Thirteen years older than Nora, Thad had been pegged by Ruby as the inevitable father figure and a mistake, not a terrible one, but a mistake nonetheless. When Nora announced that she was moving to be with Thad, Ruby begged her to live on campus and try therapy instead. She said it'd be a cheaper and easier way to deal with Nora's male-abandonment issues. She'd offered to split the cost, up to a limit. *Plus, how can you trust a man with such thin thighs?* Nora had to explain again that Thad was a cyclist, but Ruby said, *They're thinner than yours, Nora.*

At brunch, Nora nodded to the waitress; maybe a drink would help.

"Yay!" Her mother brightly smiled, wrinkled her nose as if she had won, as if she'd convinced a toddler to taste the mushrooms, just one bite.

The waitress ran a finger under the stretchy band of her watch. "Can I see your ID?"

"Oh, please." Ruby rolled her eyes. "Lighten up."

"A virgin bloody mary," Nora said.

Ostensibly Ruby had driven down during her spring vacation to break in her new car, a used red Celica she'd christened Ann-Margret, and also to see where Nora and Thad lived, take them to dinner, though of course Thad wouldn't hear of it; he wanted to impress. To be the good boyfriend he had to be extra kind to *the mother,* and with Ruby that meant a degree of flirting. When Nora brought Thad home to meet her mother for the first time, Ruby answered their knock in a bikini. "So" — she'd leaned against the door, inviting mutual appraisal — "you're Beanie's." Thad's smile switched from warm to confused and he cleared his throat, an audible question mark. Nora had to explain it was her nickname. She'd brought boys home before, but Thad was a man standing beside her, a tall man with his own business and a tan line around his wrist when he took his serious watch off at night. In the living room, in front of her mother, Thad seemed even taller, and Nora felt at risk, as if she'd been caught sneaking into a movie or using a fake ID and any moment her mom would prove her an impostor in this new life she was making for herself. But Thad-the-man loved Nora. He'd first told her on a Sunday when Nora closed the blinds in the condo so they could pretend it was too miserable to go outside. From Thad's bed, hungry and lazy, they watched the Frugal Gourmet prepare his roast sticky chicken. While the chef patted a chicken dry, mixed soy sauce and honey and garlic, Thad declared his love for the skin behind Nora's ears, her inner arms, inner thighs, all the protected places. He described her as winsome and tender and yielding, his words lingering in the air like the great frothy rain clouds that weren't outside. And Nora said she loved Thad. She loved that she had to look up words like *winsome,* loved that he would make her roast sticky chicken, that he did his laundry on Tuesdays, that he sat at the kitchen table every evening to open his mail and paid his bills right away. At night when Thad held her, he breathed steadily against her neck.

"So," Ruby said again. "You're Beanie's paramour."

"I hope that's what she told you." He crushed a paper bag with a box of crackers, Fine Herbes Boursin cheese, and a bottle of Sauvignon Blanc against his chest — grown-up snacks he'd selected at the market on the way over. With his other arm, he pressed Nora to his side. "Because I feel the same way about your daughter."

Thad held his bag out to Ruby and she shrugged, raised her tequila and orange soda a bit to show she couldn't possibly take it, and then she stepped to Nora, turning her own cheek for a kiss. "A man who knocks with his elbows; Nora, you are a Hargrove."

Nora cringed inside. She went from fearing her mother would expose her to fearing that Thad would judge her based upon her membership in this tiny exclusive club, the Hargrove women.

In the kitchen, she fanned the crackers around the cheese on a plate while Thad and her mom watched her, or rather while Ruby watched Thad and Thad watched Nora and Nora eyed them both.

"Tell me again," Ruby said. "Last summer she came with her friend—"

"Zellie," Nora said.

"She and Zellie waltzed in—"

"They did," Thad agreed. He leaned against the Formica counter, the surface dull from years of scrubbing with cleanser. The refrigerator, one they'd bought used, took up far too much room, and when Nora opened the door to look for anything to add to the plate, Thad stepped back and her mother hopped up to sit on the stove.

"Two lovely young ladies waltzed in and selected bikes. Nora chose red and we shot at the beach."

"Red shows up in photos. I taught Nora that." Ruby licked her thumb and wiped at a speck on her thigh.

"It was for the shop's summer brochure—they'll have it at the chamber of commerce, car-rental places, libraries. Bikini-clad girls, hair streaming behind them, enticing people with the Santa Barbara lifestyle. Perfect for the bike-rental shop."

The photo shoot had been fun. Zellie knew the photographer; he offered to drive them down to Santa Barbara, get them high, and take some shots at the beach. They made no money, but it was an out-of-town adventure. Zellie had a crush on the guy and he had sweet Thai sticks. Riding fat-tire bikes on the wet sand, being told to smile, laugh, smear on Vaseline to make their lips shine—it was a fantasy. Plus, Nora'd met Thad, who, when he heard they weren't getting paid, took them for surf and turf at the Chart House, then for wine on his patio. Nora's friends usually drank beer or Bacardi 151. Three months later, when her two community-college classes, Chocolate Desserts and Philosophy 101, ended, she quit her waitress job and enrolled at UC Santa Barbara.

"If you ever shoot another one," Ruby said, "I'd love to participate. All ages enjoy riding bikes."

"Absolutely," Thad agreed. "You can never have too many beautiful women in a brochure."

"I approve." Ruby winked at Nora, then hopped down and led them into the backyard, where she'd been sunbathing. Nora took a sponge from the sink and wiped the suntan oil smudge in the shape of her mother's butt from the stovetop.

Their waitress — strong arms holding a tray of drinks aloft, wide hips weaving through the crowded restaurant toward the table — looked like someone named Debbie, like a mom, with her simple, not unpretty brown eyes and a thin line of dark roots showing at her part.

Her own mother was talking to Thad. "We're closer in age than you and Nora."

"I was born under a lucky star," Thad answered.

"Yes, practically the same year as me."

The waitress set two pearl-white drinks before Thad and Ruby. "Oh." Ruby clapped her hands. "The grown-up drinks look like clouds!"

Nora's drink held a towering stalk of celery and green olives on a toothpick. She leaned forward, nibbled the droopy fronds.

"Ma'am?" Ruby touched the waitress's sleeve. "If you had to guess, who would you say is the couple?"

Nora felt herself begin to rise from her seat before an arm anchored her, and warm breath tickled her ear. "No biggie, chicken."

"I don't have to guess." The waitress tucked the empty tray beneath her arm.

Nora ordered the banana pancakes and Thad the broccoli quiche, at which Ruby snorted, one sharp *ha!*

"What's *that* supposed to mean?" Nora's body, starting with her toes, going up to her thighs, her stomach, and her teeth, clenched. She flicked Thad's hand from her shoulder, then, changing her mind, she pulled him to her open mouth and kissed him. His cloud drink tasted sweet and sharp on her tongue.

Ruby's stirring, vigorous and charged, nearly killed the fizz in hers.

On the way home from breakfast, Nora sat in back—a peace offering to her mother. She pressed her forehead against the rear window, watching the shoreline stream past, smudges of blue and yellow, ocean and sand. Ruby regaled Thad with stories of Nora's pet catastrophes, a parade of deaths: run over, mouth ulcers, head caught in the back of a drawer.

"I think we're the only people ever to have a cat commit suicide. It was horrible, the yowling. Remember, Nora? The landlord had to rip apart the entire cabinet to get at him." She laughed a little. "That cat hated you. It used to hiss when you came home from school. Remember? Are you listening?"

"You named him Attila." She felt like kicking her mother's seat.

"The landlord sent me a sympathy gift. Lilies."

He'd sent Nora a stuffed white kitten she named Willoughby. Her mom and the landlord dated briefly, and then they'd moved again.

Out the window, beyond the oil rigs, the ocean was flecked with whitecaps. When Nora moved in with Thad, she'd unpacked and put some of her things into the medicine cabinet and had been surprised to find a couple of half-empty bottles of baby oil. Too nervous to ask, she didn't mention it, and it wasn't until they came home from the beach one day and Nora discovered a quarter-size smudge of crude on her ankle that she found out what the oil was meant for. With cotton balls and baby oil in his hands, Thad had knelt before her and described the reflexive correspondence between body and foot, running a finger along her sole, saying it represented the spine, and the arch the waistline, and then, wiping away the crude, he massaged her ankle, which, he said, was linked to the pelvic zone. The kiss of cotton slick with oil on her skin drove Nora to tangle her hands in his hair. Thad carried her to his bed. She'd been glad she'd never asked what the baby oil was for, glad she'd found out in such a surprising way.

In the front seat, Thad made agreeable listening sounds for Ruby's benefit, nodding his head. The back of his neck was the exact color of a fresh croissant. One Sunday a month Thad rode his bike over San Marcos Pass, a one-hundred-mile route, and came home tan, smelling of apples and salt. His hair, damp and pressed flat from sweating beneath his helmet, revealed spots where it was beginning to thin. The mileage was yet another Thad accomplishment, like mastering the roast sticky chicken recipe. Thad did everything right and then recounted it all for Nora. His bike rides, his day at work, all in excruciating detail, because he assumed that since he was interested in everything about her, she must be interested in what he ate for lunch. It was exhausting keeping him in the loop, and so sometimes she didn't. Lately her answers were reduced to one word, *fine, good*. Because of all his kindnesses, the grocery shopping, the folded laundry — even her socks matched up — the red rose he tucked under her windshield wiper every Friday while she was in class, because of all these, she hadn't told him about her boss and his offer.

Ruby blathered on, talking about *Sweet Charity*, Nora's senior-class play. "I can hardly believe it's been two whole years! What year did you graduate, Thad?"

When Nora was little she suffered carsickness. If only she could summon it now. Instead, she closed her eyes and hummed "Good Morning Heartache" to drown out the conversation. The horrible thing was, though her mother's blatant agenda should have reinforced Nora's commitment to Thad, and on the surface did, underneath she felt a fissure growing. She would never allow her mother to take credit for her doubt.

Ruby slapped the dashboard. "I love limes!" She'd spotted a Mexican man selling net bags of citrus at a stoplight on Pacific Coast Highway. She insisted they pull over and then stop again at Warehouse Liquors for a bottle of Tanqueray and some tonic. "Now we have a plan for the afternoon." She reached back and squeezed Nora's shoulder.

In class twenty minutes early, the smell of burning dust from the radiators mixed with the briny fog that drifted in the high west windows, Nora selected an aisle seat, the better to watch people wander in. Yesterday afternoon, over gin and tonics on the patio, she'd mentally gone through her wardrobe, deciding which top flattered her shoulders best. Now, she slightly shrugged, encouraging her blouse to slip off one side, revealing her amazing clavicle. She blushed. Would it have been better to ward off the attention with a sweatshirt? She didn't want to be serving herself up on a dish, but she could feel the note, hot, all the way through her jeans. The note writer's hair was dark, he'd had glasses and the earring. He wasn't as tall as Thad. She pushed the thought away. Thad had spent the entire afternoon enduring her mother. Thinking of them, Thad and her mother together, Nora felt tethered.

Students, talking, burdened with notebooks, streamed in. Their murmuring and occasional laughter filled the lecture hall. Heads, blond of all shades it seemed, leaned over to whisper questions or peek at notes from last class. A boy with perfect teeth smiled at her, and she pinched her eyebrows together because it seemed best to appear aloof. She owed at least that much to Thad. It was ridiculous, the way her heart raced. She unfolded the Rate My Life quiz, frustrated with herself for her uneasiness, for her yearning. *Do you regularly eat fruits and vegetables* (of course). *Are you currently taking career-oriented classes* (no . . . yes, satire?). *How much do you agree with these statements: I am optimistic about my future; I have enjoyable hobbies; I like my living arrangement.* Every statement asked too much of her. *I am highly self-confident; I am a good person; I like my values; There is more good than bad in the world.* Someone leaned in so close to Nora that she couldn't turn her head without brushing against a face. All she could see from the corner of her eye was dark hair, pale skin, and a tiny slit in an earlobe from where it was pierced. She felt warm breath on her cheek.

"You smell like sugar."

"I work in a bakery."

"I like it." He sat back and she turned to see him, the boy of her note. Nora blushed again. Then the professor strode in and began talking about logical extremism or reductio ad absurdum as a satirical device. Nora lost the thread of the lecture almost immediately. *None of my senses are impaired; I exercise often and enjoy it; I believe everything happens for a reason.* Reductio ad absurdum, reduce the ridiculous to the daft, combine the absurd and the tragic, accommodate the improbable. All tools of satire. Pencils scratched, pages turned as the professor asked them to look at a passage from Evelyn Waugh, breath going in and out. *I get enough sleep at night; I can easily focus on the task at hand.* She felt the boy staring at her shoulders throughout the excruciating hour.

"You wouldn't want to go for coffee, would you?" He introduced himself as Aaron, held out his free hand, which engulfed hers.

Reflexively Nora thought what the span of a man's hand meant. When she was a little girl, back when they lived in LA, Ruby and her friend Maxine would drink wine spritzers on Friday afternoons and give each other man advice. *Never answer on the first ring; shoes reveal income; make eye contact then look away; never be coy with lipstick.* It felt as if Ruby were constantly elbowing her in the ribs. Nora looked away from the boy's large hand, up to his eyes and then down to her notebook. Her too-long bangs fell forward, half concealing her eyes. "Coffee's my only addiction."

"That's too bad," Aaron said, and Nora told him her name.

Tuesday afternoon Ruby wrestled her hulking suitcase into the living room. "Don't bother," she said, though neither Nora nor Thad

had budged. They leaned into each other on the couch, Nora reading Molière and Thad thumbing through *Bicycling* magazine. Ruby stopped in front of them, sat on her luggage, and rummaged through her purse, eventually extracting large silver hoop earrings. "You two are like an adorable old couple."

Nora lost her place and started over at the top of the page. Thad toed Ruby's suitcase with his bare foot. "Have you got our towels and ashtrays in there?"

"I wore almost everything I packed."

"And you're leaving before we've seen it all?"

"Be careful what you wish for. Besides, I've always told Nora, best to keep a man guessing."

Thad nodded. "Next time, remember: less is more."

"On the body or in the suitcase?" Ruby put on the earrings, then slung her purse over her shoulder. "Help your mother to her car?"

Nora dog-eared the page she'd now scanned twice and stood.

Ruby blew a kiss with three fingers. "Goodbye, Dad."

"Thad," Nora snarled. "And just so you both know, your witty repartee is neither. It's tragic and absurd."

"Ouch," Ruby said.

Thad unfolded himself from the couch and held open the door.

Once Nora heaved the suitcase into her mother's trunk, Ruby took hold of her shoulders. "Beanie, listen, as much as drab Thad is killing your sense of humor, I am glad you have him for the next little while. I might not be available." She stroked Nora's bangs. "Hopefully, after you finish your term, and I get out, you'll be tired of all this stability."

Nora stepped back. "Get out?" It was like Ruby to spring something on her right before leaving.

"I've signed myself up for camp. It's in the Santa Cruz Mountains, twenty-five bucolic acres, gorgeous pool, sand volleyball pit."

"What about work? You don't play volleyball."

"Personal hiatus, and now maybe I will." She bit her lip, squinted back toward the apartment. "Dad's watching."

Nora turned and there he was, standing in the window, fluttering his fingers in a small wave.

"It seems he can't bear to be without you." Ruby slammed the trunk. "Really, I have no idea what you're getting from all this." She flicked her small freckled hand out and Thad mistook it for a wave goodbye.

"Thad loves me." She jammed her fists into her pockets, willing her mother to get in her car, start her engine, and drive safely away.

"He certainly does. Yes, he does." Ruby reached out to tuck Nora's hair behind her ears, pinched the naked lobes. "You should decorate yourself."

"You're in trouble, aren't you?"

"You're so smart. Of course Thad can't resist you." She removed the silver hoops from her own earlobes, and one at a time slipped them into Nora's. "But what about tension? I don't sense any . . . flair."

"Flair?" She felt her voice crawling up into her throat. "We have tons of flair."

Now Ruby tousled Nora's hair. "Must you be so solid?"

"Stop it." She pushed her mother's hands away, patted her hair flat again. "Quit ruining things for me. How would you know a thing about solid?"

Ruby trilled, a little self-deprecating chirp. "He's still there. Mild and attentive. He'll make you soft. He doesn't make you work for it. Trust me, you'll soon be bored."

Nora enforced upon herself a haughty smile, a state of denial. She would compromise anything to spite her mother. "People with attention spans don't get bored." She turned and blew a kiss to Thad and his love-gaze — never would she keep him in the loop about this conversation. She felt her mother's moue-lipped concern press against her back. "What do you expect me to be?"

"Young."

The women looked at each other. Nora trembled with fragile defiance. A jay screeched over their heads. "I've never been young, Mom."

Ruby was the first to look away, chasing the sound with her gaze and then looking down at her hands. The sun glinted off a bobby pin in her mother's hair, pointing like an arrow toward her roots. Nora yanked the hoops from her ears and held them in her open palm. "These look better on you."

"You're right, Beanie. You don't need decoration." She clasped Nora's hand before taking them back. "So," she breathed out, a quick huff of recovery. "Camp? It's a month-long interlude — all right, it's rehab, or as I prefer to think of it, a spa vacation covered by insurance. I can watch what I eat, get lots of good sleep, no access to alcohol. Or Valium. Maybe I'll write poetry."

"Valium?"

"Even I need to relax." Ruby slid behind the wheel, adjusted the rearview mirror, touched the sides of her lips. "Do you like the car?"

"You were in an accident."

"I've been getting in fender-benders my whole life. Don't be so self-righteous. This time, I recognize I could use a little help. That's what makes me a grownup, self-reflection." She turned to Nora, her gaze frank and open. "Look at you, so beautiful and naive and, even if you can't admit it, young. Lots of men are going to love you. I've told you that before." She sighed. "And I love you and I hope you love you. You do, right?"

Nora's eyes stung. Ruby always did this, knew exactly what to say to make it seem like she was an amazing mother. "Don't rate my life."

A tiny smile, superior and sympathetic, played at the corners of Ruby's mouth. "It's hard being twenty." She closed her door and rolled down the window. "Tell me, where should a girl go to buy a bikini? I'm going to need a new bikini for camp. I was thinking gold . . ."

At the stop sign, Ruby tooted her horn, called a final "Bye, Beanie." Then she turned the wrong way. Nora cried out, "Right, go right!," but her mother with her terrible sense of direction was gone. Behind her, Thad said, "Alone at last, chicken." Nora blinked. She would not turn to look. Thad standing in the frilly green shade of the jacaranda trees, the sun beaming its cheery light down on him: she would now see it all with her mother's eyes. Nora felt stuck in a sliver of space, pressed between panes of lovely sky-blue glass. The middle of the street was the only place she could be herself.

"Another amazing, boring May-blue sky," Aaron observed.

Nora leaned toward the windshield, looked up and out over the ocean. She couldn't agree more. They were parked in Aaron's VW camper at Butterfly Beach. Supposedly they were studying for the final. Nora had her books zipped in the backpack at her feet. Aaron's elbow jutted out his window and he held a perfect Granny Smith in his hand. A jar of peanut butter rested between his thighs, which were thicker than Nora's.

"What kind of art do you make?"

"Conceptual stuff. I'm interested in the universality of foibles."

Nora nodded as if she knew what he was talking about.

"I had a piece in a gallery in downtown LA, it had this found object, like an arthritic finger, only it was driftwood. It was totally amazing—like an arthritic *what-the-fuck?*—and I painted the canvas with these vague, blurred flags from the G Seven and then I copied random candy and alcohol ads and repeated images of Ronald Reagan and then wheat-pasted the whole thing together." Aaron removed a Swiss army knife from his glove box, and while he spoke, he sliced the apple against his palm, dipped a crescent in peanut butter, and passed it to her. "I'm only in school for the parental aid. I try to take classes that will inspire my vision, like satire, because art is about disruption." His clear violet eyes, magnified by his glasses, remained fixed on her face. His voice, confident and sonorous, was perfect for a make-out song.

The assured way he spoke about his ideas made her nervous. If he asked about her, like why she was in school or what she wanted, Nora would have no idea what to say. School and work were ends in themselves. She liked baking. She was good at it. So good, in fact, that her boss wanted her to help open a new bakery. Plus, she liked reading things she wouldn't have known enough to choose on her own. Thankfully, Aaron never asked, which was fine because nearly the entire rear of his van had been converted to a sleeping platform and Nora could feel its insistent presence, like a cat rubbing against her shin. Aaron slept beneath that orange Mexican blanket. His clothing, stuffed into the net hammocks slung along the windows, gave the van a musty, animal smell. Three saucepans hung from hooks behind the driver's seat and she imagined the friendly clatter every time he turned a corner. He had a case of Top Ramen tucked under the bed. Aaron was a gypsy.

"So, Nora. I've been feeling artistically gummed up. After the G Seven piece, I haven't really been able to make anything. And this satire class, it's so—lower division. It's like, *meta*. Self-parody. Then I saw your amazing shoulders, and your amazing studentness. I bet you had a gap between your teeth, corrected with orthodontia."

Nora was so enthralled by his passion, by his penetrating stare, that she didn't correct his assumption. She watched the green sliver of apple peel in his teeth as he went on about his plans.

"My next piece is coming from that reductio ad absurdum talk. You know, like the lecture hall and the professorial professor, and you, so coed, and I'm this, like, visionary. My art has to do more than masturbate reality onto a canvas. I want to expose singular foolishness."

Nora bit her thumbnail. "So, you want to satire satire."

"Bigger. I want to hash it up." He set the peanut butter jar behind him on the tiny stove. "Let's go to the movies." He leaned in close to her, his hands resting on her knees squeezing her flesh. He smelled mostly like peanut butter, but also like his van, only stronger, and wild, as if he spent his nights on the forest floor. After the kiss, he pulled out his wallet. "Let's upset the paradigm." Forehead to forehead, he extracted a glassine envelope from between receipts and taco coupons. "This, my little friend, is windowpane. LSD."

Nora leaned away and Aaron followed, holding her wrist in the same gesture Thad used. Only Aaron didn't call her chicken, and Nora did feel the plummeting-elevator sensation in her spine.

"I love that you're afraid. That's perfect. It's totally mild . . . you know, it will just open vessels in your brain." He made a sound like a small boy imitating a bomb. The sun angled in the van, lemon yellow and sweet. His large hands drew together in front of her face like two leggy spiders, fingertips to fingertips. "Everything will *zzzp*, connect and make sense. I promise."

Nora's heart boomed in her chest. She'd never thought of taking LSD. Her main knowledge about hallucinogens came from a prevention film with a terrible song that she'd seen in sixth grade, and a story she'd overheard her mother tell at parties; something about peyote and nearly driving off the road in pursuit of a moonbeam. The movie was a joke. Her mother's story always garnered a laugh. Aaron leaned in to kiss her again. He told her it would be the most intense morning of her sweet young life. "Say you will. Be my muse." She glanced at her watch — ten thirty — then at the cracked clock on his dashboard, then at the boring blue sky. Thad was on his century bike ride and wouldn't be home until well after six. Though she couldn't quite believe it, Nora was basing her decision on time. When Aaron demonstrated sticking out his tongue, Nora responded with hers, and felt a bitter prick like Parmesan cheese where the gelatin dissolved.

They stretched out on the sleeping platform and Aaron instructed her to be alert. Coming on was always the tingly best. Looking up at the sagging water-stained liner of his van, Nora felt hyperaware. She noticed the weary *zzzz* of a fly hitting the window, the itch of the blanket against her bare arms, the heat of Aaron lying beside her, not touching any part of her but the back of her hand. Aaron told her it was important to set a tone, to build your base of happy thoughts, like drinking milk mixed with a bit of olive oil before a night of partying. So she told him about her mother's new rehab bikini.

"Have I heard of her? Is she a celebrity?"

Nora shook her head. "She called me with the address, told me to send her a SWAK package so people know she's loved."

"Wow." He squeezed her hand, said in a solemn voice, "That's tragic and absurd."

She rolled onto her side. Aaron curled around her. He got her. When she'd told Thad about Ruby's bikini, he'd roared, *Perfect!,* as if they were talking about someone else's mother. When she didn't laugh too, Thad said, *Come on . . . what did you expect? It's your mother. Exactly,* Nora had thought.

"What does SWAK mean?"

"Sealed with a kiss."

They lay together, Aaron mouthing the words *Sealed. With. A. Kiss. Sealed with a kiss. Sealedwithakiss.* He whispered it between kissing her, fast then slow; he sang it into her mouth, shouted it, said it with an accent, cried it, punched it at the air, smooched it out, and barked it like a seal. They both barked, laughing and rolling around on the bed. "Arf. Arf. Sealed with a kiss."

"Stop." He pressed his finger to her lips. "Now say *yellow.*"

She did, over and over, until the word ran together in a long string of nonsense. Aaron pressed his palm against her heart. "Everything important will happen right here."

· · ·

Nora heard the water sparkle, quivery pops, like a bowl of cereal. "Snap. Crackle," she said and Aaron nodded. They wandered down the beach where gulls pierced the air with their wings and cries. A red Frisbee trailed long ribbons of light. It felt as if she were stand-ing still and all the dogs, people, and children were gliding past, rolling by for the queen's pleasure. Her cheeks ached. Her smile was so wide that she worried her teeth would sunburn. Looking up at Aaron, she saw he was talking but his words sounded like rhythmic collisions, wave upon wave. Her heart backflipped in her chest. She took off, pounding the sand with her bare feet, pump-ing her arms, Aaron beside her. Black oysters of crude freckled the shore. The water, the color of Scope mouthwash, flew up around her ankles in tiny blisters that threatened to cut her open. They swam, they must have, because her hair was damp and when she pulled a clump into her mouth, she tasted salt. It was a great com-fort to chew on her hair. She'd been broken of the habit by her first-grade teacher. Lumpy, short Mrs. Hopewell tied Nora's hair back every morning and gave her a cherry Smith Brothers cough drop at the end of the day if she successfully resisted the tempta-tion. The cherry taste, right this minute, felt huge in her mouth. Nora spit up into the sky and dodged it coming back down. She yearned to hug the little girl who yearned to please Mrs. Hopewell with her conditional smile. She yearned to hug the little girl who arranged lilies in an empty wine jug for her dead cat. Aaron's fin-gertips grazed her wet cheeks. She pulled the hair from her mouth and asked for a cough drop. He took her hand and they ran back to the van to rest in the sun beating through his windows. They nibbled uncooked ramen noodles dipped in peanut butter and kissed with food in their mouths, sharing like hungry babies. Tak-ing off their clothes seemed unbelievably complicated. The way the zipper teeth one by one disconnected was funny and sad. They sat forever, cross-legged with their spines growing limp, eyes rigid, and sandy knees touching. A glob of black stuck to Aaron's instep.

Nora thought of cotton balls and felt vaguely sorry and tired. LSD drained from her body, like water from a tub. Aaron dragged his finger through the crude, making a smeary cyclone up his calf.

"Do you believe everything happens for a reason?"

She could tell by his voice, the way it trailed off, that he didn't want an answer. He wanted nothing from her. She was free to watch his finger or not.

"I'm a baker," she said.

"You smell like sugar. Remember?"

"Yes, but . . ." She leaned very close to him and whispered, "I have a secret in my pocket." She dug into her jeans and pulled out wet, crumpled paper. "I'm a very good baker."

"I know."

She waved the letter. "You don't know. If you did, you'd know that my boss wants me to move to Seattle in June. If you knew that, then you'd know that I bake with flair."

"It rains there."

"I like rain. My mother says it's good for your complexion." She leaned back against the door, which wasn't fully shut, and tipped backward into the parking lot, her legs flailing toward the now violet sky. The pavement came up fast. Her right elbow broke her fall. Nora was surprised and hurt and laughing. She suffered throbbing jelly pulses.

Aaron fell across the passenger seat on his belly, grasping at the air with his hands, missing her ankles.

"Ow?" She held up her bloodied elbow.

"Elbow, elbow, el-bow, there's another weird one."

Her skin was too raw to say any word more than once. From her position on the ground it seemed like she had to look a long way back to before. Her current body felt as if it had been raked over a cheese grater between then and now.

Aaron cleaned her wound with peroxide he found in a first-aid kit beneath his stove. In the failing light, with his head hovering over the pink fizz, his hair no longer smelled like the forest floor; it smelled like hot-dog water. He cleared his throat, a horrible tumbling-rocks sound, and blew on her skin when it stung. In a serious voice she hadn't heard before, he told her to bend and straighten the joint; he gently prodded.

"Can you raise your arm?" When she did, wincing, he declared that the injury was most likely soft-tissue swelling, a sprain. Then he ripped one of his T-shirts to fashion a sling.

"Nothing's broken," she protested.

He hummed a cheerful song and dropped the cotton loop over her head, then gently drew her wrist through. "First we immobilize, then RICE — rest, ice, compress, elevate."

"Are you a doctor or an artist?"

"My mom's an orthopod. My dad's an internist. I've had broken bones — fibula, ulna — a sprained ankle, and multiple cases of influenza. My mom's motto was RICE, my dad's was BRAT — bananas, rice, applesauce, toast."

"For?"

"Diarrhea." He laughed when she asked him to please not say that word over and over.

She wrapped her free hand around her wounded arm, imagined his white-coated parents extending thermometers, applying splints, listening to his heart.

"I was given remedies," Aaron said.

At Thad's, in the medicine chest, there were all sorts of remedies: different size bandages, Neosporin, Advil, and calendula oil. He would want to take care of her.

Aaron carefully rummaged through his wallet, pulling out scraps of paper, squinting. His darting insistence from earlier was missing. His voice was now sluggish. "I had coupons for tacos."

Nora's elbow hurt. She was completely unprepared for tomorrow's final. Her backpack slumped like a sad little gnome in the wheel well. She would have to lie when she got to Thad's condo. With her jeans and hair damp, her arm in the makeshift sling, what could she possibly say? She imagined opening his door to the spacious warmth, the lingering smell of dinner gone cold, freshly showered fit Thad, worried and angry, sitting beneath the bright circle of clean light on one end of the couch. He would know about BRAT and RICE. He had no obligation to forgive her but he would. Thad would tend to her and love her and she would not be bored. No, instead she would fill with self-loathing.

"Ta-da!" Aaron held up the two-for-one coupon.

"Did I inspire you?"

"I have definitely moved into a simmer mode." He tapped his forehead. "Things are composting in here." His tender eye skin was gray as raw shrimp.

In the parking lot seagulls scavenged near a tipped trash can, stabbing at foil wrappers that glinted in the streetlight. Tonight Nora would eat tacos for her dinner and sleep beneath Aaron's orange blanket. She shivered, knowing it would be cold. Tomorrow she and Aaron would say goodbye. Nora would bomb her final. Tomorrow she would call Ruby and listen as her mother described the amazing friends she'd made at camp. Tomorrow when she finally saw Thad, she would be unforgivable.

Developmental Blah Blah

MINI CUPCAKES — ICED, sprinkled, and dressed in ruffled paper wrappers — lined the pastry case like a jolly marching band. Cassie leaned forward to peer in at all the tiny perfection. "I don't know . . . He's going to be fifty."

The young woman behind the counter, bleak and gothic with kohl-lined eyes, a metal stud flashing high on her cheek like a hammered-in beauty mark, and thick black sweatbands on both wrists, was a flesh-and-blood contradiction to the buoyant mural on the wall behind her — rainbows and bluebirds.

"Little cupcakes seem appropriate for an eight-year-old girl's birthday party. Are these too hopeful?"

"You mean like too much hope?"

Cassie's daughter, Edith, loudly sighed but didn't look up from the blur of her thumbs stabbing out a text message on her cell phone. Edith had a package of Manic Panic Bad Boy Blue hair dye in her backpack and was supposed to already be coloring her hair with Pammy. Her mother dragging her along on this unscheduled stop at Hello Cupcake! on the way home from the orthodontist was just One. More. Thing.

"We sell out every day." The bleak girl shrugged. "The audacity of hope and all."

"Every day?" Comfort food was all the rage. At a recent dinner party Cassie and Ben were served poshed-up mac and cheese as the main course. The hostess said she was nostalgic for a pre-al-Qaeda evening. "Do you think it's because of uncertain times? Seeking comfort from a cupcake."

"Sometimes people buy cupcakes just because they want a tiny cake." Edith took the German chocolate samples the girl offered, passed one to her mom. "Everything isn't always about something else."

Cassie's mouth was swamped with cloying sweetness. The older she got, the less she craved sweets. And what did that mean? What was it Seth said at her last session? Cassie had asked him about developmental milestones in midlife. What should she expect going forward besides the appearance of mysterious dark neck hairs and sudden bouts of inertia sometimes with her arms halfway submerged in lukewarm dishwater or sometimes behind the wheel in her own driveway? Pausing just long enough to show mild amusement, Seth told her that the sense of one's life in a constant upward spiral vanishes. He gestured too, his finger describing a tiny tornado pointing forever higher. "That's no more," he'd said with his frustratingly unflappable tone. If Seth didn't (1) hang on her every word, (2) find her funny, and (3) sport a thick brown ponytail, which she fantasized about lopping off and stashing beneath her pillow, she might have slugged him for his cavalier nonchalance. Either that or quit therapy. What did he mean, the possibility of ascent was over? Perhaps Ben on his fiftieth birthday deserved the gravitas of a bittersweet chocolate sheet cake. To Cassie everything was absolutely about something else.

"Oh my God, I'm about to have an orgasm," Edith said.

Cassie flinched. The girl behind the counter was unfazed. Only Cassie was fazed by Edith, small and sweet, whacking her clumsy new language bat against Cassie's sensibilities.

"Dad will love them."

Truth be told, Ben would prefer whatever was cheapest. A pile of Twinkies still in their cellophane wrappers would delight him.

Ben took the joy out of gift-giving because she could see him calculate the cost of, say, a dove-gray cashmere scarf as he twined it around his neck in front of their Hanukkah bush. Whatever lay beneath the wrapping was too extravagant in Ben's view. He'd returned that scarf, bought an electric drill, claimed he was looking forward to being handy once they moved to the East Bay. The scarf, it turned out, would have been more practical. He'd used the drill only once in the new house, to attach a bookcase to the wall in Edith's room. When he severed an electrical wire, he called a handyman, who ended up earthquake-proofing the rest of the house.

But the cupcakes weren't really for Ben, they were for the women in the neighborhood who would attend his surprise party with their husbands, the women who hadn't quite accepted Cassie into their ranks, even after five years of living in Rockridge. Yes, they'd invited her to join their book club, but when she'd blurted a contrary opinion about the selection, an unsurprising novel set in Afghanistan, she'd felt them pull away. Cassie always blurted. Ben described her personality as *pungent* and then, when she let him know it hurt her feelings, he chided, "Oh, stop," with a diminishing tone, as if he had no clue why the adjective upset her.

"Honesty is admirable," Seth had agreed at another of their sessions, "but at what cost?"

At the book-club meeting, Blythe Cooper (rhymes with *supper*, she instructed Cassie at their introduction), wife of an orthopedic surgeon, gripped the novel in her manicured hands like a stone tablet and claimed it the best thing she'd ever read. Perhaps Cassie shouldn't have responded, in her quietest, most careful voice, that she found the novel's perfectly balanced shape boring, as if the novel itself had been raised in a confined space, like a veal calf. Perhaps she shouldn't have gone on to explain that she preferred messy to symmetrical, feral to polite, because isn't feral the truth? Her flushed cheeks and strong opinion were met with a long pause, furtive glances, and the sipping of good pinot noir from the surgeon's wine cellar. Then, maintaining her smile-royale, Blythe said, "If one reads only to feel better about oneself, then I suppose shitty real-life stories make sense. This novel soared." Cassie could tell by the way her hostess touched her throat that it pained Blythe to swear.

"Hello? Mother?"

Edith and the counter girl stared at Cassie, who brought her fingertips to her own throat—another moment of inertia. Then she realized what they wanted: her cupcake verdict. "You're right," Cassie said. "Orgasmic."

Edith's mouth fell open, revealing chunks of frosting in her braces. "Never-ever. Never say that word again." The counter girl too looked pained and wouldn't make eye contact as she wrote up the order.

On the way home, Edith informed Cassie that the counter girl was a cutter; that's why she wore sweatbands on her wrists, to cover up new and old wounds. It knocked the wind out of Cassie. The girl worked around cupcakes. Damn it, she'd spoken to them about hope. Edith went on to say that cutters break light bulbs and slice their skin with the thin shards. "You'd have to be so shitting strong-willed to make yourself bleed like that." The fact that Edith knew about the light bulbs and the ruse of sweatbands also shocked Cassie. Was it common knowledge because it was so common? She reached her hand toward Edith's wrist. It must be shitting awful to be a teenager today. Edith inserted her earbuds, and tinny, flea-size Nirvana music ended their conversation. But Edith let her mom's hand remain.

After the book-club debacle, Cassie hadn't gone back. She was stung by the truth of Blythe's comment. She did read to soothe the constant nattering in her head. Didn't everyone? Maybe that was why memoirs were all the rage. If you read about triumphant drug addicts, families who lived in Dumpsters, or the brutalized children of megalomaniac alcoholics, your own mundane story didn't seem so impossible. Maybe the women of the book club all lived perfectly orderly lives with casseroles and paid bills, appliqué and soccer games. Maybe Cassie was the only one with a seventeen-year-old son who no longer seemed to have room for her now that he had his first serious girlfriend. Maybe she was the only one who had a fourteen-year-old daughter who swore and had developed a taste for the vodka Cassie kept in the freezer for penne à la vodka, Ben's favorite dish. Maybe she was the only one whose husband whistled in the kitchen while making her coffee every morning and accused her of being joyless. As she pulled in the driveway, even before she'd come to a complete stop, Edith jumped out and ran down the block to Pammy's, leaving Cassie to idle in front of their home.

Thursday mornings the neighborhood women racewalked past Cassie's dining room window, a flock of house finches dressed in their serious name-brand sports gear, arms swinging to optimize calories burned, hair confined in tidy ponytails, tugging on leashes. "Come on, Phil," ". . . Wilson," ". . . Larry," she heard them say in frustration. The dogs bore manly names and were yanked away from tree trunks. Occasionally the women erupted in laughter, and Cassie felt a slight jab near her heart.

"Loneliness," Seth had suggested. "That's the cost of your honesty."

Never mind the walkers; Thursdays at noon she had Seth for fifty minutes. Should she ask about the cupcakes or would it be a waste of time? She found she'd been using her fifty minutes more and more to talk about the things one normally discusses with a spouse—a funny conversation with the butcher, the rescue of a stray dog from traffic, a social blunder at the posh-mac-and-cheese dinner party. Seth hung on her every word as if he really wanted to know her. If only she didn't have to pay someone to show that kind of interest in her life. It was pillow talk sans pillow. She sometimes left his office feeling like she needed a shower.

When she told him this, he extrapolated from Cassie to women in general, saying a woman's need to be known is as basic as a sexual urge.

Before leaving that morning, Cassie blew through her house, the usual tidy. Syrup back in the fridge, coffee spoon traces wiped from the counter, towels gathered from the floor, her son Ethan's socks and boxers as well. Edith's heavy-soled black boots and her science text splayed on the living room floor in front of the TV where she'd fallen asleep studying the laws of physics and watching *So You Think You Can Dance,* not connecting the two at all. In fact, she'd rolled her eyes with long-suffering forbearance when Cassie brought it up, the dancers' bodies arcing through space, flouting gravity and inertia. The show was cruel, its very title a taunt. It's so depressing what we consider entertainment. She placed Edith's textbook on the coffee table, carried a wineglass to the kitchen. And what about that show that makes people eat disgusting things like pig snouts. What's the entertainment value? Cassie allowed a smug smile. She had it, her entrée at Seth's office. Each week she dreaded the moment she settled on his couch, and he appraised her with his dark eyes, hands coolly resting on his thighs, then, his voice languid and, yes, sexy, asked, "So, Cassie, what's on your mind?" The first time she was taken aback. She'd been imagining incisive therapeutic questions that divined why she was quietly unhappy in her wonderful life and then specific directives to make everything better — walk in the mornings, volunteer, medication, keep a journal. "Cassie?" Was it his voice or the question? Whichever, she found it daunting, deciding what to say. The days her answers came easily were when she had endured some argument or disappointment she could rail against from his couch. Slow news weeks were hard. This was a slow news week; she had Edith's minor language infractions and disturbing knowledge of cutting, and now a diatribe on reality TV.

Throughout her quiet house Cassie gathered clothes, the bathroom rug, hurrying so she wouldn't be late. She'd start a load of wash and then head out. Downstairs, passing through Ethan's dim and cluttered room to the basement laundry, she smelled the tang of boy. Not a small boy's uncomplicated scent — grass and dirt and red vine licorice — no, a mysterious yeasty smell, skin and greasy hair. She thought to open windows. Then she heard a shivery moan and in her peripheral vision caught furtive movements on the bed, arms and legs, a bare ass, tangle of blond hair, rustling, and then an *OhmyfuckingGod,* and a startled Alice, Ethan's girl-friend, flew past her and up the stairs.

Cassie's breath escaped, her ears thrummed. Amazingly her first thought was not of what she'd walked in on but of Ethan's sheets. They were filthy. How could he bring a girl to that stinky bed? Next she thought of Alice's extravagant car. Alice drove a Saab. Ben joked with Ethan all the time that if he planned to pursue his passion for drumming, he should keep Alice by his side. He then rolled on with his favorite comic question. *You know what they call a musician without a girlfriend? Homeless.* Alice's car was cleaner than Ethan's bed. Why hadn't they had sex in the car like Cassie had with long-limbed Jeremy Deak? That's what Ethan's room smelled like, sex! A hot fistful of pennies. All of this raced through her mind and then the words came to her: *in flagrante.* The only Latin she knew.

Ethan sat on the bed in his hostile Miles Davis T-shirt; BITCHES BREW it screamed. A sheet covered his lap. He gaped at her from behind lush and greasy bangs. "Haven't you heard of fucking knocking?"

Cassie started mumbling, somewhat apologetically, about not knowing they were home. But then she thought, *It's Thursday.* Ethan was having sex in the basement when he was supposed to be at school. "Why are you home?" she demanded, mostly because she could think of nothing else to say. She picked up a hoodie from his floor and threw it at him. "Cover your boner." She winced after she said it. Where did that come from? Her inner Edith?

He winced back. "Don't converse to me about my body."

"Don't make it available for conversation. Alice has a car. With a back seat."

He wasn't listening, he was jabbing his cell with his thumbs, texting Alice, who had slammed the door when she left.

Cassie retreated up the stairs, hugging laundry to her chest. If she had it to do all over she would have knocked. Poor Alice. Cassie did not want her to be mortified. "We'll talk about this later," she called to Ethan.

"No, we won't."

"At the very least we'll talk about condoms. Again."

The first person she thought to tell about Ethan's sexual activity was not her husband, the boy's father, but Seth. And the choice didn't even seem strange.

"What's on your mind?"

Settled in the exact center of the long green couch, Cassie looked at her hands in her lap. Her nails were uneven, half bitten, half torn, and she slid her hands between her thighs. Over Seth's head, a wall tapestry of swirling gentle hues offered a safe place to rest her eyes; well, a safe place for all his clients to rest their eyes. She wondered if there were dictates for therapists, maybe even a required course on creating a haven where clients would delve and reveal. The list would include couch, chairs, pillows, rugs, and heavy curtains (all in subtle hues); a bookcase, plants, objets d'art (suggestive, rustic, and, if possible, African); a not-too-discreet clock to remind everyone that time is limited; a box of tissues and a candle or maybe a small fountain for soothing burble. Check, check, check, Seth had it all. It was sweet, someone making this effort for her.

Seth waited.

Cassie felt a smile tease against her cheeks, the words trapped in her mouth like a bee. She had a sparkly bit of life to offer up into the calculated tranquillity. "In flagrante delicto," she said.

Seth said nothing. He brought the tips of his fingers together, all ten, held right before his chest. He'd been trained to wait out silence. Cassie, whose mother was once mayor of their small town, had been trained to charm and entertain.

"Not me," she said after she'd let the pause linger. "Ethan."

"Ah." He raised and lowered his head, one nod. "And?"

She told him about walking into the basement, what she'd seen.

"I guess you're a convert to knocking now?"

"I didn't know he . . . they were home."

"What does it mean to you, having a son who is sexually active?"

"I'm old."

Seth raised his eyebrows.

"He's too young?" Her voice tilted up as if she were searching for the right answer, though of course there was no right answer. There was only her answer and why didn't Seth tell her her answer so she didn't have to do all this exhausting work? Ethan wasn't exactly young, and she wasn't exactly old. Yet there was a gaping, double-deep hole in catching Ethan in the act. Never again would he run to her, skin warm from playing, soft hair clinging to his damp face, to throw his arms around her legs. And couldn't it still be Cassie and Ben joyfully groping, having clandestine sex in the basement? She sank deeper into Seth's couch. Cassie was the center of absolutely no one's life.

Silence and Seth's fingers still pressed against each other.

"He's having more sex than I am?" That wasn't her voice, it was something Ben would say to get a laugh at a dinner party, she could nearly hear him, his swaggering voice, pride cloaked in self-deprecation. Why is it that men slap themselves on the back when their sons have sex? "Have you ever seen that show where people are challenged to eat disgusting things?"

Seth waited, unruffled by her diversion.

"I wonder, why do humans get pleasure from seeing other humans eat hideous food?"

"Voyeurism? Creepy gratification that they don't have to give in to their own strange impulses, they can watch others do it for them. No-risk pleasure."

"Creepy?" Cassie felt the bee in her mouth again. "Isn't a person with your training supposed to withhold judgment?" She shifted her gaze from the tapestry to his high cheekbones, full lips, the skin at his jaw line beginning to hammock in a trustworthy, I-will-still-be-here-in-the-morning way, and then of course to his unflinching eyes. She blinked and the tightrope appeared, strung across from her eyes to his inquisitive and velvety eyes. She felt as if she could carefully tiptoe in those special acrobat slippers, her feet caressing the wire, one deliberate footfall after another, straight across the Persian-carpeted canyon between them. Though they had never touched (did they even shake hands on her first visit?), Cassie felt more intimate with Seth than with anyone else in her life. When she first came to him she spoke of the paradox of being so caught up in the lives of her family and yet lonely when she was in the house with them. She was the voyeur, hearing Ethan's band practice in the basement, spying at the nauseous glow of the computer screen around Edith's dark outline. "We don't have game night anymore," she'd said, realizing immediately how ridiculous she sounded. She needed a life of her own, and for now, Cassie was making it in Seth's office, the only place where anyone said, Tell me about you, Cassie. The only place she could safely blurt.

"Well, not creepy." He smiled. "Human."

"So, my real question is, why do men get such a rush from their sons' first sexual experiences? Maybe I'm speaking like someone educated by sitcoms, but it seems that TV men are either taking their sons to prostitutes or slapping their boys on the back or glorifying their own first sexual acts and then lamenting their daughters' sexuality. Who do these men think their sons are having sex with?"

"Was that your situation?"

"My mother was always busy being reelected mayor. My father

preferred to look the other way. If my sister and I talked about tampons he'd turn up the volume on the TV. I told you we had a TV in every room of our house, yes?"

"What about Ben?"

"You mean what does Ben think about Ethan and Alice? I haven't told him yet. But Ethan and Alice have been together for nearly a year, it shouldn't come as a shock."

"And yet you told Ethan to cover his boner?"

Cassie winced anew. "That was messed up."

"I just wonder why you made that choice, why you didn't leave right away?"

A penetrating question followed by a pause and the tightwire between them slackened. Cassie lost her balance. Seth waited for her to come up with the insightful answer and she waited for him to do the same.

"Your threw a mini-tantrum with that line. Could it be that you're threatened by Alice? Threatened that you are losing your son and that's more than you can bear? Aren't they doing the exact right developmental thing?"

Cassie lowered her chin, offered an ingénue pout.

"How old were you when you first had sex and what did it mean to you, to your family relationships?"

She wanted to say, *How old were you?* But asking him anything was taboo. These fifty minutes were solely for her. Eighteen more minutes of Cassie, Cassie, Cassie. It was unbearable and exquisite. "I was seventeen. It completely defined me for a hideous period in my life."

His fingers came back together in front of his heart. "Hideous?"

Cassie smiled. "I've served up a mystery."

"I wonder, how is being alluring benefiting you right now?"

"It's better than being a stereotype — the clingy mother with no identity."

"And are you? A stereotype?"

It was Cassie's turn to wait out the silence, suppressing the sting at the back of her eyes.

"You and Ben decided that you would claim traditional family roles, you as mother and homekeeper; you made a huge sacrifice — your independence, your career."

"I didn't want to miss out the way my mother did. I was supposed to be lucky, staying home." In the beginning, it was as if Cassie had pricked her finger on a spinning wheel and fallen into a deep enchantment. She napped with her babies, paced the dark living room when they needed comforting at night, breathing in the vanilla and sour-milk scent of their skin. Her hand curved around a warm skull, a soft, wet mouth pressed to her night-gowned shoulder. Cassie would sway, gazing out the window at a stoplight cloaked in fog — red, green, red. Stop, go, stop. Its faint glimmer reflected off parked cars, off the cable-car tracks that marked the street like veins. Ben and Ethan asleep, Edith growing drowsy on her shoulder, Cassie's family was precious as water cupped in her palms and there was nothing she could do to stop it from seeping through her fingers except hold tight and still for as long as possible.

"Now as your children grow and engage in adult behavior, your role is shifting. You have to define yourself outside the family unit. You're all three — Ethan, Edith, and you — struggling with individuation."

"Didn't I already do that in my parents' house?"

He pursed his lips and shrugged.

Pulling out of her parking spot, Cassie grinned at herself in her rearview mirror. Seth had called her alluring.

Ethan served himself dinner, carefully segregating his food: glazed carrots far from the meat loaf, salad on a separate plate. "Mom-dude, to commemorate his half century, Dad and I are getting tatted up."

"If he does, I am def getting my nose pierced." Edith swiveled her head from Ben to Cassie, causing her bluish hair to swirl like a ragged shawl around her shoulders. The dye hadn't taken well over Edith's red hair; rather than brazen, the desired effect, her hair had come out toilet-bowl-cleaner blue after a pee.

"Smurf, this is bigger than you and your nose, it's about manhood. Me and Dad — connecting." Ethan banged his fist against his chest.

Cassie floated a wry glance in Ben's direction but he was involved with opening a bottle of Bordeaux. Ethan had been pushing the tattoo idea since last June. Both Cassie and Ben, in rare accordance, insisted he wait another year, until he was eighteen. It wasn't that they fought about parenting — Ben mostly deferred to Cassie, but he was always telling her to *lighten up*. While she erred on the side of control, Ben was more about freedom. It was the veal-versus-feral argument all over again, only this time, when it was her children and not a book, Cassie was on the veal side. Most often she and Ben settled in the center. When Ethan's tattoo yen came up, Cassie initiated an anti-tatt campaign by e-mailing him images from badtattoo.com — a man with a pickle in the center of his forehead, a pair of unicorns humping on an anonymous girl's dimpled low back. Ethan never responded to the e-mails but Cassie was enthralled by the search. The worst tattoo, she never forwarded: a penis with *your name here* tattooed up the shaft. When her screen filled with the image she'd gasped — first at the pain and then at the idea that people could be so easily swapped out.

Edith declared she hated meat loaf. Ben filled the wineglasses. Ethan sallied forth with his tattoo campaign. It was a rare pleasure, the ting of forks against plates, the smell of garlic and meat, hum of voices. Cassie made herself pause. Next year her confident, tattooed boy would be away at college and Edith would suffer under intensified parental scrutiny, and then sweet Edith, a tiny gold hoop gleaming in her nostril, would head off to college as well. She felt the speed of it pass through her and her hand went to her chest. *Pay attention now to your unsullied children.*

Out their dining room window, light leached from the day. Crows gathered to complain in the linden trees, and all along the street porch lights glowed, offering slight comfort to the deep violet sky. The neighbors' Prius arrived home. Last weekend, these neighbors had set about their seasonal decorating campaign — pots of gold and sienna mums, an autumn-leaves flag. When Mike and Carol's last kid left for college, flags became Carol's thing. Carol had a flag for every holiday, Groundhog Day, Arbor Day, and Earth Day, even National Ice Cream Day. She taught appliqué classes in her living room. Staring out the window with a bowl of cereal last Saturday morning, watching Mike and Carol heft large pumpkins from their trunk, Edith had declared, "Celebration-fucking-Nation is at it again."

Now Mike trudged past the flowerpots up his walkway. A moment later the light came on, blanching his porch with a hospital-waiting-room glare (Mike had switched out all his incandescent bulbs for energy-savers). Mike's empty-nest passion was going green. Carol had made him a reduce, reuse, recycle flag.

Cassie switched on her energy-hogging light, and the dining room bloomed in her window, an intricate diorama of their family reflected on the glass — the round oak table, mismatched candlesticks, a bough cut from the persimmon tree with clinging orange fruit, haphazard pile of newspaper, the teenage daughter staring down a hunk of meat loaf on her fork, the wry father sipping wine, the nearly grown son talking around a mouthful of carrots, the mother lingering. She imagined them part of a natural-history-museum exhibit. But what was revealed? Their diorama held no lasting evidence of any of them. It was specific and temporary.

"Don't let your meat loaf," Edith sang.

Ben shook his fork at Edith, a jokey remonstration.

Ethan slung his arm over Ben's shoulder, and Ben, cheeks

flushed from wine and attention, grinned. He was convincible about the tattoo, Cassie could tell, and so could Ethan. Ben was a sucker for his children's attention, and Cassie loved his susceptibility.

"What are you picturing, son?"

"State of California on our biceps." Ethan slapped his thin arm. Even with his hours of drumming, Ethan hadn't filled out like his father. He was lean and long, good on the basketball court, great drummer, decent student.

Ben rolled up his sleeve; he never missed an opportunity to flex his muscles. Slapping his biceps and glancing over at Cassie, he asked, "You like?" Then as an aside to both kids, sotto voce, "I drive your mother wild." Ben worked hard at staying in shape. Every day either the gym or a long run, recounted in full detail while he undressed at the foot of the bed. She had to allow he had a great body, well-muscled long legs.

"State of California?" Cassie asked.

"All the hipster kids have them on their forearms," Edith said. "They wear plaid flannel shirts, drink Peet's coffee, and smoke Camels. They're *word.*"

"Shut up, Blue Ranger," Ethan snapped, his eyebrows creeping dangerously high.

"Bite me, douche brain," Edith said.

"Hey!" This time both Ben and Cassie spoke up.

"Ethan, please say you don't smoke?" Cassie held a slab of meat loaf midair over Ben's plate. This would mean a whole new category of e-mails, cancerous lungs and permanent tracheostomies. Ethan grinned across the table at his sister. A threatening smile that said *I can tolerate you because I am better than you, termite.*

Edith stuck out her tongue, then mumbled, "Massengill."

"Please!" Cassie's throat went tight, gripped in the fist of her family. Why couldn't they be discussing the sociological ramification of tattoos, how the need to decorate our bodies might separate us from all other animals and from one another. It very well might be what makes us human, what makes us individuals. That would be interesting. That would be safe. Unlike smoking and cancer and sex and speaking like a pimp. "Can we please just enjoy dinner? I worked hard to cook a nice meal. I cut up prunes and bacon for this dumb-ass meat loaf."

Ben's fork clattered against his plate. "Where do you think Edith gets it?"

It was barely warm enough to leave the windows open. From the bed Cassie listened to the easy give-and-take of a conversation as the last of the night's dog walkers passed their house. "Does my weight feel good?" She pressed fully onto Ben, ankles to shoulders, her face against his neck.

He moaned his affirmation.

Cassie lifted his T-shirt and then hers, bringing them skin to skin. She'd read recently that newborns should have at least four hours of skin-to-skin contact each day and the recommendation made her wonder: Had she failed her own children? She started to ask Ben, "Honey, do you think . . ." but he put his hand over her mouth.

"Don't talk. Don't think," he whispered.

She was hyperaware of the sensations — warm, smooth, alive. How many hours should adults have? She felt an urge in her hips but allowed only slight pressure toward Ben. Sex was a commodity in their bedroom, with an unspoken tally kept of who instigated when. Lately, Cassie had been the initiator. She craved sex — not lovemaking, nothing tender, something brutish, two wrestlers going at each other. Was it the final cry of her ovaries? *Reproduce! Ensure the survival of the species!* Maybe that was what the cougar phenomenon was about. Middle-aged ovaries blogging and writing books and producing TV shows about their yearnings toward strong-gorgeous-too-young-to-marry sperm. Another developmental milestone.

Ben flipped Cassie onto her back and kissed her shoulder. He drifted south and she squeezed his arms. In bed their communication was effortless. Of course sex had evolved (devolved?) over their twenty-year marriage, from the initial rough and greedy consumption, to easy and comfortable (dreary?), and then to the duty of exhausted new parents, to tender nostalgia (remember how it used to be?), and now the surprise of how it used to be all over again.

Cassie wanted to say shocking, nasty things, to whisper words like *cock, suck, fuck me hard,* to throw her head back and reveal her pale, vulnerable neck. She slid beneath the covers, wrapped her hand around Ben, *your name here,* and squeezed, both her hand and her eyes tight. *A woman's need to be known is as basic as a sexual urge.* She pictured Seth's dark stare, the tightrope between them, as Ben pushed against her. *Fuck me, Seth.* Then she opened her eyes and there was Ben, his stare hungry, intent, unfocused, a hunter's concentration that embarrassed Cassie. She used to close her eyes to offer Ben privacy, but now she closed them and thought, *What's on your mind, Cassie?* She gripped the sheets and pushed back against Ben/Seth in her imaginary ménage à trois.

"Everything," she exclaimed, moving her hands up Ben's arms, groping his triceps like a rock climber seeking purchase. She wanted Ben to recall this moment the next time he was at the gym doing dips or whatever he did to develop such wonderful arms, counting off his reps, twenty-eight, twenty-nine, and suddenly be aflame with desire for Cassie. "Yes," she said. "Yes, yes." And it was only a slight exaggeration.

After, when she leaned over to turn out the light, she imagined the pale curve of her back like a Manet nude or a slice of ripe pear. She paused, wanting Ben to notice, to stroke his hand down the length of her spine and say, *You are lovely.* She tried to telegraph her longing through the absolute grace of her extended arm. But he was already gone, drifted into solid sleep. This was not the first time she'd imagined Ben admiring her back. During the middle months of her first pregnancy, Cassie lived in a constant state of amazement. She inhabited her body with another human being! She was a voluptuous poster child of strength, fertility, and energy. One morning, standing naked in a square of sunlight, reaching for a pair of green boots on the top shelf of her closet as she balanced easily on her toes, she extended her arm with such elegance she was sure Ben was astonished and overcome. She could feel his eyes, hungrily exploring her back, her ass, her newly luxurious hair. "Honey," he'd said, "even your back is fatter."

Her first time, she'd been at a keg party in Pacifica with Jeremy Deak and was suddenly freezing and dizzyingly drunk. Jeremy drove her to his house. They didn't have sex on his back seat. Jeremy hid Cassie in his closet while he said good night to his dad, anchored in his Barcalounger in the blue glow of the all-night movie channel. Jeremy's mom worked the night shift at the cannery, and their house always smelled faintly of whatever was ripe: pears, green beans, yams, peaches. She may have thrown up in his car on the way over. She probably threw up in his car. When she woke the next day, naked in his bed, her head felt as if it were painfully cobbling itself back together. Her mouth was pasty with stale vomit, and Jeremy was gone. It took several attempts to overcome the spins and stand. When she couldn't find her underpants, she pulled back the sheets and saw the silver-dollar-pancake-size spots of blood. Cassie was not on her period. *It* had happened and she didn't remember a thing. Her head throbbed so painfully she couldn't tell if she hurt down there as well, but she did feel slightly crusty. In the mirror she was too horrified by the catastrophe of her reflection to search for new womanly knowledge in her eyes. Her hair was massively snarled, her eyes smeared with mascara and iridescent blue shadow as if she'd been in a fight with a peacock. A note from Jeremy was taped to the corner — *I'll call you.* Cassie dressed; she couldn't find her purse, so she finger-smoothed her troll-doll hair, shoved his note in her pocket, and quietly opened the bedroom door. The TV was still on. Jeremy's mom slept sitting up on the couch, her hair confined in a net, her feet in a tub of water. The living room smelled sweet, like fruit cocktail. Cassie nearly made it to the door.

"Goodbye, Cassie," Mrs. Deak said.

"You too, Mrs. Deak." Cassie answered as brightly as she could and then realized she made no sense. "Thanks for having me over!" Outside she found her purse, its contents strewn across the front yard—hairbrush, lip-gloss, a mimeographed page of algebra problems, movie-ticket stub, a Bic lighter.

Cassie told this story on herself plenty of times, to girlfriends, to Ben. She even made up a name for that horrible walk across Jeremy Deak's living room, the *tramp-traipse*. She usually finished up by saying that to this day fruit cocktail made her ill. The story garnered laughs. Of course the parts she left out—the part where Mrs. Deak said, "I can smell from here what kind of girl you are" and the part when Cassie realized her first sexual experience was stolen by Jeremy and the part where she was swallowed up in shame and loneliness—those were the only parts Seth would want to talk about. Which was why she hadn't told him.

"Should I get a tattoo?"

Cassie hadn't realized Ben was awake. She wove her leg over and between his, skin to skin again. "Really?"

"If I do, when I see it—"

"Forever, you know you'll see it forever."

"I know, forever. But every time I do I'll think about Ethan catching a glimpse of his own tattoo and remembering going with his dad. It'll be like that drawing of the man holding the glass paperweight and inside it you can see a man holding a glass paperweight and inside that a man holds a paperweight, on and on." In the dark of their room, Ben's voice was soft as cotton. "It'll mean something."

Cassie closed her eyes. Yes, when Ethan was fifty he might be sentimental enough to think it. Ben was sentimental right now and for that she loved him.

The party details were coming together. Ethan promised to perform with his trio, Ménage à Trois (the name made Cassie blush), and Edith said of course she wasn't an ass-wipe and would def tone down her language for the party even though it was dismal and sad the way Cassie insisted on controlling her.

On Tuesday Cassie finalized the menu with the caterer: baby lamb chops with fig chutney, curried new fingerling potatoes, little gems of romaine with royale dressing, and the mini cupcakes. Cassie stared at the printed menu . . . baby, mini, new. Why not mature, significant, established? How about experienced fingerlings? Sensible lamb chops? Even the menu font was glaringly youthful. When asked to change it to something less frivolous, say, Bookman Old School, the caterer held up her right hand. Don't you see, she'd asked Cassie with a sad, subtle shake of her head, it would set an entirely inappropriate mood for her food. Her food — she paused to choose words even Cassie could understand — possessed an intelligent joie de vivre.

And, there it was, that word, *joie*. Ben noted its absence as he splashed delicious cream into her piping-hot, brimming coffee cup. Seth had told Cassie early on that if he were to write a mission statement for her therapy it would focus on recapturing her capacity for joy. How about we trade *jaded* for *joyful,* he'd suggested. He'd said some more after that, but the phrase *mission statement* made her deaf to everything else. Cassie responded, How about we trade *hackneyed* for *honest, trite* for *truthful*? She exaggerated her *T*s, verbally slapping him down. Seth hoisted his brows as if to say *See? This is exactly what I mean.*

Cassie, intent on proving she was not void of joie, agreed to the menu font. But she asked that the fingerlings be mashed, a nod to the nostalgia zeitgeist. Middle age does not equal morose malcontent.

The last thing that remained on her to-do list, shop for a new dress, was the thing Cassie hated most. When Blythe Cooper (rhymes with *supper*) phoned to RSVP that she and Bradley wouldn't miss the party for the world, and by the way, why hadn't Cassie been back to the book club, they missed her, Cassie found herself blurting that maybe Blythe would like to help her find a dress, and Blythe had said, "How Wonderful!"

"Cassie, I want to thank you for inviting me." Blythe clasped Cassie's hand between her smooth, expensively ringed fingers. They were standing outside Anthropologie, a shop Cassie usually avoided as much for the boudoir pillows as for the frayed hemlines of the slutty Jane Eyre dresses. Not that she was against setting a mood in the bedroom or that she was a prude — she wasn't — but Anthropologie was youthful shabby hauteur. However, today with Blythe, Cassie determined to keep her opinions to herself, even the most keenly held, that Anthropologie (the store, not the study of humankind) failed to recognize the irony of its faux gravitas name.

"Cassie, the clothes here are exactly right." Blythe kept repeating Cassie's name as if she were committing it to memory. "They're festive." She flashed a clap-on-clap-off smile, and Cassie, who did not want to be accused of a lack of festiveness, flashed a smile right back. "Go into the fitting room and let me be your personal shopper." She squeezed Cassie's hand like a delighted toddler. "This will be such fun."

Cassie found herself humming as she undressed. Blythe was being so kind! Cassie and Ben should have thrown a party years ago, right when they moved to Oakland. Standing in her underwear before the huge mirror (the dressing room was about the size of a prison cell) Cassie did a head-to-toe assessment. Her hair, recently cut in a very short pixie, looked chic, smart. Her bra and underpants — sagging, mold-colored — would have to go. She'd buy something silky, perhaps flowered or purple, before the party. Knowing she was wearing something purple next to her skin might help her with her therapeutic mission statement. It might be just what Seth ordered. This made her smile, thinking of lingerie shopping as a directive from Seth, who never spoke to her about her sex life, her desires. He'd said the word *erotic* only once and then backpedaled, explaining he meant it in a nonsexual manner. Erotic as Eros, animus versus anima, Jung and spiritual love and communication. She'd stopped listening at *erotic,* the word tumbling in the hot dryer of her mind like an adolescent boy's response.

In the soft dressing room light (thank God for soft light) Cassie grabbed two handfuls of flesh at her belly, one for each pregnancy, never to be undone, not by ten thousand sit-ups. She thought of the cruelty of Ben's flat belly. His body unaffected by their children, at least for now, pre-tattoo. She slipped off her bra. Her breasts, uncased, were significant, Rubenesque, worthy of attention. Turning, she gazed over her shoulder, appraising her ass. Two dimpled melon slices dipped beneath the sprung elastic of her underpants. Cassie believed in the adage that a woman of a certain age must choose between her ass and her face, but here she was, forty-seven, and neither ass nor face looked too bad. Standing right up next to the mirror she looked, and saw, what? What had she been looking for in Jeremy Deak's bedroom lo those many years ago when her face was trashed from the night before? Some melodramatic romanticized knowledge, carnal and mysterious, that explained who she was? Her fervent eyes were the green of moss on the glass walls of a dirty aquarium. Lines around them showed she'd been happy, had felt joy. She imagined Seth staring from across his office. Did he see her as half empty or half full? She stepped back from the mirror, sat on the stump in the corner of the dressing room (a real stump, as if she were in a forest! Oh,

Anthropologie!), and made that twirling-finger gesture of his, *the upward spiral is no more.* The woman in the mirror still looked like a human with a sense of potential.

"Voilà." Blythe passed in seven dresses. "Remember, color is the new black, and with your skin and elegant hair, something here will be perfect." Half of Cassie's void-of-joy wardrobe was black. "I particularly like the . . ." Blythe stuck her head in the room and took in Cassie's reflection. Her expression froze but did not waver on her smooth-as-a-fitted-sheet face. "I'll find you a slip, something slightly alluring."

The first dress she would not try on could best be described as a getup, a Hostess Sno Ball–pink number that would be perfect for offering mini cupcakes. The next was yellow. No one looks good in yellow.

"How about something a little darker," she called to Blythe, hoping she'd understand the code for black.

"Humor me. Slip on the turquoise."

Cassie reluctantly stepped into the turquoise and tangerine dress. It was better than she thought, two giant blocks of color, turquoise skirt with a tangerine bodice. She looked like a walking Rothko painting. When she stepped out, Blythe held her hand before her mouth and said, "You look exactly like Susan Sarandon." She walked around Cassie as if she were considering a major purchase, a car or a sofa. "With the right accessories . . ." And she glided out into the store again, Cassie in tow. Blythe gathered a scarf, crystal earrings, gold bracelets. Cassie glanced in a mirror. In the brighter light of the store she saw that the dress wouldn't do at all, it was puffy in the wrong places. Beyond the mirror was a clear day, an extravaganza of rust and gold leaves against a bright sky. Cassie truly hated shopping. She thought she might go ahead and buy the dress just to be done with it and then wear something she already had in her closet.

Across the street, pedestrians strode past Peet's Coffee holding white paper cups, and Cassie yearned for one herself. She would offer to buy a latte for Blythe and then maybe they would talk about trips, GPAs (if Blythe asked after Ethan's, Cassie would refrain from her stock answer: *It's π*), college searches, the faux-safe subjects that held secret treachery, hidden hierarchies for middle-aged, middle-class women. She looked up and down the street, seeking the clump of plaid-clad teens that Edith mentioned. What had she called them? *Word*? Ah, her charming kids! A blue head caught her eye. Her first thought was, *Why so many blue heads?* How ridiculous. But then the way this blue head turned was too familiar. Edith. Standing on the corner at one-thirty on a Wednesday. Cassie's heart revved up. Why were her surprises always unhappy?

"I'll be right back." She shoved her handbag at Blythe and bolted out the door, setting off the rhythmic bleat of Anthropologie's alarm system.

Edith and a boy ambled up the street away from her. She noted the good-news detail that they weren't touching. It mattered. She needed to handle this in the best possible way and so suppressed the urge to scream Edith's name, which would be wrong and bad and she'd have to admit it later when she told Ben and Seth about this moment. Following after them, she called out Edith's childhood name, nonchalant as possible, "Fred."

Edith didn't respond so Cassie ran, barefoot, she realized, when she stepped in something dank and damp, until she caught Edith's shoulder and spun her around. "Why aren't you in school?"

Rather than resist, Edith totally surprised her by throwing her arms around Cassie and saying, "Mom, Flood's so psyched about coming to Dad's party."

"Why aren't you in school?"

"Sweet! What are you wearing?"

Why was Edith talking so fast? What size were her pupils? Her eyes were hidden by ponderous smears of kohl shadow, both above and below her lashes, as if King Kong had applied her makeup.

"We had a short day. I told you this morning."

Perhaps she had, Cassie couldn't remember. She took her daughter by the shoulders and held her still. Edith wore sweatbands on her wrists.

"Fuck-ola, Mom." Edith tried to shrug Cassie's hands away. "Chill."

Flood, the boy beside her daughter, laughed out a "Cracking dress." He had a pierced tongue. Wasn't that for sexual enhancement? Flood, Edith was explaining, worked at Peet's and went to school at night to get his GED. "He's, like, a latte genius."

Another young man, this one in a Day-Glo-yellow vest with a badge on his left chest, stepped up to Cassie and clamped his hand on her shoulder. "Ma'am?"

"WTF, Mom?" Edith stared at the security guard.

"I'm required to escort you back to Anthropologie."

Now it was Cassie's turn to shrug a hand away. The four of them created a small roadblock standing in the dappled shadows of the elms that lined the sidewalk. Pedestrians craned their necks as they sidled past, some stepping out into the street.

"Now," the guard said, tightening his grip as if Cassie were a flight risk. Cassie turned her slit-eyed, mouth-thin-as-a-pianowire expression toward him, and he added, "Please."

"I need a moment with my wayward daughter," Cassie explained. She must have said it very loud because Edith's face went pale and she stage whispered, "Fuck my life, Mom. You're a spectacle."

"Take off the sweatbands."

"Who's the criminal here?"

"I need to see."

Edith slid the ugly black bands from her wrists and threw them at Cassie. She held up her unscathed arms. "Satisfied?"

Cassie both was and wasn't satisfied. She was relieved Edith's skin was untouched, but why did her daughter posture toward emo? All the drama and upheaval and plaintive music. What happened to her sunny child? A woman in a cooking store held a whisk midair and stared out at Cassie. Stared at the shoeless woman ranting at a blue-haired teenager on this lovely autumn afternoon.

Blythe, waiting by the door when Cassie and the security guard returned, asked if everything was okay and then added, "I guess that's what you meant by feral."

Cassie flipped through *Real Simple* magazine in Seth's waiting room, eavesdropping on the clients before her. She couldn't hear anything distinct, just the rise and fall of three voices that left her feeling territorial and excluded. When a great wave of laughter erupted from the inner room, she added discouraged to her emotional inventory. How could she follow whatever was going on in his office? She was like a standup comedienne having to go on after someone really funny, say, Eddie Murphy, before he started taking all those hokey movie roles.

She'd decided to wear her Rothko dress to the appointment, mostly as a sight gag for when she told her Edith/Blythe story, but also as a sort of penance because it was expensive and she absolutely would not wear it to Ben's party. The dress swooped and clung, looking both absurd and kind of sweet, like a balloon bouquet.

"What's on your mind?"

All signs of joviality were banished from Seth's face. She wondered how he did it, how he shifted from being the vessel for one client's messy life to being available for the next in just a few short minutes. Tai chi? Silent primal scream? Did he have some cleansing ritual? If he did, that's what he should share with her. Enough of the weighty prolonged silences, repeating her words, the self-actualization crap; she needed to know how to be less herself, not more herself.

She had sort of worked out her story so it was a joke: shopping, sighting Edith, the wild conclusions that raced through her mind — cutting school, cutting her flesh, ecstasy, sex — the forced purchase of the ugly dress. But once on his couch, she didn't have the energy. "I want . . . to be less vivid."

He nearly smiled and then stopped himself when she didn't join in. Yes, she got it; less vivid in her Technicolor dress, it seemed like a joke.

"Go on."

"I heard you laughing with your last clients, and now look at you. You're sort of . . . amorphous. You have no clear outline."

"I'm not certain what you mean by *outline*."

Cassie stared over his head at the womb-colored tapestry. She wasn't certain what she meant either. In fact, she had no idea what she was saying or where it came from. Sitting on the couch, fiddling with pillow fringe, she wondered if she was telegraphing information to him by crossing her legs, looking out the window, by needing to do something with her hands. God—therapy, this business of revealing and concealing, was hard fucking work.

They sat in silence for a bit and then Cassie launched into her story. "Well," she said, the word carving a space in the room for her mind-dump to begin. She mentioned Blythe, the cost of honesty, and her decision to keep opinions to herself, trying on the garish clothing, seeing Edith and Flood on the street, the security guard, the dog shit she'd stepped in and then tracked through the store, Edith's claim that she would never cut, she just thought sweatbands were *tight*.

Seth's expression was pliant; it could go in any direction, smile, frown, or compassionate furrow. He brought his fingertips together in front of his chest the way he did. The story was good, but for some reason Cassie had no joy in the telling. Diminished capacity and all.

"I suppose what I meant about your absent outline . . . you have no agenda. I always have an agenda: hold the kids to a standard that I know is best for them, be a good wife, love my husband." Her eyes stung and then spilled over. Why had she put on mascara today? It was shitting awful to be her.

"It sounds exhausting."

She nodded.

"I'm wondering why you feel you have to work so hard."

Cassie released a faltering sigh. "Last night, after the Anthropologie escapade, I called Ben and asked him to bring home Chinese. He brought Ethan's spicy shrimp, Edith's sesame noodles, his favorite — pepper beef — some sweet and sour pork, and white rice. He didn't bring one dish that I really like. He forgot. We've been married twenty years and Ben couldn't remember what I like to eat."

"How did you feel?"

"I scrambled myself an egg."

Seth lowered his gaze and waited for Cassie to answer his question.

"It sounds so pathetic, but I want to matter."

Seth waited.

"Aren't you going to tell me everything isn't about something else? It's what Edith tells me."

He raised his eyes; the tightrope appeared. Only this time, he was stepping onto it. "I have no personal agenda in my office because I'm trained to be receptive. To become what best serves my client. To help them see clearly how patterns in their lives may not be serving them. I guarantee you that that is not the way I am in my personal life. We all have agendas."

Cassie gave a tiny nod. "Thank you," she whispered, both tensing and relaxing at the same time. Seth offering this kind of sympathy, describing anything about himself, was slightly unsettling. She yanked three tissues from the box and blew her nose, loud and ugly. "Excuse me."

"I'm used to phlegm."

"This is the dress."

"It's lovely."

"Really? I feel like a Rothko. *Untitled Number Forty-Seven* or something."

"Do you know how many times you've told me your age?"

"If you are going to reduce me to a midlife crisis, I wish you wouldn't."

"I would never reduce you." She wasn't sure, but she thought his smile smoldered. He took five or so steps along the tightrope. Cassie had the disquieting sense that Seth was seducing her, only she had a co-pay.

"I feel like a john."

"So that makes me a gigolo?"

"Why must I pay someone to show interest?"

"You've said that before." His eyes, her refuge, would not release her. And then he was beside her, gently taking the pillow from her hands and laying it on the floor. His hands were warm and moist, as if he were the nervous one. "Cassie, relax. You have no idea how amazing you are."

She mumbled something about transference.

Only of course that wasn't what happened at all. They had a terrible rest of the session, consisting mostly of great walled silences while Seth waited behind half-closed eyes. She couldn't tell if he was looking down to offer her privacy or if he was avoiding her. Either way, the tightrope never appeared.

Finally he said, "If I were describing your subtext, it would be, *Hello? Over here. Care. Cherish me.* Does that feel true?"

"*Cherish*? That's a song I danced to in seventh grade."

Seth looked down and to the left again. Didn't that particular gesture equal something in the big book of body language? A lie? Love? Disdain? Silence pumped into the room, filling it until Cassie felt pressed against the wall. At last she told him that therapy consumed too much of her thoughts. She felt that she would have to work through her self-indulgent issues on her own.

"I don't know what *self-indulgent* means."

"I'm sick of my own whining when, really, I have nothing to whine about. Sometimes after I've been here, I cringe at the things I've said."

"You're talking about Maslow's hierarchy of needs. Your basic needs of food, shelter, and safety are met, so you can focus on your emotional needs."

"Whatever. You've become a sort of raison d'être for me. I mean, I go through my week looking at myself and how I act to see if anything is therapy-worthy."

"That's called self-awareness."

"Or maybe boredom. I'm just . . . itchy, all over. I think I need a career."

She stood to go, and he stood as well.

"We can talk about your itchiness next week. If you decide to discontinue therapy, we can have closure at our next session."

Cassie never wanted to be on the receiving end of that type of sentence again. Have closure?

He must have seen it in her face because he quickly said, "My door will always be open." She looked up and he leaned in and they were kissing. Seth awkwardly, far more awkwardly than she'd ever thought possible for him, conveyed her back toward the couch, leaned her against the cushions, bent his knee between her legs, made them fit together just so.

Only of course he didn't and Cassie didn't even want him to, she just wanted him to want to.

The centerpieces were adorable. Cassie had stayed up late printing black-and-white baby pictures of Ben onto vellum and then gluing them into frames placed before votives. Ben, wise and cherubic, a buttery sage of a baby, glowed at each table. The setting was perfect, lighting optimal, Ménage à Trois played just loud enough to make it feel as if the party were a happening, food stations were dotted throughout Ben's photography studio, both upstairs and down, same with the liquor, so people mingled. Check, check, check. It was all good.

Real-life Ben looked adorable too. After the tattooing (yes, it proved to be the perfect distraction), Ethan had convinced Ben to stop by his studio to document the experience. When Ben stepped in and threw on the lights, Cassie saw confusion, then recognition, and then glee. Ben adored all eyes on him, and here was his party, in his space, on his fiftieth birthday, with all his friends and neighbors singing "Happy Birthday" and applauding. Egged on to unveil the tattoos, Ethan hugged his dad loosely from behind and whispered in Ben's ear. They were nearly the same height, with the same avid smiles, same toast-colored hair; they hung together easily. Cassie, standing in the midst of the clustered guests, looked around for her daughter. Edith kept her promise and didn't bring Flood, but as her mini act of spite she'd brought Pammy and René-René, a pale, sullen-sullen boy from her school with a thick-linked chain looping from his ear to his lip piercing, who piled his plate high and then sat on the floor, picking his teeth with the sharp ends of lamb bones. Cassie in her own mini act of spite suppressed her displeasure and told René-René the way he'd slit his T-shirt with great gaping holes was *off the hook.*

"My dad says hold tight on the tatt unveiling," Ethan said, and a collective groan rose from the crowd. "Maybe if we get him drunk enough," Ethan added. "Beer pong?"

"Son, remember, I'm fifty."

Good-natured, comfortable laughter rolled like a wave through the room. Cassie stepped forward with two beers for her men. She was both in the moment and not. She knew that this was what she should be doing, stepping into her family, looking too-too in her black dress, adoring smile, only her smile was slightly ironic. In her mind she was the self-mocking party thrower.

"Termite," Ethan called out, extending the circle of magnanimity, "get up here."

Edith emerged from the guests and hugged Ben. Her bluish hair worked perfectly with the color palette of the Rothko dress. Cinched with a black studded belt to show off Edith's waist and personality, the dress looked great. She stood with them, holding Cassie's hand. Her smile had a hint of mockery as well, only unlike

Cassie's, Edith's was other directed. She leaned forward for what Cassie thought would be a peck on the cheek and fiercely whispered into Cassie's ear she was def getting her nose pierced tomorrow. "It's my time to shine."

The tattoos ended up being the theme of the night. Ben and Ethan relished denying everyone the pleasure of seeing what they'd committed to.

"You pulled it off." Ben nuzzled Cassie, his hand sliding along the plunge of silk on her cut-low-in-back dress.

"I guess I'm amazing."

"If you're lucky, I might show you my skin ink."

Cassie said, "Broccoli with fermented black beans." When Ben pulled slightly away, squinting at her, she added, "That's my favorite dish."

"Cassie, you're amazing." Blythe Cooper stopped her on the stairs, enveloping Cassie in her exotic cinnamon-and-bourbon perfume. "I don't know how you kept this fabulous party a secret from your husband."

Cassie maintained her serene, good wife expression.

"Ethan's band is Wonderful, your Edith looks perfect in the dress. And you, you look just like Rita Hayworth with a pixie. Bradley, doesn't Cassie look like Rita Hayworth with a pixie? Wonderful? And after what she's been through this week."

"How did that lucky husband of yours convince you?" Bradley's hand on Cassie's arm was so soft and warm it felt as if he'd kept it in the pocket of his cashmere blazer for the last twenty years. Cassie waited for Bradley to continue his inquiry but he seemed to have nothing more to say. Of what had Cassie needed convincing? What had she been through? The conversation was a confusing mishmash of half revelations. Cassie gulped more wine, waiting for Bradley to explain.

"They're permanent, you know."

Well, of course. Cassie hoped for just a second that when finally unveiled, the tattoos would be ridiculous: pit bulls, vaginas, marijuana leaves.

The bartender had no rum, and Mike and Carol let Cassie know they were disappointed. She apologized and motioned for them to follow her. Apparently drinking was also an empty-nest passion of her neighbors. "Ben keeps a supply of booze to relax people, you know, when family portraits aren't going well."

"Does he give it to the babies?" Carol placed her damp hand on Cassie. Why was everyone touching her?

"He's been known to soak the corner of a blanket in Manischewitz." She winked and stepped sideways, ditching Carol's hand. "You're having a good time?"

"What a party," Mike boomed. "Ben is a lucky, lucky man."

"I made him a flag, a camera with a big lens."

"Yep, a lucky, wasteful man."

Cassie turned to look at Mike but he wasn't looking at her. He was staring at the ceiling, his hands thrust deep into his pockets.

"Leave it, Mike," Carol warned. And then to Cassie in a loud whisper, "Now you see why I need a drink."

"Just that I saw the new weather stripping around the doors . . ."

"Who goes to a party to look at weather stripping?" Carole asked.

"If Ben'd switch out all these incandescent bulbs, he'd save a bundle on electricity."

Cassie opened the cabinet: whiskey, gin, vodka, and a gap where Ben normally kept the rum. "Will whiskey do?" She gave them the bottle. "The bartender is wonderful. He'll fix you right up."

From the balcony, Cassie scanned the room for blue hair. Ethan's trio played "Song for My Father," the cue that Ethan's toast would be up next, and then Edith had something prepared as well. Where was Edith? No doubt with the rum.

"Excuse me," Cassie murmured two, three times, placing a hand on a shoulder, offering a mild smile. Striding through the room, purposeful and casual, she felt the sway in her hips, the air against her back. Cassie fit inside her body.

The weatherman had predicted the first frost. The end of the marigolds, he'd said. Hurrying down the driveway, Cassie wrapped her arms across her chest against the chill. The moon, a giant cocktail onion in the inky sky, lit the street. She peered between houses, inside cars, and heard them before she spotted them sprawled on a lawn, the bottle, their teeth, and the whites of their eyes gleaming in the moonlight. They were singing the Barney love song between spasms of laughter. Cassie paused. It seemed innocent, friends lingering on one of the last nights before winter. She stepped behind the Coopers' Escalade listening to the kids' voices make a round out of the smarmy song, Edith's raspy voice cutting below René-René's tenor and Pammy's reedy soprano. Even when Edith was in preschool, her sweet voice seemed to harbor repressed desires: "Twinkle Twinkle Little Star" had sounded vaguely smutty, as if Lil' Courtney Love was in the classroom. Pammy lay flat on her back, singing up to the sky. Edith propped herself up on her elbows, and René-René stood smoothing down his dress. Yes, René-René was now in the Rothko dress, and Edith had on his red pants and dangerously slit T-shirt.

Cassie stepped out from behind the car and Edith caught sight of her.

"Mayday, mayday. Shitstorm approaching."

"Edith." Cassie closed her eyes and the name came out a discouraged lament. Default mode would be to yell, to grab the bottle and hiss at them about brain development and stupidity and grounding, but in her clearest moment of the night so far, she simply held out her hand for the bottle and told the three of them to go inside and get some coffee. All that other stuff could come tomorrow.

"Doesn't your dress look *sick* on R.R.?"

He did a pirouette in his yellow Converse high-tops, which set them staggering with laughter. Cassie followed behind, wondering if there was a right thing she should be doing. Pammy, near to tears, turned around to face her and said how sorry she was. She held a finger to her little bow of a mouth and slurred, *Shhh*. If Cassie were Pammy's mom, she wouldn't let her hang out with Edith.

"Straight to the coffee and eat some cupcakes."

"Cupcakes are comfort food . . ." Edith's voice swelled; she waggled a finger and heaved herself at her mother. Cassie bent her knees, braced for her daughter's clumsy force. Holding Edith in her arms was unwieldy, like trying to flip a mattress. Damp warmth radiated from Edith's skin to Cassie's bare shoulder, only now, unlike those long-ago nights in their San Francisco living room, her daughter smelled of rum, and Cassie's fingers, instead of offering tender protection, felt like claws, ready to tear. "I can smell what kind of girl you're becoming."

Edith pulled back far enough to stare sloppily into her mother's eyes. "Well . . . you don't smell like anything."

The door opened; laughter spilled out. Cassie felt the sting, sharp, in the center of her chest, behind her eyes, and she gripped Edith's tender arms so hard it was nearly the same as pushing her away. "Don't. Don't ruin your father's party. I mean it. Don't." Before she followed the kids inside, she took a long pull from the rum bottle.

Everyone was listening to Ethan, who was pleased with himself, telling a story about his dad. Cassie smoothed her hair, took a glass of wine from a tray that went past. Edith politely maneuvered toward the front of the room. This story of Ben's childhood was Ethan's favorite. He held up his hand and made flicking gestures with his thumb and index finger. "It was a piece of inside-out Scotch tape stuck to the end of his" — now he wiggled his pinkie down near his fly — "and it was all linty and schmutzy. My grandparents freaked; they thought it was a tumor."

Someone called out, "How old was he?"

"Sixteen!" Ethan's grin was wide, wide, wide.

"Two! I was two." Ben fake slugged him, pretending embarrassment, but he glowed.

Then, as if they'd choreographed it, Cassie's two men unbuttoned their cuffs and rolled up their sleeves. On the pale skin of their forearms they each had a mud-flap girl, one of those nude, big-busted, big-bummed, flippy-haired silhouettes you see on sixteen-wheelers rolling down the highway. Ben's girl sported a pixie haircut and was reading a book. A whoop went up. Cassie could feel all eyeballs turn to her as if magnetized. What would the wife say? Everyone was caught up in the delicious spectacle. What happened to the state of California? Truth be told, she didn't really care about Ben's tattoo; it was Ethan's that made her bristle. What kind of woman would marry a man with a mud-flap tattoo? There went her grandchildren.

"Mine is an homage to my smart, lovely wife." Ben opened his non-tattooed arm, called Cassie's name. The gathered guests parted so she could step toward his embrace.

"I hope she's reading *Divorce for Dummies*," Cassie deadpanned.

Ben leaned down and whispered in her ear, "You're so sexy."

Cassie whispered back, "What were you thinking?" before she bit his ear hard enough for tears to spring to his eyes. The party sang the birthday song again, then Edith jumped onto the band platform and Ethan settled himself behind the drums.

Launching into "My Heart Belongs to Daddy," Edith sang like a cat licking herself, languid and intent, the microphone pressed against her lips, her eyes closed. Cassie could feel Ben's rising vigilance as he watched Edith. Whether he was nervous for her, singing in front of sixty people, or could sense that she was drunk, or was just now noticing Edith's twin-edged power and vulnerability, Cassie wasn't certain, but she was grateful for his tensing muscles. Yes, it would take two of them to see Edith through. In the tight red jeans and boots, blue hair and pale skin, she looked like a modern-day Norma Jeane. Cassie ached.

"'And though you're perfectly swell . . .'" Edith, coquettish and confident, let the words hang in the air. Then she turned to Ethan, her eyes now open and bold, and the music suddenly thrashed. Ethan swept into a raging drum solo. That the two of them had practiced this, found something to do together, for their father, increased Cassie's pleasure and guilt. *I can smell what kind of girl you're becoming.* Ben unwound his arm and fist-pumped the air. Edith nodded vigorously, the rhythm jolting her body until she was jumping, a crazy pogo worthy of Patti Smith. She let out a throaty, ragged scream that was met by René-René hooting from the back of the room while all the adults in the middle seemed trapped in amber. Blythe would be there, looking at Cassie, ready to offer up smug concern. Cassie forbade herself to take her eyes from her children.

Her skin luminescent, Edith shouted, " 'My heart belongs to my daddy . . .'" She moved with the confidence of a jungle cat, wild and fierce with rage and love. "Da-da-da-da-da-da-da-da-dad."

Cassie's hand covered her mouth. Her ribs could barely contain the huge beating within. Her daughter caught her eye and for a moment the tightrope appeared, the two women stepping onto it, knowing everything about each other. Cassie's swelling heart split wide and Edith mouthed something: *I love you* or *fuck you,* or both. All Cassie knew for certain was that Edith was everything.

ACKNOWLEDGMENTS

For finding me and championing my work, I offer giant thanks to Heather Schroeder. For bighearted dedication to these stories, and for careful and keen suggestions, I thank Andrea Schulz. Thanks as well to Nicole Tourtelet and Christina Morgan for shepherding me through. Thanks to the many people at Houghton Mifflin Harcourt who worked to make this book everything it should be. Thank you to my mom, Ellen Hart, for nights spent reading *Winnie-the-Pooh* at my bedside and instilling in me the love of stories. Also, great thanks to my uncle Joe Hart for his belief and pride in me. Sarah Hart, Molly Hart, Carole Hart, hooray for you! Barbara Johnson, for your friendship, early reads, and trademark gushing, thank you and a big fat hug. To my teachers Antonya Nelson, Robert Boswell, Charles Baxter, Judith Grossman, Rick Reiken, thank you for your generosity and wisdom. To Debra Spark, thanks for your early and continuous encouragement. Jay Ponteri, friend and believer in my work, I am grateful to you. And to the rest of the Cougars! Jesse Lichtenstein, Scott Nadelson, Van Wheeler, Erin Ergenbright, Willa Rabinovitch, thanks for your smarty-pants readings of these stories. Jerry Kay and Cathy Warner, thanks for reading early drafts. Susan Hill Long, my pal and sounding board for all things writing, I am grateful to you. Guy

Burstein, thank you for listening, reading, and helping to sort things out. For the gift of money and time, I am grateful to Money for Women/Barbara Deming Memorial Fund and the Ragdale Foundation. Finally, a giant thanks to Kirby Wilkins, my very first writing teacher, generous and smart and possessor of possibly the kindest eyes on the planet.

CREDITS